For Jen:
None of this would be possible without you.

For Laura, Abby, Caroline, and Elizabeth (our little women)

For everyone who has been touched by cancer:
Life is precious; you know that better than anyone.
You are an inspiration to me!

Acknowledgments

So much of my life, my experiences, was poured into this story. And since I don't live in a vacuum, I certainly can't take all the credit. If I were a glass vase, I'd be frosted from all the fingerprints on my life, all the hands that have helped to shape and form and polish me.

My foremost thanks go to my wife, Jen. Not only was she a wife and mother during our battle with cancer, but she was also my nurse, my counselor, my coach, and my rock. I know what caregivers go through because I watched her. It ain't easy.

Thank you to my four daughters. They inspire me every day and make getting up every morning a new adventure. I have a hard time imagining what my life was like before they came along.

Big thanks to my parents, who are ever ready to encourage and support me. I know their prayers are ceaseless because I feel them every day.

Thanks to Les Stobbe, my agent, who supported this new endeavor and continues to guide me with his wisdom and experience.

Many thanks to my editors—Debbie Marrie, Deb Moss, Adrienne Gaines, and LB Norton. Without them I'd be a disheveled, unkempt, ragamuffin trying to make an impression with ruffled hair and stains on my shirt. They are all excellent at what they do.

Thanks to the marketing, publicity, sales, and design teams at Charisma House for taking our projects seriously and sharing my desire to change the world one reader at a time.

Thank you to attorney Chris Menges, who offered advice

regarding the legal aspects of the story. I had it all wrong until I asked him.

Humble thanks to my readers who make all this worthwhile. You don't know how much you mean to me. Every day I wish there was something more I could do for you to show my appreciation. I hope you enjoy this story.

Lastly, but most importantly, endless thanks to my Rock, my Guide, my Counselor, my Friend, my Savior, Jesus for seeing us through the toughest year of our lives and bringing us out stronger and more sure of His love than we've ever been.

I am so undeserving of all the beautiful people God has brought into my life!

Foreword

N MARCH 17, 2008, I was diagnosed with colon cancer. Later we would find out it was stage three and had infiltrated my lymph nodes. Being thirty-five with a wife and three young daughters, that's a tough pill to choke down. Honestly, I remember most of that yearlong battle, but certain memories are more vivid than others.

I remember the day I received the news. I was at work and got a phone call from the doctor: "Michael, I'm very sorry but you have colon cancer." I called my wife, told her, then finished my workday. Later that evening we argued. Jen thought I should be more upset; I didn't see what the big deal was.

I remember the day I found out what a big deal it was. We sat in the surgeon's office as he gave me the playbook for how we'd attack this foe. Surgery, chemo, ileostomy, follow-up surgeries, the whole deal. I felt like someone had sneaked up on me and sucker-punched me in the gut.

I remember the first time the full weight of what was to come hit me square in the chest. It was on my way to work, and I thought about my wife and girls and what would happen to them if this enemy claimed my life. I didn't want Jen to be a widow and my daughters to grow up fatherless. Right there in the car, doing forty-five down Lehman Road, I sobbed so hard I could barely see.

I remember the moments right before surgery and the peace I felt. I remember waking up from surgery and seeing Jen's face. I remember the first chemo treatment and that feeling of uncertainty and fear. The side effects of chemo were terrible; the ileostomy was gross; I fluctuated between being an emotional wreck and being stalwart. Like I said, I remember most of it.

Many of my memories and the emotional blueprint formed by them have worked their way into this story. I suppose many of you who have been touched by cancer will relate in some way or another. I hope you will, anyway. This story may be fictional, but the experience is certainly not. It's shared by millions who have faced that monster called cancer, whether personally or vicariously through a loved one or friend.

Cancer changes you. It's one of those landmarks in life that everything is referred to as either before or after. I still think about it every day, how it changed me, how I see life differently now, how I see others differently, God differently, my work differently.

It's odd to say, but in many ways I'm thankful for having been through cancer. It was a trial that turned into a blessing in more ways than one, an irritant that was transformed into a pearl. I had the privilege of seeing a side of God few people get to see, to see him as Daddy and fall into His arms, lean on Him for strength, rely on Him for courage.

I hope you find this story not only moving and inspirational but also deeply personal. I firmly believe that stories are not just for entertainment, but they serve to show us something of ourselves, something of others, something of the world around us and of God above us. And I hope that after you read it, you will find it worthy of passing on to someone else so that hopefully they too can find something there that might encourage or inspire or give hope and courage where it is needed most.

Thank you for allowing me into your life for a few brief hours. Please know I consider it an honor and don't take it for granted, not for one second.

PROLOGUE

The St. Claire Ranch, Virginia, 1976

NENA ST. CLAIRE TOOK EVEN, determined steps across the farm as if an invisible string connected her chest to the porch of her family's sprawling ranch house. Shoulders back, chin high, she kicked up dust with her boots as she passed the last of the stables with its freshly painted columns. Inside a horse whinnied, and one of the hands, a young Mexican named Pedro, emerged, leading a mare by a rope harness. He tipped his hat and said, "Afternoon, Miss Nena."

Nena ignored him, not because she didn't like Pedro—she did, she liked all the hands—but because her mind was on one thing only.

The sun beat down on the ranch like an angry taskmaster, making Nena's hair and skin uncomfortably warm. Perspiration dotted her chin and upper lip and stuck her shirt to her chest. Normally she liked warm weather, hot even, but not today.

The black willows lining the lane to the main road stood motionless, as if they sensed the anger building in Nena's chest and anticipated the confrontation that was about to occur.

Walking in front of the covered, wraparound porch and blooming wisteria framing it, she marched up the steps and crossed her arms. Her pulse thumped in her neck. She stared at the porch boards. They too had been freshly painted a glossy battleship gray.

Her father stood there, in deep discussion with Howard McGovern. Mr. McGovern was a tall, imposing man. Roundish

1

in the middle, he always wore a gray suit and white shirt cinched at the collar with a black leather bolo tie. He cradled his white Stetson in one hand as gently as if it were a newborn. Sweat wetted his thinning white hair and dripped down the back of his thick neck.

Nena's father glanced at her, whispered something to Mr. McGovern, then shook the big man's hand.

Mr. McGovern turned and nodded at Nena. "Good day, Nena."

She ignored him too and, arms still crossed, drilled her father with a steely stare.

"Yes, well then," Mr. McGovern said. "We'll talk later, Jack. Good day to you."

"Thanks for stopping by, Howard."

When Mr. McGovern was gone, Nena's father took a long sip of his tea and placed the glass back on the wicker coffee table. "I wish you wouldn't treat our guests so rudely, Nena."

"Why was he here?"

"You know why. Business."

Nena placed her hands on her hips. "Is that what you call it?"

"Nena, I wish you'd be reasonable about this. The McGoverns are a good family, well respected, honorable. Their roots in this land go back to the 1700s. Howard's ancestors were friends with Thomas Jefferson. They're good people."

"And they're rich."

He stopped in his tracks, as if she'd placed an invisible hand on his chest, and looked at her, eyebrows raised. "Yes, they're wealthy, and he's offered to help us out so we can keep the ranch."

Nena knew the ranch had taken a downturn in recent years, though she had no idea how bad it was. "Is he buying us out?"

Her father shook his head. "No, no, nothing like that. He's helping us out, partnering with us." He turned his face toward the stables, those four magnificent structures Nena spent so much time in.

"If I marry Ted." She said the words like she'd been given a handful of arsenic to swallow.

"Yes. But Nena—"

"And you call it business."

"Nena, that's not what I meant. Be reasonable."

"Reasonable? You want me to be reasonable? What is this, the seventeenth century, and you're arranging my marriage to unite kingdoms?"

Her father hit the porch railing with an open hand. "It's not like that, and you know it."

"It's exactly like that."

"You know Ted, Nena. He's a good man; he'll make a good husband."

Tears sprang to Nena's eyes, but she did nothing to wipe them away. "You don't know him like I do. I won't marry Ted. I won't have anything to do with him."

"Nena, without their partnership we'll lose everything eventually. The ranch is unsustainable. This is the best way."

"No!" Tears now poured down Nena's cheeks and dripped off her chin. She clenched her fists. "You can't make me marry Ted McGovern. I don't love him and never will."

"But you did. Everyone thought you did."

"I thought I did too, Daddy, but I didn't really know him. He's a—"

Her father jabbed a finger toward the stables. "It's that ranch hand, isn't it? Jimmy."

Defiantly, as if she were making her last stand and willing to give all on this mountain, Nena pulled her shoulders back, sniffed, and stared her father in the eyes. "I love Jimmy, Daddy."

"I heard about what happened between him and Ted. Howard wasn't very happy about it. Demanded I let Jimmy go."

"That? Ted had it coming. He provoked Jimmy."

Her father lifted his chin and stroked his mustache. "It'll never work, and you know it. He's not good enough for you."

3

"Not good enough? Listen to yourself."

"You know what I mean. He could never take care of you, provide for you. And what will happen to the ranch, did you ever think of that? Do you ever think of anything besides yourself? This ranch has been in our family for three generations, and you're willing to throw it all away over some childish crush?" He sat down hard on the wicker love seat and dropped his head into his hands.

"Maybe I should talk to Mom about it," she said.

He lifted his head. "Don't worry your mother with this, Nena. She's not been doing well. She doesn't need the added stress."

"Fine. Jimmy and I can make it work, Daddy. I know we can."

"You can't."

"Don't you want me to be happy?"

He lifted his face as if he'd been slapped. "Of course I want you to be happy. And you're happy here, aren't you? On the ranch?"

It was where she was happiest. She loved everything about the ranch. The way the branches of the willows moved in the breeze. The anticipation for the wisteria to bloom in April. The stables and their aged, worn wood. The horses, the aroma of hay and manure. The hands who would come and go with stories from Mexico. She couldn't lose it. She didn't intend to.

Chapter One

NENA HUTCHING LOVED BEING OUT on the porch first thing in the morning; it was her favorite time of day. On clear mornings the sun peeked above the black willows and painted the sky brilliant shades of pink and orange. Sometimes deer would gather in the front lawn as they crossed from one pasture to the next. She'd seen upwards of thirty or forty at a time. And if the temperature gradient was just right, a low mist would settle across the ranch, hovering like slow-moving water, giving the whole property a dreamlike appearance.

But Nena's dream had long ago been shattered.

Gathering her legs under her, she pulled the blanket up to her shoulders and took a long slow sip of her tea, letting the mug linger at her mouth so the steam could warm her face.

As a child she used to sit here with her father and watch the sun rise, listening to the sounds of the ranch stirring. The smell of cut grass and her dad's coffee, the sounds of Spanish chatter and horses nickering for their morning meal, the hum of truck engines and men shouting...it had all been so familiar, so comforting. There was a sense of peace here, of purpose and rightness that she had come to rely on.

But now the place was a ghost town. The pastures were overgrown, the stables empty. The hands had moved on long ago, finding work and fulfillment elsewhere. The black willows, once the landmark of the St. Claire ranch, had aged without care. Some had died and been cut down; others were in desperate need of pruning. And the ranch house, once so noble and pristine, the signature of the success of Jack St. Claire, had fallen into disrepair. Porch paint peeled like an old sunburn, one of the steps needed a new board, and the wisteria had long ago stopped blooming.

Jim did his best to keep up with the place, but it was just too much work for one man.

Nena took another sip of tea and listened to the silence. There had been no sunrise this morning; the sky was heavy with dark gray, furrowed rain clouds. A storm was on the way, and in her bones Nena felt it would be much more than just a meteorological event.

The bleeding had started three weeks ago. At first it was spotty, nothing too alarming. But as the days passed it increased, until finally an appointment was scheduled, a colonoscopy performed, a tumor found. Now Nena could do nothing but await the results of the biopsy. Nothing but sit here haunted by regrets, sipping her tea, reminiscing about the better days the ranch had seen.

The sound of tires rolling on dirt broke the morning silence, and Nena saw an SUV making its way down the lane. She knew immediately who it was—Dr. Les Van Zante—and called for Jim to join her on the porch.

Les had never made a house call before. Of course, she told herself, maybe it wasn't a house call. Maybe he was just stopping by to say good morning and tell them he hadn't gotten the results yet, so she should stop fretting and breathe easy. He'd been their family doctor for well over thirty years; more than just a physician, he'd been a friend. But the lump in her throat and the chill that crept over her skin told her this was more than a cordial visit.

Jim emerged, coffee mug in hand, hair still disheveled, face unshaven. "What's the matter?"

Nena nodded toward the vehicle halfway up the lane.

Jim sipped his coffee and said, "Les."

"Why do I feel like an innocent defendant about to receive a guilty verdict?" Nena said.

Jim rested his hand on her shoulder and squeezed. "Don't do that, Nena. You don't know why he's here."

The SUV stopped in front of the house, the engine shut off, and the door opened. Les stepped out and closed the door behind him. He nodded. "Jim, Nena."

Nena noticed the absence of a "good morning." Clearly it wasn't a good morning.

"Morning, Les," Jim said.

As Les made his way up the steps, avoiding the rotting section of the first board, he neither smiled nor frowned. His face was as stone-still as any world-class poker champ. He shook Jim's hand then Nena's.

The knot in Nena's throat tightened, preventing her from swallowing, but her mouth had gone so dry there was nothing to swallow anyway.

"No 'good morning'?" she said.

Les was a tall, handsome man, with a long face and sharp nose framed by a thick crop of woolly white hair and a neatly trimmed beard. His deep-set eyes were such a light shade of blue they almost appeared to be gray. Creases outlined his eyes and mouth, and deep frown lines appeared when he was in thought. He shoved his hands in his pockets and rocked on his heels. "Nena, Jim, we received the biopsy results." He scanned the land around the house as if searching for a way out of delivering the news.

Nena tilted her head to one side. "And?"

Les rubbed his nose, ran his hand through his hair. "I'm sorry, Nena. You have colon cancer."

The last two words that registered before everything blurred were "colon cancer."

Les kept talking, but Nena heard little of it, just bits and pieces, like scattered raindrops that occasionally land on your nose, catching your attention. She heard "MRI" and "ultrasound," "surgery," and "chemotherapy." But they were just isolated words, foreign almost. Her ears picked up the sound of them, but to her brain they made no sense.

She looked at Jim, her husband, the man who had fought for her all those years ago and risked his life and won. The man who had never left her side because he'd promised he never would. His eyes were glassy and distant. He nodded in time to what Les said, but he too appeared to be in some other place, a place where couples grew old together and enjoyed reasonably good health, where they traveled and spent lazy afternoons walking outside or sitting on the front porch, where they spoiled their grandchildren.

A place where people weren't blindsided by cancer.

He held her hand, but she didn't feel it. Her body was numb, paralyzed. She wanted to get up and run off the porch, find a safe place in the stables, but she couldn't. It was as if she were glued fast to the seat of the wicker chair.

Memories came clanging into her head, just images really, her father sitting atop Warlord, his prized Arabian. Her mother hanging laundry as her hair blew in the breeze and a smile crinkled her eyes. Her three children, running, laughing. Rocking her baby girl, her youngest daughter, and singing her a lullaby—*Baby, my sweet, don't you cry. Baby, my sweet, don't you fear. Mommy will take care of you, I'm here.* Her children, grandchildren...how long had it been since she'd seen them?

As these thoughts drifted in and out, that word, that awful word clamored like an old noisy cowbell. She hated that word. It had taken her father and her grandfather, the only man she genuinely admired (except for Jim, of course). The word itself sounded like a sentence, like Les was not really telling her "You have colon cancer" but "You're going to die."

The porch began to spin then, slowly at first, in a perfect circle, then faster and faster and off-center. Her head suddenly felt as light as helium, and she thought she would vomit.

"Nena, honey, are you okay?"

Jim held her with both arms. She'd slipped from the chair. Had she fainted?

Somewhere in the distance, in the pasture behind the house, she heard a horse whinny. Or was it only her mind playing tricks, hearkening back to a time of simplicity and innocence?

"That's enough for now," Les said. He too was near her, his hand on her shoulder. "Nena, we're going to fight this thing. We're going to throw everything at it."

Jim helped her to her feet, but her legs were weak, and the porch undulated beneath her.

"We'll set things up for the MRI, CAT scan, and surgeon," Les said. "Someone will call you with the appointment times." He bent forward and looked Nena right in the eyes. "Nena, are you sure you're okay? We can bring you into the office and check things out right now."

She shook her head. "No. I'm fine. I just need to get back in the chair, have some tea."

"Are you sure?"

"I'm fine. Jim can help me."

But could he? Could he help her this time? It was cancer, after all, the same cancer that had taken her father and grand-father. A monster that had tasted blood, and not just anyone's blood, but her family blood.

She drew in a deep breath, but the air was so heavy with moisture and the promise of rain she had a difficult time filling her lungs.

Les said his good-byes and left, promising to call later and see how she was doing.

When the SUV had disappeared down the lane, Jim stroked Nena's hair and said, "Nena, it'll be all right." His other hand rested on hers, but she still couldn't feel it.

It would be all right. How did he know? He didn't. That was the plain truth. Those were the words everyone said, the words everyone *would* say to her. *It'll be all right.*

Jim said, "Did you hear what Les said?"

She shook her head. "No." Her throat felt like it was the size of a straw.

"He's going to set you up for tests to see if it's spread to any other organs. Then we'll see a surgeon and talk about getting it out of you."

It. He couldn't bring himself to say the word: cancer.

"The surgeon will set us up with the oncologist," Jim said.

"And then what?"

"Radiation, chemo."

"More tests, prodding, poking, cutting."

"Probably. But I'll be right next to you the whole time. We'll beat it, Nena. We will."

"Maybe it's not that bad," she said. "Maybe it'll just be a matter of cutting out the tumor and being done with it." The words sounded so hopeless, like someone lying there with a compound fracture, bone jutting through the skin, leg cocked at a sickening angle, saying maybe it was just a sprain.

Jim looked out over the ranch, his eyes so distant and worried. "Maybe."

Chapter Two

ENA WAS IN DENIAL. JIM knew it, and he supposed that deep down Nena knew it too. She'd watched her grand-father go through this, then her father. She knew what kind of a beast the disease was, how unforgiving. She knew the effects of chemo, how it ravaged the body and toyed with the mind. She might be stubborn and prideful, but she wasn't ignorant.

He looked at his wife, at the worry lines etched into her fore-head, the creases around her eyes and mouth. When had she gotten so old? The stress of the news had aged her ten years in a matter of minutes. In some strange way he felt like he was looking at her for the first time again. That thought couldn't help but lead to another thought, the terrible events that had led to the first time he saw her, all those years ago...

Jimmy Hutching pulled open the screened door and entered the kitchen just in time to see his father's hand connect with his moth-er's cheek. He'd hit her with an open hand, and the impact made a hollow, smacking sound, like the sound of slapping a cow's haunches to get her moving. His mother reeled to the side, never letting out a sound. Her knees buckled, but she caught herself on the counter.

"Dad!"

Ed Hutching whirled around, the look in his eyes one of con-fusion and anger. The veins in his neck bulged, and one wormed straight down the middle of his forehead like a fault line splitting his skull into equal halves. Dark sweat stains blotched his shirt, and a string of saliva connected his upper and lower lips. He pointed a soiled finger at Jimmy. Dirt crusted the underside of his chewed fingernails.

"Stay outta this, boy. This is 'tween your momma and me."

At twenty-one Jimmy was almost as tall as his father, but the elder Hutching had at least thirty pounds advantage, most of that labor-hardened muscle.

Dad had been out fertilizing the east field and, as had become his habit, must have been passing the time by downing beer after beer.

He curled his fingers into a meaty fist and shook it at Jimmy, then turned back to his wife. "You ain't good for nothin', you hear?" The words tumbled out of his mouth like so many misfit blocks. "I work all day out there"—he jabbed his finger at the window—"and you can't even have my supper ready for me when I come in?"

Mom had crouched closer to the countertop, hiding her face. She knew not to argue with him when he was like this.

Dad picked up an empty plate and threw it against the far wall. The plate exploded into a thousand shards of porcelain, which littered the floor like fragmented hail.

Jayne flinched and pressed herself closer to the countertop.

Jimmy took a step forward, closer to his father. "Dad, c'mon."

But Ed straightened up, his facial expression relaxing a bit. "Oh, I see, you're sidin' with her now, huh? You two teamin' up against me. What? You gonna do the cookin' now, so she can sit in there and watch her stories on the TV? Is that it?" He walked toward Jimmy, shoulders back, making himself as big as he could.

Jimmy didn't back down. As much as Dad hated to be challenged, he hated a coward even more. If he found even a hint of fear in your eyes he'd be on you like a wolf on a jackrabbit.

Dad stopped only inches from Jimmy. When he spoke, his voice was low. "You two tryin' to bump me out, is that it? You tryin' to take my place as man a' the house?"

Jimmy had to turn his head up slightly to look his father in the eyes. In them he found a stranger. This was not his dad, not the man who raised him and taught him how to farm the land

and care for the livestock. This was an imposter who'd shown up a year ago when the slip from the bank came stating he'd missed yet another payment on the farm equipment and if he didn't pay up soon, they'd repossess the tractor and combine. And that would just be the start. They'd managed to make some of the payments, enough to keep the bank off their doorstep, by selling off a few acres of land on the east end of the farm. But they couldn't keep doing that or they'd have nothing left to farm.

"You know that's not the case." Anger tightened Jimmy's throat. "Don't lay another hand on her."

"Jimmy—" His mother stood upright now, her arms folded protectively, holding herself tight. "Jimmy, don't. It's okay."

"No, Mom, it's not okay. He's got no right to treat you like that. No right at all."

Dad shoved Jimmy in the chest, pushing him back two steps. "No right? Who're you to tell me what my rights are in my own home?"

Sweat dotted his upper lip and brow. He was trembling now, teetering on the edge of control. A man his size, there was no telling what he was capable of if he ever really lost it, and the alcohol had pushed him to that threshold.

"Easy, Dad, calm down, okay?"

Ed swung around and punched the cabinet door above the countertop. The wood buckled and splintered in the center. "Don't tell me to calm down. Don't tell me to do anything in my home." He hit his chest with an open hand. "This is my home. My land."

Ed spun on his heels, stumbled once, then grabbed Jayne by the arm and yanked her close to the stove. "Now do your job and make me some supper." He raised his hand as if to slap her again, but Jimmy was quick and caught his father's arm. With his other hand Ed swung wildly and caught Jimmy on the chin. Jimmy lost his grip and staggered back, falling to the kitchen floor. He heard Mom scream and Dad say, "Leave him be. He wants to be a man, he needs to take his punches like a man."

Jimmy shook the fog from his head and pushed himself to his

knees. From there he stood and faced his father, the Ed Hutching imposter.

In one clumsy but quick motion, Dad swung his hand around and caught Mom along the side of her face. "How are you raisin' this boy?" he yelled. "He ain't got no respect."

Jimmy threw himself at his father, both fists flailing. But even in his drunken state Ed was the more experienced fighter. He ducked left and swung with his right, catching Jimmy in the gut. Jimmy folded over at the waist and hacked loudly. Nausea spread throughout his belly like fire.

Dad reached for Mom again, but Jimmy held up a hand. "No, stop. Please stop." His voice barely made it out of his mouth. "I'm sorry."

Dad stood over Jimmy, fist clenched, a bull ready to charge if provoked. "Get outta this house, boy. You hear me?" His voice was deep and gruff, but clear. The confrontation had sobered him some.

Jimmy glanced at his mother. She stood with both hands over her mouth, tears running down her cheeks.

"I said get out. I'll give ya ten minutes to pack your stuff."

Mom's face twisted into a mask of hurt and sorrow. "Ed, no."

"Shut up, Jayne. He's near twenty-two. He needs to grow up and be a man sometime."

Jimmy knew this wasn't about growing up, and it had nothing to do with becoming a man. He thought of arguing, maybe even apologizing and pleading, but it would do no good. Without a word he turned and headed upstairs where he emptied his drawers into a large duffel bag.

Ten minutes later he stood in the kitchen again. Dad sat at the table, head in his hands, fingers laced through his thick hair. Mom stirred something on the stovetop. The spoon trembled in her hand.

"I'm leaving now," he said and hated how the words sounded. So final. A wave of sadness pushed over him. His dad didn't look up, but Mom came to him and put her arms around his neck. "Shh. I'll be okay, Mom. Really. I'll be fine. I'll stop by and see you."

He didn't care if he ever saw his father again, but he'd miss his mother. "You'll be okay too." And he truly hoped she would. He hoped that by removing himself from the situation, Dad's burden of provision would be eased, if even a little, and he'd ease up on the drinking. He hoped. But the reality was that with Jimmy gone, Dad's share of the farm work would nearly double.

Jimmy tried to pull away, but his mother clung to him. He whispered in her ear, "Come with me, Mom. Just walk out and let him be alone."

She shook her head, sniffed. "No. He needs me more than you do."

"If he hits you again, I want you to leave. Promise me."

She paused as if running the scenario through her head, weighing her options, then nodded.

Jimmy kissed her on her reddened cheek, then on her forehead. "'Bye, Mom. I'll come by and check in." But he wasn't sure if he would or not. He had no idea where this journey would take him.

He glanced at his dad and almost said good-bye, but the man didn't even look up. Turning his back toward his father at the table, Jimmy said in a low voice, "When he sobers, tell him I said good-bye."

Mom put her hand on his chest. "I will."

He pushed the screened door open. On the back porch a sob rose in his throat, but he drew in a breath and forced it down. Not here, not like this. He took a step, then two, and before he knew it he was halfway down the sidewalk, putting distance between the only life he had ever known and a whole world of uncertainties. Only when he hit the dirt lane that would take him to the main road did he let the tears come.

CHAPTER THREE

NENA SAT ON THE SPRAWLING, wraparound porch her grandfather had built and allowed the breeze to ruffle her hair. The morning air was still cool, so she had moved to the porch swing where she could sit in the sunlight as it slanted in from the east. But she was anything but comfortable.

She looked out over the pastureland, overgrown with witchgrass and thistles. The fencing had deteriorated over the years, the paint faded. Rails here and there had rotted and broken and now sat cockeyed like broken limbs left to mend at odd angles. The pastures were empty, the last of the horses sold five months ago. She'd kept one, her own quarter horse, Ike. He'd lived to be thirty-four; then one day six weeks ago, a Thursday, he just died. No warning. Nena mourned, but she knew it was for the best. She would have had to sell him eventually as well. And who would want a geriatric horse? Only a butcher. A natural death in his own stable was the best and most gracious exit for her dear Ike.

The barrenness of the surrounding land reflected her soul. She felt so vulnerable, so...so abandoned. Like she'd been left on a rocky outcropping in the middle of the ocean, with a beast of a storm brewing. She could see the dark clouds on the horizon inching closer. Despite the quilt she'd wrapped around her shoulders, Nena shivered.

She had cancer. It was something she had to keep reminding herself because it still felt so much like a dream.

"I have cancer." She said it aloud, allowing the words to roll out of her mouth, feeling how her tongue formed them and how foreign they sounded to her own ears.

She had a tumor, a grotesque thing growing in her colon. The thought of it disgusted her. She imagined it a misshapen and discolored thing, every bit the monster within, scheming and devising to take her life. Even now, if she concentrated, she could feel it in there. Maybe it was just her imagination. She didn't care. All she cared about now was getting the thing out of her before it could sprout tiny tentacles that reached to other organs and spread their poison throughout her body.

Suddenly Nena stood, crossed the porch, and walked down the steps. Quickly, feeling she had to keep her legs moving or she'd go crazy, she crossed the yard and entered the nearest stable. Its cavernous interior welcomed her as it had her entire life. Horses hadn't been housed in this stable for years, but the smell of hay and oats and sweat was still in the air. With the exception of paint chipping on the exterior siding, the structure was in pretty good shape. Termites had yet to find the massive beams.

She turned at the sound of footsteps in the dry dirt behind her. Jim came up to her, hands in his pockets, a look of fear in his eyes—a look she hadn't seen since they sold the first of the thoroughbreds twenty years ago. They thought they'd lose the ranch then, but Nena fought hard, sacrificed everything, and managed to keep it this long. Everything else was gone—the horses, the help, their children—but the land remained.

"You doing okay?" he asked.

Nena looked around the stable. Most of the stall doors were open, the floors swept clean. She drew in a deep breath and closed her eyes. "Do you remember when this place was at its peak? The smells, the sounds, the people." She opened her eyes. "So many people, weren't there? There was always something going on."

Jim smiled. "I remember it well."

"And look at it now, falling apart around us." Her eyes met his. "I'm afraid I'm going to wind up like the ranch, Jim. What if even now, while we're standing around waiting for things to happen—tests, more appointments, results—this thing is growing inside me, spreading to other parts. I don't want to deteriorate like this land. I don't want to be the person no one can care for, left to die a slow, lonely death. I won't allow that."

Jim put his arms around her. She'd grown so cold over the years, she knew that. The strain of dealing with the financial nightmare her father had left her, the exhaustion of fighting to keep the ranch, had sucked every last ounce of passion and warmth from her. And Jim and the children had suffered for it. But after all the years of struggle, after she'd pushed so many people away from her, being in Jim's arms still felt right.

"I won't allow it either. You won't be alone, Nena," he said. "Not as long as I'm around."

She knew there was nothing he could do but stand on the sidelines and offer support. This was her war to wage. And truthfully, she wasn't sure she had it in her to fight.

Jim pulled away but put a hand on her cheek. His palm was softer than it used to be; arthritis in his back and knees forced him to do less manual labor. "I'm going to call the kids and let them know."

"Why?"

"Because they're our children and you're their mother. They deserve to know."

She shook her head. "Don't bother them with this. They have their own lives, they're happy."

He cupped her face in both his hands. "Nena, they'd want to know."

"And what can they do? Nothing. There's nothing they can do. Don't bother them with it."

"I'm calling them. They *need* to know."

Nena turned away and walked to the stable wall. She ran her hand over the wood. Time had weathered it to almost a silky smoothness. "I want this thing out of me, Jim."

"They'll get it out."

"No, now." The panic was there again, like bony fingers clutching her chest and squeezing. Sweat broke out on her forehead. "It's spreading, I know it is."

Jim came up behind her and put his hands on her shoulders, but she pulled away. She felt like clawing at her abdomen, getting in there and tearing the tumor out herself.

"Nena—"

"No! They're fooling around and taking too much time. They have other patients, other things on their minds. I'm just another cancer patient. They don't care how long it takes."

"Of course they do. Their job is to save your life, to fight for you, to make all the right calls and do the right procedures. But it takes time. They want to make sure they get it right."

"And while they're taking their time, this thing could be spreading in me."

Jim tried to take her in his arms, but again she pulled away and fled the stable. There was nowhere to run, she knew that. This wasn't some fairy-tale ogre she could hide from. It sprang up from within her, her own cells gone rogue. It was her fault somehow, some way. Her body was in rebellion, and she couldn't control it.

Nena ran to the nearest pasture, fell against the fence. Sobs pushed their way up her throat and came forth in a gush of tears and coughing. She was going to die, she knew it. This cancer was going to take her life.

Chapter Four

THE STUDY SEEMED SMALLER, AS if the walls had inched closer, eating up floor space. Paperwork, mostly old invoices and sales receipts, cluttered Jim's desk. They'd sold off everything they could and were still in a hole deep enough to fit a horse trailer. He clasped his hands together to stop the shaking. He had to be strong for Nena.

Jim flipped through his Rolodex. Whether their children cared or not, they deserved to know, they needed to know. He hoped—hope was all he had to hold on to at this point—that the kids might find it in their hearts to visit their mother.

He found Kenny's number and picked up the phone. His thumb hovered over the buttons. Maybe he should call Barbara first. She was the oldest and the one most likely to remember the good times, the laughter and love, when the ranch was alive with activity and Nena was committed to being a mother.

No, Kenny was his only son, the one to whom Jim could talk man-to-man. Jim would tell him first. Then Roberta, the youngest and most calloused. Poor girl, she'd never really known the tender side of Nena. Then Barb.

The study shelves held dusty trophies and faded photos of horses. It was a history of the St. Claire horse ranch and the champions it once raised. At the tail end were pictures of Barbara seated high on Shadowfax, a brilliant white Arabian. She was the only one of the kids who'd taken to riding. Growing up, Kenny was content to work in the stables and follow the vets around, assisting them wherever needed, and Roberta wanted nothing to do with the horses. She knew they had replaced her.

Jim's thumb still hung over the phone's buttons like a

guillotine ready to fall, finalizing the death of the family. The kids had all left, run from home, and started their own lives. There had been nothing to keep them here on the ranch or even in Virginia. They had jobs, families, friends, homes of their own. They made plans and kept schedules, talked on the phone, went to the park. He wondered if they even thought of their parents, of the ranch, if they ever wondered how Mom and Dad were getting along.

Nena was on the porch again. She wouldn't be happy if she knew he was making the calls. It wasn't always like this. Times had been simpler a lifetime ago, before the children, before he and Nena were married. Before the one awful event he'd never told Nena about. He'd been young once, naïve, innocent. A young man with a fire in his belly.

Jake's Tavern wasn't five miles from the Hutching farm. Dad frequented it often in the evenings, after the chores were done and sun was gone. He'd say he was running out for supplies, and in a way he was, just not supplies for the farm. He thought he was being sneaky, hiding something from his family, but Jimmy knew where he'd gone and what he was up to. Sometimes Dad would come home with a black eye or swollen lip, say he'd gotten into a tussle with the bull, Otis, or tripped in the darkened barn. But Jimmy knew he'd gone to Jake's, mouthed off to the wrong patron, and been force-fed a healthy helping of humble pie.

Mom knew it too; she had to. Jimmy wondered if his father's charades embarrassed her or if deep down she was glad when he took a beating.

The tavern wasn't anything to look at, just a one-story, flat-roofed building along a barren stretch of State Road 197, a mile outside the town of Monroe, Virginia. If you were going for the atmosphere, you'd be sorely disappointed.

Jake's was mostly populated by farmers and ranchers, and it was

21

common knowledge that the cowhands and horse hands often got into it. Jimmy had been in there just once, several months back when he turned twenty-one. He proudly showed the bartender his ID and ordered a beer. It took only two or three sips for him to realize how awful the stuff tasted. Besides, he'd seen what it could do to a man, a marriage, a family. It just wasn't worth it.

It took Jimmy nearly an hour to walk the four miles to Jake's, carrying his hastily packed duffel, and he needed a cold drink and something for the road. His intention was to get to Monroe, hop a bus, and head for Richmond. He had a little over a thousand dollars he'd saved from doing odd jobs for neighboring farms and figured that would get him far enough away from home that the smell of his father's alcohol would be well out of mind. He had no real plan for finding a job, though. He'd be a sail-less boat drifting in the ocean, letting the current take him where it pleased.

He pushed through the door at Jake's, and the smell of cigarettes and body odor almost pushed him back out into the heat. A dozen other men were there, sweat-stained and weary from a long day of toiling under the sun. Some sat at the bar, some in booths, sipping their beers and smoking. The conversation was light and jovial with laughter coming from every corner. A light blue haze filled the air, giving the place an otherworldly feel. Jimmy walked up to the bar and sat on a stool.

The bartender, a middle-aged man with a trim beard, pocked face, and squinty eyes, wiped his hands on a towel. "What'll it be, kid?"

"Just a Coke, please."

He turned away without saying a word and returned momentarily with a large glass full of ice and soda. He glanced at the duffel bag on the stool next to Jimmy. "You goin' or comin'?"

"Going." Jimmy took a long sip of the Coke.

"Where ya headed?"

He shrugged. "Don't know yet."

"Well, I'm sure you'll have no trouble findin' your way." He smiled and showed how many teeth he was missing.

"Just getting away from here."

"Ah, runnin' away from troubles, huh? The police ain't after ya, are they?"

Jimmy took another sip of Coke. The cold carbonation burned his throat as it went down. "Nothing like that. Just looking for work."

"Where ya live, kid?"

"Down the road apiece."

To his right a big guy with a thick chest and broad shoulders turned on his stool. "You Ed Hutching's boy?"

Jimmy nodded.

The man stood and stretched to his full height, well over six feet. He clenched his big, cannonball hands in front of his chest. "Your dad's got a big mouth."

Something told Jimmy this brute was no family friend. The man took a step closer and watched Jimmy through narrowed eyes. He was no doubt waiting to see if Jimmy had inherited his old man's mouth.

"It's not any smaller at home," he said.

The brute relaxed his hands and took a draw on his cigarette. "You say you're lookin' for work?"

"That's right."

"You had enough a' your old man's mouth?"

"Something like that."

"Can't blame you." He pressed the butt of his cigarette into the nearest ashtray, blew out a long, thick puff of smoke. "The St. Claire ranch is lookin' for a hand to help in the stalls and around the grounds."

The St. Claire ranch was one of the largest horse farms in Virginia.

"Go on."

The man nodded. "Be a good place for you to work. Nice people there, good pay."

"Thanks for the tip." Jimmy downed the rest of the Coke, fished some money out of his wallet, and laid it on the counter. "One for the road too."

"If you're interested," the big guy said, "find a man called Cricket; he'll hook you up. Tell him Bill Mosley sent you."

"Cricket?"

"You'll see when you meet him."

"Thanks."

"Don't mention it." He looked around the tavern, found who he was searching for. "Hey, Juan."

A Mexican man in a booth by himself turned his head.

"When you're ready to split, would you mind takin' the kid here—"

"Jimmy."

"—Jimmy here with you? Help him find Cricket."

The Mexican nodded, emptied his glass, and pushed a sweat-stained Stetson onto his head. "Sí, I'm ready now."

Juan was a short guy, stocky, with a thick black mustache and brown leathery skin darkened even further by the sun. He walked up to Jimmy, hands in the pockets of his jeans. "You lookin' to take the job in the stalls?"

"I'll take any work I can get."

"Hard work, long days, you up for that?"

He was up for anything if it meant a place to stay and a steady paycheck. And he'd be close enough to home that he could check in on his mother from time to time—once the dust settled and Dad forgot about his tirade.

"I'm up for it."

Juan shrugged and tipped his hat forward. "Okay then, follow me."

There had to be some hope of reconciling the family, some way to bridge the divide between himself and Nena and their children. Nena's intentions were good, they had always been, but still the wounds were there.

Still holding the phone with his thumb resting on the buttons, Jim leaned back in his chair and looked at the ceiling. Thick, exposed beams ran lengthwise across the room. They'd been taken from an old barn a few miles away and installed when Nena was just a girl. Her father had completely renovated the study, mounted the shelving to house the trophies and photos, installed mahogany paneling on the walls, and had the beams added to the ceiling.

Those family wounds ran so deep and had been festering for so long; deep down he wondered if anything could fix their family. But he had to try. Without further hesitation he punched in the numbers to Kenny's home phone.

Chapter Five

IT LOOKED TO BE A long day, and Ken Hutching was tired already. He'd gotten home late last evening, did some work in his home office, then tossed and turned all night. Lately every day at the law offices of Hertzel, DeGuardo & Shea was a long one. Dealing with other people's problems was exhausting, especially when Ken had problems of his own. And ambition, lots of ambition. John Hertzel, one of the firm's partners, told Ken that if he put in some additional hours and won a few more cases, he'd be up for partner next year. At twenty-nine that would make Ken the youngest partner in the firm's hundred-year history and give him a nice financial boost. Maybe he could get that yacht he'd been eyeing.

Ken stared at himself in the bathroom mirror. His eyes were glassy, his hair prematurely graying. One of his clients, Dale Henderson, was currently in the midst of a nasty battle with his soon-to-be-ex-wife over their thirty-foot yacht. Seems Dale wanted it for sentimental reasons, but his wife wasn't about to let go of it. Funny, the power an object could hold over two people. Dale was young, early forties, and was also gray before his time.

Ken opened the bathroom door and stepped into the hallway. Downstairs he could hear Celia in the kitchen, smell the aroma of bacon and eggs. He still had work to get caught up on from yesterday and wanted to do a little here at home before heading into the office.

He descended the stairs and was greeted by Amber, their golden retriever, her nails clicking on the hardwood floor, tongue hanging from the side of her mouth.

"Hey, girl. How are you?" He rubbed Amber's head as the dog wagged her tail and sniffed his pant leg.

Ken ducked into his office, turned on the light, then followed his nose back to the kitchen. Celia was scrambling eggs on the stovetop. Maddy, their one-year-old, was in her high chair and squealed when she saw Ken.

He gave Celia a peck on the cheek. "Sorry I got home so late last night. How was your day?"

"Busy," she said. "Yours?"

"Busy." He kissed Maddy on the forehead. "And how are you, Princess?"

"Dah!"

"Where's Robby?"

"In his room, I think. He brought something home from school yesterday and wanted the two of you to work on it together. You should see what it is."

Ken draped his tie around his neck. "I will later. I have to get started on some stuff before the day starts. I'll be in my office."

"You should at least say good morning to him; he was pretty upset when he had to go to bed without seeing you. It was the third night in a row."

"I will." He looked out the back windows at the pool and pool house. The landscaper had been there yesterday and the yard looked great. They'd recently bought this house in Chicago's northern suburb of Kenilworth, and he was glad they did. It was a good purchase.

Ken turned and headed through the kitchen, past the dining room, and into his office, a room in the corner of the house with two large floor-to-ceiling bookshelves and a sprawling oak desk. He closed the door behind him and opened his briefcase on the desktop. The O'Leary case sat on top in a manila envelope.

Married thirty-three years, four kids, five grandkids, Jack O'Leary decided to run off with his wife's male assistant. Now he wanted a divorce, the house, the classic MG Midget in the garage, and the couple's giant Schnauzer, Thor. And it was Ken's job to see he got it. Jack's wife, Loretta, was all too willing to grant him the divorce and the car, but she wouldn't budge on the house and had already declared that Jack would have to pry Thor's leash out of her cold, stiff fingers. Ken had been going back and forth with Loretta's lawyer via letters and phone calls for weeks and was getting nowhere. He needed to avoid having the case taken to the courts for adjudication.

Word around the firm was that if Ken could pull this off, the promotion would be sooner rather than later. He sat behind his desk and rubbed his temples. There had to be something they could use as leverage, something Loretta was hiding. Everyone had secrets.

The door of the study opened, and five-year-old Robby walked in. "Hi, Daddy."

Ken slid some papers from the envelope. "Hey, buddy, how was school yesterday?"

"Good." He had something in his hand.

"Yeah? Did you learn anything new?"

Robby's eyes widened. "A man came and showed us how to make these."

Ken glanced up. Robby held a multifolded piece of white paper. "That sounds interesting."

"Wanna fly it with me?"

Ken looked at the paper again. "What is it, bud?"

"An airplane. It can do real cool tricks."

"Oh, a paper airplane?"

"Yeah, it flies really good. Wanna see?"

The documents were all out of order; he'd have to talk to Michelle, his secretary, about that. "Uh, I'll tell you what. Let Daddy do a little work here, then you can show me a little later. Right before I go to work, okay?"

He went back to organizing the papers and didn't notice when Robby left the room. A few minutes later the door opened again. This time Celia stood there, her hand on the knob. "What's wrong with Robby?"

Ken shrugged. "I don't know. He was just in here, showed me his paper airplane."

"Did he show you how well it flies?"

He set the documents aside. "Huh?"

"Did you see it fly?"

"Uh, no. I told him he could show me later."

Celia crossed her arms. "You didn't let him show you?"

"No. He can show me later, I said. Before I leave for the day."

"He's been looking forward to showing you since he came home from school yesterday."

"Well, I'm busy right now, Celia. These documents are all out of order. I can't make sense of any of it. Michelle has to do a better job or she's finished."

Celia sighed deeply. "Breakfast will be ready in a minute."

Ken shuffled the pages, trying to find the forms that belonged together. "Can you bring mine in here?"

"You're not eating with us? We didn't see you at all yesterday. The kids—"

"Celia, please, don't, okay? Look, if I eat while I work, I can get a head start on this stuff, and then I'll be able to come home earlier and have more time later for Robby."

"So now it's after you come home this evening?"

"Yes. I don't know. Maybe. We'll see how things go. I have a lot of work to do, and this"—he held up the stack of disheveled papers—"doesn't help any."

Another sigh. "Ken—"

"Okay, look, send Robby back in and I'll take a look at his airplane. Then can I eat in here without all the sighs and guilt stuff?"

She left and shut the door behind her. Ken put his head in his hands, rubbed his face. Didn't she understand that he worked so hard for her, for the kids? He wanted them to have a good life, a comfortable life, to have anything they wanted. He sacrificed for them, and it felt like she was just fighting him on it all the time.

The phone rang, and he picked it up on the first ring. "Hello, Hutching residence."

"Kenny?"

"Dad."

"Hello, son."

"Hi, Dad. Is everything okay?" When Ken moved his young family to Chicago five years ago to join the firm, Dad had called every week to check up on them. But over the years the calls had become less frequent. Now Ken couldn't remember the last time his father had called him. Three months ago? Four? Maybe as many as six. His voice sounded much older than last time they spoke.

There was silence on the other end of the line. "You okay, Dad?"

"Yeah. How's the family, how're the kids?"

"They're fine, growing, you know."

"How's Celia?"

"She's fine too. Dad, what's wrong?"

A sigh filled the earpiece. "Kenny, your mother has cancer."

Celia's father had died of lung cancer when she was just a young teen. His own grandfather had died of colon cancer. "What kind?" he asked.

"Colon."

"Is it bad?"

"Doesn't look good. We'll know more after tomorrow."

"What's tomorrow?"

"A CAT scan."

"To check for metastasis?"

"Yeah."

Ken held the phone to his ear, a pen in his hand. He should feel something, anything—anger, sorrow, fear, even pity—but his emotional slate was blank. All he could think of was what would become of the ranch if she died. They could finally sell it and pay off the banks. The ranch had been losing money since he was a kid, just after Grandpa died. It was a weight that had pulled them all down and had destroyed their home. But Mom had refused to do what needed to be done. She'd put that cursed land ahead of her own family and had gotten nowhere with it. There would be a ton of legal stuff to wade through too. "Will she need chemo?"

"That'll start as soon as we meet with the oncologist."

"How are you doing financially, Dad? I'm sure your insurance won't cover the full expense of the treatments."

Dad sighed again. "I don't know. Not good. I wasn't thinking about that."

"Look, whatever bills you get, you send them to me, okay? I'll handle it."

"You don't have to do that, Kenny."

"I want to." He had to do something.

The study door opened, and Robby walked in carrying his paper airplane. Ken waved him off, shaking his head. He put his hand over the mouthpiece of the phone and whispered, "Not now, buddy. I'm on the phone with Grandpa."

Robby put the airplane on the desk, next to the photo Celia had taken of him on the first day of kindergarten.

"I can't put that burden on you," Dad was saying, and Ken knew he meant it. Dad had always been the self-sufficient type, didn't like accepting help from anyone.

"It's what I can do, being so far away and all. Just send me the bills and I'll take care of them."

"We'll see." That meant he would but didn't want to come right out and say it. Too humbling. "To be honest, though, I'd rather you'd come out and see her."

Ken paused, scribbled small circles on a piece of paper in front of him. He picked up Robby's airplane and scanned the folds. "I can't, Dad. Not now. I'm right in the middle of a big case, an important one. If I nail this, I could get promoted to partner."

"So you can get more important cases?" There was a hint of sarcasm in Dad's voice.

Ken didn't say anything. He didn't want to argue.

"How is everything in Chicago?" Dad had changed the subject, which meant he didn't like where the other one was going.

"It's fine, Dad. It's a big city, lots going on all the time." He put down the plane. "Listen, keep me updated on Mom's condition, and send those bills, I mean it. I want to help. You have enough on you. I don't want you burdened with a bunch of medical bills."

"All right, son. I'll call you when we get the results of the scan."

"Good. 'Bye, Dad."

"'Bye."

Ken put the phone in its cradle and looked at the plane. The creases were sharp and straight, the lines symmetrical. Robby had done a good job.

The door opened, and Celia stood there again, head tilted to one side. She didn't look happy. "We need to talk."

Chapter Six

ROBERTA HUTCHING PEELED ONE EYE open, then the other. A buzz sounded in her head, monotonous, constant, like the steady drilling of a determined dentist waging war with a monstrous cavity. Bars of early morning light slanted into the room through half-shut blinds. Her eyes closed, and her mind began to fog again with the remnants of sleep.

But the buzzing was still there. Persistent.

Opening her eyes again, she drew in a deep breath through her nose and pushed the sheet to her waist.

It was only then that her mind registered where the buzzing came from. The alarm clock. It was six o'clock. She reached to her side and hit the snooze button. She'd give herself ten more minutes to clear the haze from her brain and adjust her eyes to the light.

Feeling to her left, she found only sheets, no Thomas. Sorrow overcame her then, that familiar feeling of abandonment, that he'd gone to work without saying good-bye again. No, he had the day off. He told her he'd taken the day off so they could spend some much-needed time together. Erica and Nikki would run the coffee shop for the day.

He must be in the bathroom or kitchen. Or maybe he'd gone out for an early morning run. Or for some fresh-brewed coffee.

Roberta rolled to her left and placed her hand on his empty pillow. The indentation from his head was still there. They'd been dating for three years, and where had it gotten her? In bed beside him, but that was about it. Next week they'd celebrate their dating anniversary. Every year she convinced herself that this would be the year he'd propose.

They'd talked about marriage plenty, and Thomas seemed interested. He was definitely the kind of guy who wanted to settle down someday. But every year so far she'd been disappointed. He'd given her necklaces, bracelets, even a beautiful and expensive sapphire ring, but never *that* ring. No worries, though. Sooner or later he'd propose, and she could wait. Or could she? What if she'd figured him all wrong? What if all that talk about marriage was just to keep her around?

The alarm sounded again, and Roberta rolled over and hit the off button. She sat up in bed and rubbed at her face. If he didn't propose this year, they'd have to talk, seriously talk. She'd spell it out for him.

"Thomas?" Her voice sounded small and weak in the empty room.

She got up and walked to the window, opened the blinds all the way. Their Santa Monica apartment overlooked Mother's Beach and Marina del Ray. Sunlight glittered on the water and reflected off the hulls of so many yachts lined in rows as neatly as if they were keys on a piano. She'd always wanted to live in California, and being with Thomas had given her that opportunity.

Leaving the window and the bedroom, she wandered into the kitchen area. "Thomas? You here?"

She noticed a piece of paper on the countertop. She crossed the small kitchen and lifted the note.

> Good morning, babe, had to go to the café this morning. Will probably be there all day. We'll catch up later, and I'll get a day off next week. Promise.
> Hugs and kisses (but more kisses), Thomas

Roberta let the note flutter to the countertop. He'd done it again, put the coffee shop ahead of her. She hadn't seen him in three days. Every day he'd left before she awoke and got home long after she'd gone to bed. She'd tried staying up to wait for him, but after a long day of work at the newspaper she was exhausted, and by the time eleven o'clock rolled around, she couldn't keep her eyes open any longer. And she was such a sound sleeper she never even heard him come home and get in bed beside her. The only proof she had that he'd even come home was the indentation his head left on the pillow and a few telltale strands of hair.

Of course she wondered if he was seeing another woman. That thought was always there. But other than the long hours away from her and the apartment, away from their life, he didn't show any of the other signs of cheating. But how would she even know? She rarely saw him anymore.

Tears pushed behind her eyes, and those nagging questions were there again. Would he ever propose? Where were they going? Had she wasted three years of her life already, following Thomas to California? At least to the last question she could answer a firm no. She hadn't wasted her time. She'd landed a good job with the *Los Angeles Times* as a beat reporter and was on the fast track to becoming a feature writer. Her editor loved her work and had all but promised a promotion next year.

Her mobile phone rang on the counter where it had been recharging overnight. For an instant she thought it might be Thomas, calling to apologize, to say he was leaving the shop right now and she should be ready when he got home because he was taking her out and they were going to spend the whole day together. She picked up the phone and looked at the caller ID.

Her father. She hadn't spoken to him in months.

She let the phone ring three times, unsure if she wanted to answer it or not. What could he be calling about? She glanced at the clock on the microwave. It was nine thirty on the East Coast. The phone rang again. Once more and her voice mail would pick it up.

Forcing her thumb to move, she hit the talk button and said, "Hi, Dad."

"Good morning, Berty." He hesitated. He was the only one who ever called her that. "I wasn't sure if you'd be awake yet." His voice sounded thin, tired. Worried, even.

"Being out of bed and being awake are two different things. I haven't had my coffee yet."

"Do you want me to call back in a half hour?"

"No, no. It's fine. What's the matter?" She knew this wasn't just a cordial phone call to check in, see how she was doing. Dad hadn't done that in…she couldn't remember the last time. Then again, when was the last time she'd called him?

There was silence on the other end, and for a second she thought she'd lost the connection.

"Berty, your mother has cancer."

That was it. No preparation. No *How are things in California?* Of course, she'd asked what was wrong. She wasn't exactly Miss Small Talk herself. She didn't know what to say.

He waited, then said, "It's colon cancer, and it doesn't look the greatest."

Look the greatest? As if there was a type of cancer that looked great? Dad never was that good with words.

Finally she found her voice. "Is it treatable?"

"We're not sure. She needs to get a CAT scan to see if it's spread to any other organs. She's looking at surgery to remove the tumor, then radiation, chemo, the works."

Tumor. Radiation. Chemo. CAT scan. The words sounded so alien, so cold and malicious. And yet she felt nothing. "And the prognosis?"

Again, the silence. "It depends on whether it's spread or not."

"When's the CAT scan?"

"Tomorrow. Eleven o'clock."

"How…how are you?"

"We're hanging in there." His voice cracked. "Your mother,

you know how she is, she doesn't want to believe it. She won't accept it."

Yes, Roberta knew exactly how she was. "She's in denial."

"Yeah. But reality will hit soon enough." He paused, and she heard him draw in a deep breath. "Berty..."

Roberta knew what was coming and shut her eyes. *Don't do this, Dad.*

"...do you think you can come out here and see her?"

That was the real reason he'd called, to ask her to come to Virginia and see her mother. The mother she hadn't spoken to in over a year. The mother with whom she had no relationship and never had, at least not that she could remember.

She hesitated, tried to collect her thoughts, form her argument. "Dad...I don't think it's a good time right now."

He'd expected that answer from her, of course he had. He'd have to be delusional if he thought she'd just spurt out *Well sure, Dad, I'll hop on the next flight out of LA and be there by this evening.* No, he wasn't dumb. Her father had spent his life working with his hands, but he was one of the smartest men she'd ever known.

Still he said nothing, and she felt compelled to explain further. "The newspaper, they need me. I can't just drop everything and leave them high and dry."

Yeah, they really needed someone to cover the upcoming city council meeting.

"And Thomas's coffee shop is really taking off, and I need to be here for him."

As if Thomas even knew she was there.

"And...and then the price of airline tickets. Reporting isn't exactly the highest-paying job."

As if she spent her money on anything else.

He said, "I understand."

She believed he did; he understood completely the friction that existed between his youngest daughter and his wife. No, more like the gulf. There was no *friction*, because they were too far apart, physically and every other way. He didn't argue with her, that wasn't his style, didn't even try to lay on the guilt. But the disappointment in his voice was evident.

She should have said she'd ask off work next week, get some money together, kiss Thomas good-bye, and be there for him if not for her, but she didn't. Instead she just said, "I'm sorry, Dad."

"Berty, I love you. I want you to know that. I know you and your mother don't see eye to eye—"

"Dad—"

"No, let me finish. It wasn't always like that, though. You don't remember, but she was a different person, a different mother. You're so much like her when she was your age. Independent. Full of life and dreams. She loves you too. She does. She loves all you kids. She's just not good at showing it."

"I love you too, Dad." And she did. She'd always gotten along well with her father. At home she was Daddy's little girl. It wasn't until she up and followed Thomas to California that their relationship deteriorated.

"I'll keep you updated," he said. "Good-bye, Berty."

"'Bye, Dad."

The phone went dead, and Roberta placed it on the counter. Her mind spun in circles so fast it made her dizzy. She sat on a barstool and put her head in her hands. Her mother had cancer. Dad wanted her to fly to Virginia to see her. Why? It must be worse than he was saying. But through all the mental debris one thing kept running through her head. *You don't remember, but she was a different person, a different mother.*

No, she didn't remember. Or did she? She'd had a recurring dream for the past year or so. It was a simple dream, really, nothing elaborate, and only lasted moments. She was just a child, maybe one or two, sitting on her mother's lap while they rocked and her mother sang a lullaby.

Baby, my sweet, don't you cry. Baby, my sweet, don't you fear. Mommy will take care of you, I'm here.

But it was more than the image and sound that remained with Roberta after she awoke each time; it was a feeling. Love, security, a vivid sense of belonging, comfort. She was in her mommy's lap, and there was no place on earth she'd rather be.

She'd always thought the dream was her damaged psyche conjuring what should have been, what it had longed for as a young child.

She needed to talk to someone. Thomas. He'd listen to her, offer some advice. He might be busy with the coffee shop, but he'd stop to talk to her. He was there for her when she really needed him.

So why did she feel so alone?

Chapter Seven

ELIA SHUT THE DOOR BEHIND her and leaned against it, keeping her distance from Ken's desk. She folded her arms across her chest. Ken knew that look. It meant trouble was on the horizon. He wasn't in the mood for a fight.

"Celia, look, I'm not up for this, okay? If you want me to eat breakfast with the family, then fine, I'll eat with the family. I'll just have to stay at the office a little later this evening getting stuff done." He lifted the pile of documents and let it fall back to the desk.

The look he received didn't change. "You think this is about eating breakfast with us once in a while?" she said. "Boy, you really are out of touch, aren't you?"

"What's that supposed to mean?"

"Ken, when's the last time we actually sat down and had a meal as a family? Any meal. Do you even know? When's the last time you did *anything* with the family?"

Ken pointed a finger at his wife. "That's not fair, Celia, and you know it. I've been very busy lately with—"

"Yes, with your cases. Always the cases. Your job is always more important than your family."

"I do my job *for* my family." He felt blood rush to his face. "You think I get up early, go to bed late, and put in long hours in between because I like overworking? I do it for you, for the kids, so you can have a comfortable life."

"But we don't want a comfortable life, Ken. We want you. Are you willing to give up some of your status at the firm, even the promotion, to save your family?"

Was she giving him an ultimatum? "'That's not fair." He nearly yelled it. "You can't make me choose."

"Why not? You have no problem sacrificing us for the job, no problem clearing your schedule for meetings, phone calls, research, more meetings. You make work a priority—*the* priority. Are you willing to do the same for us?"

He didn't say anything. He felt like a witness who had just been cornered by a slick trial lawyer. Celia should have been the attorney.

She dipped her head, put both hands to her mouth, and choked out a sob.

"Oh, come on," Ken said. "There's no need to cry."

He started to stand to cross the room and do his husbandly duty of yielding to her tears, but she stopped him. "No, stay there." She took a moment to compose herself, wiped at her tears, brushed back her hair. "I can't take it anymore, Ken. I feel like a widow. You're here but you're not here. Present but miles away. I miss you, your kids miss you. Robby just came to me in tears because he was so excited to show you the airplane he'd made, and you brushed him off."

Ken sat back in his chair and let her talk. She needed to get this off her chest; he'd let her say it.

"You've chosen what's more important to you, and it's your job."

Ken nearly knocked his chair over standing up. "Now wait a minute. You can't say that. I told you, I do what I do *for* my family, not *instead* of my family."

"Why don't you ask us what *we* want, Ken? Whether we'd rather have a big house and fancy pool in a ritzy neighborhood, or if I'd rather have my husband around and the kids have their daddy to play with them, read to them, fly their paper airplanes with them, for Pete's sake? They don't care if you're a big-time lawyer or a ditch digger. They just want their daddy to be there. To be *here*."

Ken drew in a deep breath and closed his eyes. He wasn't the yelling type. He was a lawyer; he reasoned with people, made his arguments and proved his point, showed them where they were wrong and he was correct. But with Celia there was no reasoning, especially when she got angry.

Celia turned halfway to the door and put her hand on the knob. "I'm leaving, Ken. Today."

"What? What do you mean, leaving?"

She looked him directly in the eyes, and what he found in hers put chills up and down his arms. "When you come home from work tonight, we won't be here."

"You're taking the kids from me? You can't do that. Where will you go?"

"To my parents." Her parents lived an hour's drive west, in Barrington Hills. "We both need the time apart, you know we do. You need time to think about what you really want in life, what really matters to you. I need some time away too, to think."

"And what about the kids? What do they need?"

"A daddy. One who will be there for them, who's willing to put everything aside to do something with them. One who's willing to sacrifice for them and doesn't ask them to make the sacrifice."

Ken shook his head. If he weren't so angry he would have laughed at the irony of the whole thing—the divorce attorney whose own marriage was on the rocks. One would think after dealing with so many couples who didn't know how to make marriage work, he would have learned from their mistakes.

Celia looked away, then back at him, tears in her eyes. "I'll tell Robby we're going on a vacation to Pop-Pop and Grammy's. We'll take Amber too, of course. Feel free to call us in the evenings to say good night." She opened the door to go out, but Ken spoke.

"Celia, wait."

She rested her forehead against the edge of the door and shut her eyes. "What."

"That was my dad on the phone. My mother has cancer. Colon."

She opened her eyes, turned her head. "Is it bad?"

Ken shrugged. "Don't know yet. She gets a CAT scan tomorrow to see if it's spread."

Celia stepped back into the room and shut the door so it was open only an inch or two. "I'm sorry, Ken, really I am, but it doesn't change any of this."

"I know. I just thought you'd want to know. Do what you feel you need to do."

"Don't make me the bad guy here."

"You're the one leaving, taking the kids from their home."

"This?" She waved her hand above her head. "This isn't a home; it's a house. There is no *home*. I'm doing what's best for our family."

"I disagree."

"Oh, do you? And I guess you're going to cross-examine me now, counselor? Is that right?"

"Knock it off. I just don't think taking the kids away is the answer." He wasn't about to beg her to stay, wasn't going to make promises he couldn't keep. He wouldn't stand in her way, either; that would only make things worse.

Celia slumped her shoulders. He could tell she was weary of the arguing, weary of the constant tension between them. Too bad she didn't realize she was partly to blame. If she would only try to understand where he was coming from, to see things from his viewpoint. But she only saw what she wanted to see.

"This isn't a punishment, you know," she said. "I just... I need some space, some time to think. And you do too."

"Why don't you let me be the judge of that?"

She hesitated, then was out the door, pulling it closed behind her.

Ken tilted his head back and looked at the ceiling. He felt like he'd totally lost control of everything in life, like it was spinning in wide, wild circles and there was nothing he could do to corral it. Frustration boiled up within in, and he snatched his pen off the desk and threw it across the room. It hit the far wall and bounced to the floor.

Chapter Eight

JIM CLICKED OFF THE PHONE and put it back in its cradle. His heart ached for Roberta, not because she wouldn't come to Virginia—he knew she wouldn't—but because she seemed so lost, so starved for attention. He'd tried to give it to her, tried to make up for what was lost in Nena's preoccupation with the ranch, but he was a dad, and what did a father know of raising a girl to become a woman? She needed her mother, but Nena was too busy.

He didn't blame Nena. He couldn't; he loved her too much. She was only doing what she thought was best for the family and for the ranch, and in a way Jim admired her for that. She was such a strong woman, so determined, so focused.

Pushing back from the desk, Jim stood and headed out of the study and through the back door of the house. He crossed the yard and entered the mare stable. At one time every stall had been occupied by a mare and her foal. The smells came back to him then, and the sounds of horses snorting and foals whinnying, people's voices as they came and went, hooves tamping the dry ground. He loved this place.

Walking to the end stall, Jim ran his hand over the smooth wood. It was right here that he first met and fell in love with Nena.

The St. Claire Horse Farm was located a good twenty miles west of the town of Monroe. They drove with the windows down and Mexican music blaring at ear-bursting volume. Juan was a careful driver, taking his time and staying within the speed limit. He said

little during the drive except to point out when they had entered St. Claire land. It took thirty more minutes to reach the entrance, a straight lane lined with black willows, their branches hanging motionless in the still air. At the far end Jimmy saw the stables, four large, columned buildings painted pale yellow.

The sight of the farm and the stables put a rock in his belly. He was really doing this, leaving home and branching out on his own. The farm had been the only life he'd ever known. He knew nothing of thoroughbreds. The Hutchings had one horse on their farm, Miss Molly, and she never did anything more than graze and eat her oats.

Juan stopped the truck in front of one of the stables and shut off the engine. He looked around, drew in a deep breath, and smiled, his eyes crinkling at the corners. "The smell of the farm," he said. "I love it; don't you?"

Jimmy did. The scent of hay and manure, it was what he'd grown up with. But here, there was no manure odor, just hay and barley, dirt, and fresh, clean air. He smiled. "Sure do. Can you point me to Cricket?"

Juan stepped out of the truck and motioned for Jimmy to come closer. Partially covering his mouth with his hand, he said, "You know, Cricket, he don't like funny business, you know?"

Jimmy nodded. "Sure, no funny business."

"Okay. This way, follow me."

Jimmy grabbed his duffel bag. "Wait."

Juan turned and raised his eyebrows.

"What's funny business?"

"Horsin' around," Juan said, then burst into laughter, pointing at Jimmy like he'd just pulled off the practical joke of the century on the new kid.

Jimmy shook his head and followed Juan to the far stable building. To the left of it was an office, and in the office was the man they called Cricket. He looked to be about sixty, with leathery, tanned skin stretched tight over his gaunt face. Tall, thin, with wiry legs *that seemed disproportionately long, it was immediately apparent how he'd gotten his name.*

Juan motioned with his thumb. "This is Jimmy. He wants the job in the stables."

Cricket eyed Jimmy up and down as if he were the insect and had been placed under a magnifying glass. "Jimmy who?"

Juan shrugged. "I don't know, Jimmy the kid?"

"Hutching, sir." Jimmy said. "Jimmy Hutching."

"You have any experience with farm work, son?" Cricket's voice was high and raspy.

"I grew up on a dairy farm outside Monroe, sir. Been doing farm work my whole life."

"Well, you got the build for it. Ever work around horses?"

"No, sir." He didn't think mentioning Miss Molly would help his cause. "But I'm a fast learner and good with animals."

"You good with people too?"

"I try to get along with everyone."

Cricket nodded. "Good. Don't need no troublemakers stirring things up around here. We deal with million-dollar horses, you hear? They come first. Can't have a buncha rowdies gettin' the horses all spooked."

"Yes, sir." Jimmy immediately took a liking to Cricket. He seemed tough but fair.

"Good. How'd you find out about the job?"

"Bill Mosley sent me."

Cricket's eyes brightened. "Mosley? How is he?"

Jimmy shrugged, remembering what Mosley had done to his father. "He's in good health. Tough guy."

"The toughest." The older man paused, crossed his arms, and leaned against his desk. "Well, you seem like a good kid. Let's give it a go. Come by here first thing in the morning, and we'll get all the papers signed and get you on the payroll. Sound okay?"

"Yes, sir. Absolutely."

"Good." He stuck out his hand, and Jimmy shook it. "Juan, show

Jimmy where the bunkhouse is. And son"—he drilled Jimmy with a look—"don't disappoint me. Just do your job and keep to yourself and you'll do fine."

The bunkhouse was a long, squat building that housed stable hands and grounds workers, fifteen in all, thirteen of them Mexicans. Jimmy had a small room he was to share with another hand. It included two beds, two dressers, a small black-and-white TV, a standing swivel fan, and a small closet. There were two shared bathrooms with showers, one at each end of the building.

After dumping his duffel on the bed, Jimmy walked to the window and put a hand on the screen. Little air moved outside. It would be a hot night, and he wasn't sure the fan would do the job. From where he stood he could see the stables and workers coming and going; their day would wind down soon.

For the first time since he entered Jake's he thought of his mother and wondered what she was doing at that very moment. He imagined her standing by the kitchen window, gazing into the distance, wondering where he was, what he was up to. He could see the tears on her cheeks and almost feel the pain in the pit of her stomach. He'd hated to leave her, but his dad was right. It was time for him to make his own way in the world. Ed Hutching had suggested it for all the wrong reasons, but he was right nonetheless.

Jimmy was glad he'd found work so close to home though. He'd go back, maybe next week, stop in and see how his mom was making out. He'd try to find time to do it during the day so he wouldn't run into his father.

Exiting the bunkhouse, Jimmy headed to the stables to get acquainted with his new environment. Outside the sun was almost gone, and a moody orange light dusted the farm. For as far as he could see in any direction, rolling hills of the greenest grass, like the sea frozen in mid-undulation, spread to the horizon. The western sky was alternating shades of orange and pink with fingers of color protruding into the deepening blue above it. He drew a deep breath and took in the aroma of grass and hay, of freedom and a new beginning.

The stables closest to the bunkhouse housed the mares, twenty in each building. Some had foals in the stall with them; some were still obviously pregnant. Jimmy stopped by one stall and peered through the iron bars. A mother, dark brown, was there with her foal, a lighter shade of brown and balancing itself on long, spindly legs. It teetered and wobbled and nudged its nose under the mother until it eventually found its source of food.

A commotion to his left caught Jimmy's attention—shuffling feet, hushed, urgent voices. A group of people had gathered around one of the stalls.

Someone caught his arm. "Hey, you the new guy?"

Jimmy turned and faced a young woman, he guessed about his age, sandy brown hair, green eyes, a smattering of freckles across her nose and cheeks. A dog circled his feet and sniffed at his pant leg.

"Uh, yeah, Jimmy Hutching." He reached down to pet the dog's head.

"That's Hickory. You ever see a foal being born, Jimmy Hutching?"

"No. Plenty of calves, but no horses."

"You're a farm boy?"

"Dairy farmer."

She started toward the far stall, where more people had gathered. "Well, c'mon. You get a front-row seat to witness the miracle of life."

He caught up to her. "Do you work here too?"

"Sure do. Wouldn't have it any other way." Her steps were quick and smooth, the walk of someone who felt comfortable in her environment.

"What's your name?" Something about her immediately attracted him. Sure, she was beautiful; anyone with at least one working eye could see that, but there was something else, an aura about her, a confidence that he found appealing and made him want to get to know her better.

"Nena. And this"—she spread her arms and turned to face him—"is my element." Her face beamed like a summer sunrise.

They arrived at the stall, and Nena pushed her way through a group of men. Jimmy stuck close and soon found the wall with his new friend. The mare was on her side, breathing heavily.

"We knew she'd foal tonight," Nena said.

"How'd you know that?"

"She hasn't eaten any of her oats all day; that's a sure sign."

The mare rocked back and forth, tried to stand, snorted, and dropped her head to the straw bedding.

"She's in active labor," Nena said. "Poor girl. But this is her third foal, so she's been here before."

Again the mare lifted her head. Her eyes rolled back in their sockets, and she snorted loudly.

"This foal is quite the celebrity already."

"Why's that?"

"The sire was Mercury's Dream, undefeated as a two-year-old and a consistent winner as a three-year-old. One of the flat-out fastest runners ever. And the mother here, Devious Driver, has the endurance of ten horses. They say her heart is the size of a basketball. So this little foal is getting the perfect combination of speed and endurance. You ever hear of Secretariat, Jimmy Hutching?"

"Uh, I guess. Sure."

"You guess, sure? He's only the greatest racehorse of all time. He was a machine when he was running."

"Okay."

"Well, word is, this little foal is going to make Secretariat's records look like child's play. There's a lot riding on this little one."

Suddenly a burst of liquid shot from the mare's tail end, and she moaned, chuffed, snorted. Her abdominal muscles contracted fiercely and relaxed.

Nena leaned closer to Jimmy. "That was the water breaking."

Nothing new there. He'd seen it happen a hundred times with cows.

"She needs to get the foal out soon now."

The mare pushed again, rocked back and forth, tried to stand, but fell back onto the hay, exhausted.

Seconds ticked by and nothing happened; the mare lay nearly motionless, the only movement being the contraction of her abdominals and an occasional snort.

"So what brings you to our ranch?" Nena said, keeping her voice low and eyes on the mare.

Jimmy wasn't about to spill his family's problems during their first meeting, tell her how his dad had become a drunk and beat his mother, how he'd taken his frustrations out on his family and ordered Jimmy to pack his stuff and hit the pavement. "I just needed a change of scenery."

"Geographically or philosophically?"

That was an interesting question. "Both, I guess."

"Oh, look." Nena pointed at the mare, a look of wonderment and excitement brightening her face. A single hoofed foot now protruded from just below the tail. "The other foot should come soon. Horses are born feet first, did you know that?"

"Nope."

"Front legs, then head, then hind end. Like they're diving out."

The leg inched out farther, but the second one didn't follow. Two women in jeans jumped into the stall and approached the horse cautiously. One wore a rubber glove up to her right shoulder. The tension in the small group that had gathered around the stall increased noticeably.

Nena's hand went to her cheek. "That's the vet and her assistant. She's going to have to push it back in and try to get the other leg to come out."

The vet grasped the protruding leg and gently pushed it back into the birth canal. Her arm went in as well. The mare groaned and knocked her head against the ground. Minutes passed, every tick of the clock crucial now. Finally the vet eased her arm out and backed away. The mare rocked and tried to stand again, then relaxed and slumped to the ground. She groaned and chuffed, contracted her abdominals. Moments later the foreleg appeared again, but this time it was followed by the second leg.

Nena clapped. "Come on, little horsey, you can do it. Come into the world." She was in her own place, eyes wide and puddled with tears, hands at her mouth, rocking back and forth on her heels. Jimmy said nothing, not wanting to ruin the moment for the horse or Nena.

Eventually the head slid out, and the vet ran into the stall again. She grasped the forelegs just above the hooves and pulled the foal toward the mother's hind legs. Slowly, inch by inch, while the mare groaned and snorted, the vet worked at the foal until its hind legs appeared and slid out easily. The foal moved erratically while the vet's assistant went to work cleaning it up.

Tears streamed down Nena's cheeks, and Jimmy couldn't help but tear up. She looked at him and smiled. "Jimmy, you're crying."

He smiled back at her but said nothing. He didn't want to disrespect the moment by making some excuse about dust getting in his eyes. He sniffed, blinked away the tears, and straightened his shoulders.

Nena cocked her head to one side. She'd made no attempt to wipe at her own tears. They left long, silvery tracks to her jawline. "I'm glad you're here, Jimmy Hutching."

Jimmy nodded. The moment had gotten to him and stirred up emotions simmering just beneath the surface. The foal, Nena... after such a day. A lump formed in his throat. He wasn't the crying type, but the contrast between this place and the dairy farm was so stark, and the tension released after the birth and thinking about his mother back home with his drunk father was just too much. He knew if he opened his mouth at that moment there would be no stopping the tears. And he didn't want to cry in front of Nena.

She patted his arm and grinned. "You have a good night, you hear?"

Again, he only nodded.

Jimmy headed back to the bunkhouse, walking along a path worn to the bare soil by the boots and sneakers of men and women from all walks of life but with one common love: horses. He felt unworthy to walk where they had trod. Above the sky had darkened, and stars made their appearance.

He thought again of his home and wondered what his parents were doing. No, he knew exactly what they were doing. Mom was on the sofa knitting a new pair of mittens or a scarf or maybe a sweater, and Dad was glued to the TV, working on a beer while he drifted in and out of sleep.

At the bunkhouse Jimmy met his roommate for the first time, a tightly muscled, middle-aged man with a wild crop of wiry, graying hair and a handful of gaps in his teeth. He lay on his side on the cot, head propped by one hand.

"Hey, name's Jumper." He had a lazy Southern drawl and looked Jimmy up and down with narrowed eyes, as if he were an extinct creature only just now discovered to be still alive and well.

"I'm Jimmy." He extended his hand, but Jumper didn't even look at it.

"You the farm boy they just hired?"

"If I'm the only one they hired."

"Saw you gettin' tight with the boss's daughter. You plannin' on makin' a move?"

"Boss's daughter?"

"Pretty little thing, ain't she?"

Jimmy shrugged, trying to hide the fact that he'd been caught off guard. "Sure, she's attractive."

Jumper sat up on the edge of the bed, lifted a tin cup, and spit a wad of black saliva into it. "She didn't tell you she was a St. Claire, did she?"

"Does it matter?"

"Does it matter? Does it matter if a horse's got four legs or not?" He spit again. "Not only is she a St. Claire, which puts her off limits for grunts like us, but she's engaged."

"Good for her." He couldn't ignore the twinge of disappointment in his chest.

Jumper shook his finger at Jimmy. "I'd stay away from her if I's you. She's to marry Theodore McGovern. The third. Two a them's been datin' since they were old enough to know what it was. It was like some kinda arranged marriage or something."

"Who's he?" Jimmy had never heard the name before.

"Only the son of one of the richest horse owners 'round here. Ever hear a' Mercury's Dream?"

"The sire of the foal that was just born."

"Yeah, and guess who the owner was."

He didn't have to guess. "The prince of Arabia."

The finger wagged, and Jumper spit into his cup again. "You watch yourself, farm boy. The McGoverns are some powerful people, you know?"

"Sure." He stripped out of his clothes and slipped into a pair of shorts and a clean T-shirt. The cot, though small and bumpy, felt good, comfortable enough.

Jumper lay back down and stared at the ceiling. "She is somethin' else, though, ain't she?"

Jimmy didn't answer, but silently agreed. She was something else. Nena St. Claire, the boss's daughter, engaged to the prince of Arabia. Off limits. Cricket's words came back to him: Don't disappoint me. Just do your job and keep to yourself and you'll do fine.

Words to live by, indeed.

Jim ran his hand over the smooth wood once again. That was some evening. He'd lain awake most of the night thinking about Nena and those green eyes and that wide smile. He thought he'd never talk to her again. Surely she was out of his league. What would she want with a farm boy when she had Ted McGovern, the prince of Arabia?

But how things had changed, how they had gone against

everything he'd expected. He'd never spoken about all of it, not even to Nena. It was a burden he carried, a secret he'd kept tucked away for decades.

Jim made his way out of the stable and back across the yard, into the house, into the study. He took his seat behind the desk again and picked up the phone. He still had one more child to call.

Chapter Nine

LIFE HAD SUDDENLY GOTTEN VERY complicated for Barb Mackey. She sat on the barstool by her counter, holding the little white business card in her hand. She didn't want to make the phone call, knowing what would follow, knowing the pain and suffering it would cause her and her family. Life would be turned on its head and shaken violently. She thought of her two children: Kara, so independent at thirteen and yet still so childlike, and Mikey, just ten and such a momma's boy. How would they deal with it? And Doug…what a support he'd been already, but how would he hold up when things got much worse and the bulk of the responsibility fell on his shoulders?

Suddenly the card seemed to be made of lead. She dropped it, staring at it as it lay there, a lifeless cut of paper with the power to wield such fear and anxiety. She imagined a mouth forming and laughing at her, taunting her about the pain it would inflict, the disruption, the mayhem.

But this was a valley they all had to traverse. There was no way around it, only through. She and Doug planned to tell the kids tonight, after she made the call and had everything set up.

Barb's hand trembled ever so slightly, as if a cold wind had given it a shiver. Picking up the phone, she pushed the numbers before she could talk herself out of it. Before the other line could ring once, her phone buzzed, signaling a waiting call. The screen said it was her dad. She hit the button to disconnect from the one number and connect to her father's.

"Dad?"

"Barbara, it's me."

"Is something wrong?" His voice didn't sound right; it wasn't strong and sure like it usually was.

"It's your mother."

"Is she okay?"

He paused, sniffed. "She has cancer, Barbara, in her colon."

Tears puddled in Barb's eyes, as if someone had given a spigot only a quarter turn, just enough to allow the water to seep out. Her chest tightened, throat constricted. "How bad?"

"We don't know yet." He told her about the CAT scan and the plan to meet with the oncologist.

Barb fingered the card in her hand. "Dad, I'm sorry. How's Mom doing with it?"

"She hasn't said a whole lot. You know how she is. She's angry and scared. I don't think she wants to face the reality of it."

"Did you tell Roberta and Kenny?"

"I just got off the phone with them. I wanted to call you last."

"And how did they react?" She knew her brother and sister had no real relationship with their mother, especially Roberta.

"As I expected. Berty with apathy, Kenny with offers of money."

"Can you blame them though?"

"She's still their mother."

"I know."

There was another pause, so long that Barb had to ask, "Dad, you still there?"

"Yes." His voice was small, distant.

"What is it?"

"Barbara, can you come see her?"

Barb and Doug had moved their family to northern Pennsylvania four years ago. They were a seven-hour drive from her parents but had only been to see them twice. She stared at the business card still in her hand. The office name, the bold black letters, appeared to grow until they filled her whole field of vision.

"I…I'm sorry, Dad, I can't right now. I have something I need to do here first." She knew the one call she needed to make would set off a series of events that would keep her from going to see her mother for months, possibly.

"Are you okay?"

"Yeah, I don't know. No, I'm fine. Please, don't worry about me. Take care of Mom and yourself, and let me know when you hear something about the scan."

"I will. Are you sure you're okay?"

"Yes, Dad, please...I'll be fine. Really."

"Okay. I love you, Barb."

Her dad's words brought a lump to her throat, and she had to force the words past it. "Love you too."

Barb clicked off the phone and let the tears come again. Like a summer downpour they came in waves, robbing breath from her lungs. After a few minutes she'd settled enough to get a glass of water, dry her eyes, and pick up the card again. She still had a call to make.

Chapter Ten

THE SUNNY BEAN, THOMAS'S BABY and first love, was located on the Ocean Front Walk overlooking Venice Beach. Vendors selling wares of every kind dotted the walkway, finding minimal shade under the tall palms. Shirtless men in board shorts and bikini-clad women roller-skated along the concrete walk, bopping to the rhythm of whatever tunes their earbuds fed them. Roberta loved the Walk and its carnival-like atmosphere. Thomas couldn't have found a better location for his coffee shop.

Outside the shop an elderly vendor in traditional Rastafarian clothing had a wide array of paintings spread on the concrete and a sign that read ALL ARTWORK $15. Roberta wondered if he was the artist or merely the peddler.

Dry heat rolled off the sun-bleached sand and brought out a warm sweat on her forehead. But as soon as she swung the coffee shop's door open, two things hit her: the cool relief of the air-conditioned interior and the smell of coffee. She could even pick out the aroma of the French vanilla cappuccino, her favorite. The small interior was furnished with cherry café-style tables, each accompanied by two simple brushed steel and cherry chairs. The walls were painted milk chocolate with white trim. The contrast had been her idea, and it looked beautiful. Thomas worked behind the counter while Erica, his summer college help, ran the register and charmed the patrons. She was young, attractive, and got to spend more time with Thomas than Roberta did.

Roberta scolded herself for being so jealous. But it was more than jealousy, wasn't it? She was suspicious. Was Erica the woman stealing Thomas's heart and time?

Again she chided herself. Thomas had to hire help. The coffee shop had really taken off, and he simply couldn't handle the register and the orders by himself anymore. What was he to do, turn Erica down because she was pretty and fit and had those gorgeous brown eyes?

Roberta had waited until midafternoon to visit, knowing the morning rush would be over and Thomas would more likely be able to slip away for a few minutes. All morning she'd fretted over her father's phone call, alternating between anger and remorse. Anger because she felt like her dad was using her mother's cancer as a ploy to get her home, away from California, and remorse because she felt so bad that it had come to that—using an illness like cancer to attempt healing. And then there was the disappointment in her father's voice when she'd soundly rejected his plea with such lame, even trivial excuses.

There were only a handful of customers at the tables, sipping coffee and chatting quietly. Not one had looked up when she walked through the door. No one recognized her as the owner's girlfriend. Erica was taking money from a man at the register, smiling prettily and batting those dazzling eyes. Thomas had his back to her, mixing a smoothie.

Roberta caught Erica's eye and smiled and waved. Erica smiled back, glanced at Thomas, and said something. He turned around and handed the customer his drink.

His eyes found Roberta. At six two and just over two hundred pounds, Thomas was nicely built and athletic. His cropped hair only highlighted the gray that dusted his head. In the café's light it seemed to glisten like silver.

"Hey, babe, how are you?" He busied himself with cleaning the counter while he talked. "What brings you this way?"

She shrugged. "Just out for a walk. It was supposed to be our day, remember?"

"Yeah, I know. So sorry about that. Nikki was supposed to help out, but she called in. Something about her dog having to go to the vet. Are we good for another time?"

A couple entered the café and stood in front of the menu board.

"Afternoon, folks," Thomas said to them, putting on his best smile, the one that had won Roberta's heart. "Whenever you're ready, Erica will be glad to help you out."

Roberta stepped closer to the counter and lowered her voice so it felt like their conversation was just between the two of them. "How's the day going?"

"Busy. We had a killer morning. Something going on out there today?"

"Not that I know of. Just a normal day in Venice. Hey, can we talk?"

He looked at the customers. "Now? Babe, I have to work, you know."

"Can't Erica handle things for a few minutes?" She knew she was pitting herself against the café, and maybe against Erica.

Thomas knitted his brow. "Babe, I'm sorry. It's not like that. I have to spend some time in the books this afternoon. You know—" He lowered his voice even more. "Countin' the cash and all that." His grin widened.

"Tonight then?" Roberta didn't try to hide the disappointment in her voice and didn't miss the quick glance Thomas cast Erica's way before answering.

"I'll be home as soon as I can, like always. As soon as we get things closed up here and all the books squared away." Again, the smile. "I promise. Then we can sit up and talk into the wee hours of the morning. Deal?"

She nodded and forced a smile. "Sure. Deal. Wee hours."

Roberta walked back to the apartment, dropped onto the bed, and buried her face in her pillow.

Chapter Eleven

HE EVENING WAS COOL ENOUGH that Jim needed to slip on a jacket and brew a mug of hot tea to go outside and sit on the porch. It was late, and Nena had already gone to bed. Despite the chilly temperature, he left the front door open. Closing it didn't feel right, as if he were closing the door of his heart to his wife while she slept upstairs.

Across the front lawn a low mist moved with the speed of the tide, so slowly it was almost imperceptible. The light from the porch reached out maybe ten, fifteen yards, then was swallowed by the thick darkness of the evening. Beyond the veil of black he could see nothing. The lane just disappeared, the trees faded, as if the earth really was flat and the ranch positioned just feet from the edge, as if Jim could descend the porch steps and take no more than fifteen strides before he'd vanish into nothingness. For a moment, an instant only, the thought appealed to him. His wife had cancer, an ugly, deformed monster growing inside her, spreading its venom, poisoning her cells, and his children all made excuses for why they couldn't come see her. He loved his children—more than life itself—and didn't blame them for the expanse that existed between him and Nena and them. But their apathy still cut deep.

He remembered when times were happier, when laughter was abundant, when Kenny raced around the front lawn with a cowboy hat on his head and six-shooters at his hips. Sheriff Shooter, that's what he called himself. He remembered Roberta crawling around on the porch picking up Cheerios. He remembered the first time Barbara sat on a horse. She was only three, but he could see in her eyes that she was hooked. After that all she wanted to do was "ride the horsey." He remembered when Nena laughed often and smiled all the time. She loved this ranch, loved the horses, the action, the workers, the business side of it. This was where she belonged.

Jim sipped at his tea and shook his head. And now look at them, a family fractured. But were they irreparable? Only time would tell.

Through the open door he heard Nena call his name. He glanced at his watch. It was after eleven. She'd gone to bed two hours ago.

Leaving the porch, Jim entered the house and shut the door behind him. He set his mug on the table in the foyer and headed up the stairs. Floorboards whined under his weight. At the top of the staircase he stopped and listened, said his wife's name, but there was no answer.

Suddenly a morbid thought shoved its way into his head. What if the monster inside Nena had claimed its victory already? What if the cry of his name had been her final breath, her final plea to be rescued from the grip of death? He bolted for the bedroom. Nena was on her back, arms at her side. Enough moonlight filtered past the blinds to see her face, the closed eyes, the mouth slightly agape. Jim's heart paused its beating while he reached toward her. He rested his hand on her forehead and felt the warmth. She moaned and rolled over, pulling the covers to her shoulder.

Jim shut his eyes and clenched his jaw. *Get a grip, Jimmy.*

After stripping out of his clothes and slipping into his pajamas, he got into bed next to Nena and spooned his wife, his hand on her hip. She stirred a little and moaned again, a pathetic sound of sorrow and loss. He had no idea if she dreamed or not, but he supposed that if she were dreaming, it was anything but pleasant. He brushed her hair to the side and lightly kissed the back of her neck. "I love you."

It didn't take him long to slip into those warm waters of sleep.

But the dreams that found him there were disjointed and violent, filled with flames and writhing bodies. Several times he awoke (or maybe he wasn't awake, he couldn't tell) and thought he saw Nena standing in the corner of their bedroom. One time he even said her name out loud. But each time he was quickly pulled back under by sleep's firm grip.

At 3:12 a.m. Jim startled, snapped awake by something in his dream, an urgency, but he immediately forgot what it was. He tried to remember, but his brain was still in a sleep fog and churned slowly. But it was there, right before him, just out of memory's reach: that needing to do something or go somewhere or warn someone. To his right Nena rolled to her back and mumbled something incoherent. She raised an arm and thrashed at the air, grunted from the effort. Then she began to weep. Jim had never seen her cry in her sleep before. She spoke again.

Jim rolled to face her. "What is it, honey? Say it again." He spoke quietly so as not to wake her.

Tears seeped from Nena's closed eyes, cascaded over her temples and got lost in her graying hair. She whimpered then said, "I'm at the end of it all."

She said it a few more times, each time more declarative than the previous. Jim did his best to sooth her. He combed her hair with his hand, kissed her cheek, her forehead. Eventually she settled back into a comfortable sleep.

It had been four days since Jimmy Hutching left his home on the farm and embarked on a new life on the St. Claire horse farm. Yesterday Jumper had slapped him on the back and said, "Well, what do ya think? Is the dairy princess ready to fly solo?"

Solo meant working without Jumper peering over his shoulder and breathing down his neck, and Jimmy knew he was. The work wasn't much different from what he was used to on the farm, though the horses were a bit more testy than dairy cows. Thoroughbreds were known for being high-strung, especially when they were as spoiled as the St. Claire thoroughbreds.

Jimmy lifted a shovelful of manure and dropped it into the wheelbarrow. He'd spent the last two hours mucking out the stalls and laying down a fresh bed of straw. Outside in the sun the heat was nearly unbearable, but in the stables, with a breeze moving through the center alleyway and the direct rays blocked from reaching the horses, it was cooler. But still, sweat soaked his shirt and matted his hair to his forehead.

He hadn't seen Nena since they'd watched the foal's birth the other night, but Jimmy had looked for her. He couldn't get her image out of his mind. Those bright green eyes, the freckles, her quick smile, the way she tilted her head to the side when she studied him...he longed to see her again, to catch even a glimpse of her walking in the distance. He wondered if he'd scared her away with his crying the other night. He was sure Theodore McGovern the Third, the prince of Arabia, never cried over the birth of a foal. He'd no doubt seen it a hundred times. It was probably best that she kept her distance anyway. She was like royalty and she was engaged, and he was just a common ranch hand. A grunt, like Jumper said. A nobody.

He dumped another load of manure into the wheelbarrow, stopped and wiped sweat from his brow, took a swig of water from his thermos.

"Hey, Farm Boy."

Jimmy looked over his shoulder. Nena. She wore blue jeans and a faded T-shirt that fit her perfectly. He lowered the thermos and dragged the back of his hand across his mouth. "Hey."

Nena hooked her thumbs in the pockets of her jeans. "Looks like you've been earning your keep."

Picking up the shovel, Jimmy said, "Where've you been?"

She tilted her head. "You been looking for me, Jimmy Hutching?"

"No. Not intentionally. I mean, I just noticed you haven't been around." He sounded like a fool.

"You just noticed, huh? What else have you noticed?"

There was a moment of awkward silence until Jimmy turned and put the shovel to the floor of the stall. "Why didn't you tell me you were a St. Claire?"

"Does it matter?"

"You said you work here."

"I do work here. I help train the horses. We just got back from racing one of the two-year-olds in Florida."

Jimmy kept working while he talked. "Florida. How was that?"

"Hot."

"It's hot here too."

"Not like it's hot in Florida. Florida is a whole 'nother class of hot. Have you ever been there?"

Another shovelful of soiled straw hit the wheelbarrow. The smell was pungent but not overpowering, nothing Jimmy hadn't dealt with before. "Nope. Never been out of Virginia."

"Never been— Farm Boy, we need to get you out more."

Jimmy stopped and leaned on the shovel. His breath was shallow and clipped. Sweat poured down his forehead and stung his eyes, but he didn't wipe it away. "Us farm boys can't afford the luxury of romping around the country. We have cows to care for and land to tend."

Nena stepped closer and rested her hand on the stall. "Did I say something wrong?"

"Why didn't you tell me you were engaged?"

"You didn't ask."

"That's not a common question to ask a girl the first time you meet her."

"No, I suppose it isn't. But I am wearing a ring." She flashed a rock the size of a small marble. Jimmy hadn't noticed it the other night. "Besides, is there a law against an engaged girl talking to another guy?"

Jimmy didn't answer. He knew he'd overreacted, but there was no way to take it back now.

"Even a girl"—Nena peered over the wall—"engaged to the prince of Arabia?"

Jimmy's face flushed, his cheeks burned. "Jumper shouldn't have told you that."

Nena laughed. "You're blushing, Jimmy. That's cute."

"I'm sorry."

"For blushing?"

"No. For the prince of Arabia thing. It was stupid."

"I think it's funny."

Jimmy leaned the shovel against the wall and wiped his face with his shirt. "Look, you seem nice, got your head on straight and all..."

"That's a good thing. Wouldn't want to walk around with a cock-eyed head."

"But—"

"But I'm royalty..."

"And I'm a grunt. You probably shouldn't be here talking to me."

"You've been listening to Jumper too much, Jimmy Hutching. I can talk to anyone I want to. Ted and I are engaged, but he doesn't own me, and Jumper isn't my social coordinator. I like talking to you. You're real, honest. I like that."

"Good." He paused, took a drink of water. "But I don't want to cause any trouble. Cricket told me to keep my nose clean."

"Cricket tells everyone that. Don't worry; you're not dirtying yourself by talking to me."

"That's not the way I meant it."

"I know. I'm just ribbing you."

"I don't want Ted getting, you know..."

"Jealous? He's not the jealous type. And he's not the confrontational type, either."

"You sure?"

She smiled, her cheeks pushing those emerald eyes into crescents. "You're such a farm boy." And with that she spun on her heels and headed off, hollering over her shoulder, "See you around, Jimmy. Keep that nose clean. You wouldn't want to make any trouble for Cricket."

CHAPTER TWELVE

ROBERTA CLOSED HER BOOK, ROLLED over in bed, and looked at the clock. It was almost midnight. The clock's green numbers laughed at her, told her how gullible she'd been. Thomas said he'd be home as soon as he could, and they'd talk into the wee hours of the morning. And she, like an idiot, had believed him. Well, it was almost the wee hours, and he still wasn't home. She couldn't help but think he was with Erica, holding her in his arms, having a real conversation with her.

"Stop it, Berta," she said out loud, as if the sound of her own voice would jar her from the tortuous thoughts.

She *should* stop it, though. She was probably being too hard on Thomas. He was an entrepreneur, after all, trying to build a business from scratch. He'd only opened the café six months ago, and already business was booming, the money pouring in. He had to invest a lot of time to get the project off the ground. Once it was established he'd be able to spend more time away from it. At least that's what he constantly told her. And like always, she believed him.

Roberta picked up her cell phone and hit the buttons to bring up Tiffany's number. Since moving to California, she'd made only one friend, Tiffany Summer, another reporter at the *Times*. The two had hit it off famously from the first time they met, and, besides Thomas, Tiffany was the only person Roberta talked to on a regular basis.

Tiff would still be awake; she was a night owl who liked to watch the late-night shows.

The phone rang once.

Roberta liked Tiffany. She was a good listener, which made her a great reporter.

Another ring.

And she was even-keeled, a boat that never rocked no matter how great the storm.

Three rings.

C'mon, Tiff, pick up.

Tiffany was married, had gone through a divorce, married again, had a miscarriage, wrecked her car, and lost her sister in a bizarre shooting, yet she exuded a level of peace that Roberta couldn't fathom.

After the fourth ring Tiffany's voice mail picked up and instructed Roberta to leave a message. She didn't. She'd try again tomorrow if she didn't see Tiff at the office.

Roberta dropped the phone on the bed beside her and picked up the novel she'd been reading. It was a story about an Amish woman torn between love for her people, her culture, everything she'd ever known, and love for an "Englisher" who'd stumbled into her life and stolen her heart. She smirked. If only she could escape to the simple life of the Amish.

The apartment door opened and closed. Roberta heard Thomas shuffling around in the kitchen, opening and shutting the fridge, turning lights off. Then he appeared in the bedroom doorway and looked surprised to see her.

"Oh, hey, babe. Didn't expect you to still be up."

Roberta placed the book on her bedside table. "You said we could talk when you got home. Remember...wee hours of the morning?"

"Oh, yeah. I did, didn't I? What time is it?"

"Midnight."

He slipped off his shirt. "You okay?"

She pushed her lips into a smile. "Just tired."

Pulling open a drawer of his dresser, he reached in and got

out the old jogging shorts he slept in. "You didn't have to wait up, you know."

"I know. But I wanted to talk to you about something. I got a phone call today."

"From who?" Thomas walked into the bathroom. "Keep talking. I'm listening."

"My dad."

He opened the door to the linen closet and pulled out a towel. "Really? What's up?"

"Can we talk face-to-face? It's kind of important."

He stepped out of the bathroom, towel in hand. "Can I jump in the shower first? I'm tired and smell like the café."

"You smell like coffee. I like that smell."

"I'll only be a couple minutes. I can be in and out in five."

"Why are you so late?"

The irritation must have been evident in her voice, because he tilted his head to the side and said, "Babe, c'mon. Don't be upset. It took me longer to reconcile the books. There was a discrepancy between the receipts and the register. I needed to figure it out before I left."

"And did you?"

"Of course. Sorry it took me so long. I'll be just a few minutes. Promise."

He shut the door, and seconds later Roberta heard the shower turn on. She didn't know why, but she couldn't help but feel a deep sense of hurt. Yes, she did know why. Thomas used to always give her a kiss when he saw her. It was the first thing he'd do. He hadn't at the café, but with customers around she understood. Thomas was never one for showing affection publicly. But he hadn't just now either. In fact, he'd stayed on the other side of the room, kept his distance from her, as if he didn't want to get too close because she might...what? Smell Erica on him?

Stop it, Berta. You're being silly. Stupid.

But the thought was still there, niggling at her like an itch that couldn't be reached.

Finally she turned off the light and pulled the sheet up to her shoulders. She couldn't sleep, though, no way. So when the water shut off and Thomas eventually emerged from the bathroom, she faked it, kept her eyes closed. He got in bed beside her, gave her a peck on the cheek, and rolled over. Minutes later she heard the deep, even rhythm of his sleep breathing.

Her eyes popped open. Slivers of moonlight slipped past the drawn blinds and cast the room in a lunar glow. The windows were open, so she could hear the sound of traffic on the street below, someone talking in the distance, a dog barking. For a long time she lay there, looking at nothing in particular, her eyes only half focused on the ceiling. Her mind turned with thoughts about Thomas cheating on her, lying, sneaking around; about her mother and the cancer that had found her body, the treatment she'd go through; about her father and how disappointed he'd sounded on the phone.

Eventually, somewhere in those wee hours of the early morning, her eyelids grew heavy and she drifted to sleep. The dream came again: she was on her mother's lap, rocking back and forth, back and forth. Those comforting arms were around her, holding her and singing that same lullaby. Her mother's voice sounded like the warmest breeze on a spring day. That feeling was there too, the sense of belonging, of being home, secure, safe. Like there wasn't a thing in the world that could harm her when she was in those arms.

Roberta's eyes opened into the darkness of the bedroom. She was on her side, facing the clock. Its green numbers glowed 2:32. The emotion from the dream lingered like the sweet aroma of something homemade, pie or biscuits. If only she could hang on to that feeling, gather it and hide it away. But within seconds it faded, and she felt again the pain inflicted by

Thomas's apathy. She rolled over to face him and reached out her hand to touch his arm.

But Thomas wasn't there.

CHAPTER THIRTEEN

ROBERTA TYPED THE LAST SENTENCE of her article and scanned it again. It was as good as it was going to get. She clicked the mouse, brought up the e-mail window. Her editor's address was just another two clicks away. Attach the file and hit send; it was that easy. The article would run in tomorrow's paper. Nothing groundbreaking, just the highlights of another city council meeting. Roberta loved journalism, but the beat she'd gotten stuck with was boring enough to almost make her want to try something else. *Almost*, if she hadn't been boringly employed with the *LA Times*, one of the largest papers in the country. Journalism was a ladder career; you paid your dues doing the mundane stuff, and if you did a good enough job and made nice with the right people, you'd get to take a step up.

She gathered her purse and laptop, grabbed her soda can, and headed for the exit, mumbling, "Another evening by myself. Gee, can't wait to get started on this one."

As she left the newsroom, a woman's voice stopped her. "Berta, wait up."

Roberta smiled and adjusted the laptop case's strap on her shoulder. "Tiff, hey, good to see you."

Tiffany was just arriving for her second-shift police beat. She had the exciting stuff—chasing the cops, reporting on murders and shootings and gang wars. In LA there was always something happening to get the adrenaline going. Police reporting wasn't feature writing, and it was nowhere close to having your own column, but in Roberta's opinion it was as high on the beat-reporting ladder as one could get.

Tiffany caught up to Roberta and took her hand. "Oh, I'm

glad I ran into you. I'm sorry I missed your call last evening. Busy shift, and I had to stay late. Was it important?"

Roberta diverted her eyes and hesitated, knowing her body language spoke volumes. "Yeah, sort of. You have a couple minutes?"

"Sure, I do. It's about Thomas, isn't it?"

"Boy, cop chaser *and* clairvoyant. I bet that comes in handy."

"How do think I landed this gig?"

"You mean it wasn't your charm and good looks?"

"You're too sweet. Here." Tiffany led her to a sofa in the lobby. "What's going on?"

Roberta told her about Thomas's obsession with the café, his long hours, empty promises, apparent apathy toward deepening the relationship, his avoidance of any kind of commitment. She didn't mention Erica with the flirty eyes or Thomas's suspicious behavior last night. He'd returned to the apartment a little after three and said he couldn't sleep, so he went for a walk. Since when did people go for a walk in the middle of the night? Allegedly the stress of the café had given him restless legs, and the only way to alleviate that was to walk it off. Roberta mentioned none of this to Tiffany. She didn't want to come off as a jealous girlfriend seeing things that weren't there.

When she finished, Tiffany sat quietly on the sofa next to her, legs crossed, fingers laced on her lap, and stared at a spot on the floor. Finally she lifted her eyes and said, "Do you think he's cheating on you?"

So much for not coming off as the jealous girlfriend type. Roberta shrugged. "The thought's entered my mind. He has this employee, Erica, young college girl, beautiful, great shape, who's always making eyes at him. I see the way he looks at her."

"You suspect something."

"I don't know if I do or not. I don't want to be like that, but..."

"But you don't feel like you can trust him."

"I guess."

Tiffany was probing Roberta's wound and getting into some painful areas.

"So why do you stay with him?" It was an honest question, one Roberta had asked herself on different occasions, more lately than usual.

Again the shoulders rose and fell. "I don't know. I'm a glutton for emotional punishment?"

Tiffany smiled and took Roberta's hand. "I don't think you're a glutton for anything. You want to know what I think?"

"I don't know, do I?"

"You can decide after I say it. I think you're afraid of being alone. You're all the way out here in California, don't know anyone but Thomas and me, you have a broken relationship with your family, and a neglectful Thomas is better than nothing."

It was as if Tiffany explored deep into that wound and hit the central nerve source. Tears pushed their way to the corners of Roberta's eyes. The flesh on the back of her neck tingled.

"Am I on the right track?"

Roberta nodded.

"Listen, girl. I know being alone seems like the worst sentence possible, worse than covering city council even, but it's better to be sure about a man before committing your life to him. Take it from someone who's been there."

Tiffany had never told Roberta what went wrong with her first marriage, just that it didn't last even a year, and she had to get away from the man who said he loved her but knew nothing of real love.

Roberta nodded and wiped at a stray tear making its way down her cheek.

"Oh, dear." Tiffany reached into her purse for a tissue. "Now I've gone and made you cry. I'm sorry."

Taking the tissue and dabbing at her eyes, Roberta said, "It's fine. I needed to get some tears out. I've been so confused lately."

"Do you love him, Roberta?"

"Yes. I do."

"And that's what makes it so hard. Do you think he loves you?"

More tears came. Roberta blotted her eyes with the tissue. "I think he's in love with being in love, but I'm not sure he knows what real love is."

"Well, at least you can admit that much. Look, I'm not telling you to cut it off with Thomas. Don't see me as a wedge. Be sure; that's all I'm saying. And know your own worth. You're a beautiful, talented woman with a ton going for her. I want to see you wind up with a man who deserves you, not just someone you're willing to settle for." Tiffany's phone buzzed. She pulled it from her pocket and looked at the screen. "Oh, man, I'm sorry. Gotta run. Someone's shooting up a jewelry store in Inglewood, on East Florence."

"Sounds boring," Roberta said. "Not nearly as heart-stopping as listening to Councilman Torres read the minutes from last month's meeting."

"Just be glad Torres isn't the type to pull out a gun and start shooting the place up."

"At least it would give me something to report. Be careful."

Tiffany stood and patted Roberta's hand, gave it a squeeze. "You're a smart girl. I know you'll make the right decision. Do you mind if I pray for you?"

Roberta knew Tiffany was religious, but she'd never mentioned praying before, let alone offering to pray for Roberta. "Sure. Thank you."

"Promise me you won't do anything rash."

"I won't," Roberta said. She stood and gave Tiffany a hug. "I promise. Thanks for listening and for the free advice."

"Just think it over, okay?"

"Of course."

"And the advice wasn't free. You owe me a latte when we both have the time."

Tiffany left, and Roberta sat back on the sofa. She was

drained, like she'd just run an emotional marathon and hit the wall. She and Thomas had a lot to talk about. The time would have to be right, though. Rushing things would only make the situation worse, more volatile. She'd give it a little more time, and if the situation didn't improve, then she'd spring some questions on him, confront him point-blank. She stood, feeling exhausted but empowered, and left the building. Thomas better see what he had soon, or he'd lose it.

Chapter Fourteen

KEN'S OFFICE FELT LIKE A crypt. The hour was late, nearly nine o'clock, and as far as he knew, the rest of the firm's suite was empty. Everyone else had gone home to be with their families, to kiss their wives and husbands, get their kids into bed. But there was nothing at home for Ken. Of course there was nothing here for him either. With the darkness outside pushing against the large window, his tenth-story office felt empty and cold, like a tomb from some old horror flick.

Ken pushed away from his desk and walked to the window. It reached nearly from floor to ceiling and provided a spectacular view of Lake Michigan. On clear days, when visibility was good, he could see all the way to the Indiana Dunes National Lakeshore and Michigan City. This evening, though, beyond the pane of glass and the blackness of night, the dark waters of Lake Michigan churned and writhed a hundred feet below. They beckoned him, and for a moment he thought of driving out to the pier and throwing himself into those waves. Quickly he brushed the thought away. It was nonsense. Celia would come to her senses sooner or later and realize what a good husband and father he was, what a good provider he'd become. She'd appreciate his sacrifice.

He thought of Robby and Maddy. He missed them, but they were young and resilient. A few years from now, when this was all in the past, they wouldn't even remember it. By the time Maddy was in school, he'd be a partner and financially secure enough that he could scale back and spend more time at home. Besides, he truly enjoyed his job; why couldn't Celia understand that? He wasn't like other guys who spent their free time on a golf course or in a bar. He liked the challenge of his work, and he was good at what he did. One client last year, who'd walked away from an ugly divorce with everything but the family's Maltese, quipped that Ken could negotiate the teeth out of a shark. He was that good.

So why was he so miserable? Why was he contemplating ending it all in the cold waters of the lake?

He was missing something, more than his kids, more than Celia. Something else.

His hand went to his face and rubbed the stubble on his jaw. He couldn't quit now, he was too close to making partner. Celia and the kids would have to wait. They'd be thankful they did once he got that fat bonus and pay raise. Maybe he'd buy that yacht so they could spend time together as a family cruising the lake. The kids would love that, and Celia had always said she'd like to have a boat one day.

Ken looked at his watch and was startled by a voice behind him saying his name. He spun around and found Ed DeGuardo standing in the doorway, tie loosened and shirt untucked. "You putting in a late night, Ken?"

Ed was in his sixties but looked much younger. Tall, fit, a full crop of dark brown hair, he was an imposing man anywhere he went. Ken had seen him in action in both the negotiating room and the courtroom, and he was the type of man people listened to.

"Yeah, working on this O'Leary case."

"How's it coming?"

"Fine, I just need to do a little more digging." Truth was, he wasn't working on the O'Leary case, and it wasn't coming along fine. Unless they came up with a rock-solid bargaining chip or dug up something to hang over Mrs. O'Leary's head, it was looking more and more like she'd get the house and the Schnauzer.

"Great." Ed tapped the doorjamb with his fist. "That's what

we like about you, Ken. You're a fighter. You don't give up. How's the family?"

Ken hesitated and hoped Ed didn't pick up on it, but Ed was a good lawyer. He was trained to notice if someone was lying. "They're well. Celia probably has the kids in bed by now."

"How old is your youngest now…Maddy, right?"

"Yes. She just turned one."

Ed smiled. "I always loved that stage. They grow up too quickly, don't they?"

Ken forced a smile. "They sure do."

"Hey." Ed tapped the jamb again. "Make sure the lights are out when you leave. And keep up the great work."

"Sure thing. Thanks, Ed."

Ed left, and Ken was alone again. He had no reason to stay here. He gathered his jacket and briefcase, switched off the lights, and headed out the door. Maybe he'd swing by Boyle's Pub on North Lincoln and grab a few drinks before going home.

Ken fumbled with his keys and finally found the keyhole. He pushed open the front door and stumbled into the foyer. The house was so still and quiet, he almost thought he'd broken into the wrong home. He felt his way through the darkness to his study, found the desk lamp, and switched it on. Soft yellowish light illuminated the desktop. He usually kept it neat and organized, but lately things had gotten away from him. Papers lay in haphazard piles; bills, some overdue, sat unattended in their envelopes. A half-full coffee mug from last night sat on one corner, near the photo of the family at the beach. They'd flown to Panama City, Florida, and swum in the Gulf of Mexico. The water was much warmer than Lake Michigan. They were all smiling; Ken's arm was around Celia, his other hand draped casually across Robby's shoulder and resting on the boy's chest.

They looked so happy, so content. The perfect family. That was just four months ago. What had happened?

His head felt a little woozy, so he sat in his chair and rested it on the desk. For the past few nights he'd stopped at Boyle's on the way home and put back a few drinks. This evening he'd had one too many. He couldn't hold his alcohol like he could in college.

Ken lifted his head and reached for the mug. It didn't matter that the coffee was probably ice cold and stale; he needed some caffeine. Taking a sip, he noticed the red light blinking on the answering machine. Celia? The clock said 10:17. He'd missed the kids' bedtime again; she'd probably left a nasty message. But she would have called his mobile phone. He didn't remember seeing the blinking light this morning or last night.

With a shaky finger he pushed the button. There was one message, and it was left earlier that evening.

"Daddy, are you there?" It was Robby's voice. Ken picked up a pen and tapped it on the desktop. "Daddy, I want to say good night. We're havin' lotsa fun, but I miss you. Call me."

That was it. It was too late to call now. Robby would have been tucked into bed hours ago. Celia was probably still awake, but Ken didn't need any scolding and belittling.

He stood and crossed the room while unbuttoning his shirt. He slipped off his shoes, grabbed the pillow from the wingback chair, and sat in the recliner, his bed for the past several nights. Sleep was what he needed more than anything now; he'd feel better in the morning, have a clearer head. He'd call Celia then.

If she'd even talk to him.

Chapter Fifteen

The sound of the ringing phone woke Ken from a deep sleep. He startled, turned in the recliner, pulled the lever to fold the leg rest down, and stood. Throbbing pain pulsed through his head, and his eyes went blurry. The room spun in tight circles.

The phone rang again.

He sat back down, rubbed his face, slapped his cheeks. The room settled and eventually stopped. Standing slowly, he walked to his desk and reached the phone on the fourth ring, just before the answering machine picked up.

"Hello?" His voice cracked.

"Why didn't you call last night?" It was Celia.

Ken glanced at the clock. It was almost nine. "Well, good morning to you, too."

"It's not good. Robby woke up crying this morning because he didn't get to talk to you last night."

A weight sat in the pit of Ken's stomach. "I, uh, I stayed at the office late. Sorry I missed the kids again."

"Yeah, *again*. Even from a distance nothing changes. You still don't have time for them."

He could hear the disgust in her voice. "I said I'm sorry, okay?"

"No, Ken, it's not okay. Not at all. Robby kept asking why you didn't call him back after he left you the message. What am I supposed to tell him? I won't keep lying for you. He misses you, you know."

"Well, whose fault is that? You're the one who took him from me."

"So you're putting the blame on me? Really? He thought you didn't care about him, Ken. He even asked me if you still love us."

A lump rose in Ken's throat. He forked his fingers through his hair and sat in the desk chair. "Is he around? Can I talk to him now?"

Celia's sigh came through the phone as static. "I'll get him."

There was a pause, then, "Daddy?"

"Hey, buddy, how are you?"

"Good."

"What have you been up to?"

"Pop-Pop showed me how to ride a bike, a real two-wheeler."

Again the knot was there in Ken's throat. That was his job; it was every daddy's job. "Really? How did it go?" He had to force the words from his mouth.

"I almost did it, but I falled two times."

"Did you hurt yourself?"

"One time I scraped my knee, but it's okay now. Grammy put a Band-Aid on it with some creamy stuff."

"I bet you were brave. That's great. Hey, listen, I'm sorry I didn't call last night. I had to stay at work late. Sorry, bud."

"That's okay." But Ken could tell by his son's voice that it wasn't okay.

"Be good for Mommy, all right?"

"I am."

"Great. Can you put her back on now?"

"Okay. I love you, Daddy."

"I love you too."

"Wait, Daddy?"

"Yeah."

"When will we see you again?"

Tears came to Ken's eyes now. The sound of Robby's innocent, sweet voice was too much. "Soon, bud, soon. Be good for Mommy."

"Okay, Daddy."

And then he was gone. There was another short pause until Celia came back on. "Hello?"

"I'm here."

"Maddy's still sleeping, so you'll have to talk to her tonight."

"That's fine."

"So where were you really last night, and the night before that, and the one before that?"

Ken sat back in the chair and rubbed his eyes. "I told you, at work."

"And that was it?"

The fact that she didn't believe him, even if he was lying, irritated him. He wasn't fooling her at all. "Yes."

"Because I ran into Joey Maguire's wife at the store yesterday. You remember her?"

Ken didn't answer. He'd met Joey at Boyle's the other night. They hadn't seen each other since college. Joey always had a big mouth.

"She said Joey saw you at Boyle's two nights ago. Shared a few drinks. Said how nice it was to see you again. Do you remember any of that, Ken?"

Again he didn't answer. Opening his mouth would only push him farther into the hole.

"What's going on? I thought you stopped drinking five years ago."

"I've been a little stressed, all right? There's a lot of pressure with this case at work, and then you up and leave and take the kids from me—"

"So you're passing the blame my way again."

"I'm not blaming it on you. I'm just saying how it is."

"You need to stop." She used the same tone she used with Robby when he got mouthy with her.

"I will."

"No, I mean it. Stop it right now, Ken. You know how far you've come. To ruin all that now would be insane."

"Okay."

But he'd already ruined it. Even now, at nine in the morning, he craved a drink. He'd started drinking in college, and it had quickly become a habit. By the time Celia was pregnant with Robby, Ken was drinking more than she was comfortable with. She'd made that very clear on several occasions. He'd convinced himself, though, that he could work better with a little alcohol relaxing him, clearing his mind. When Robby was born, Ken was so overcome with pride and love for his son that he swore off drinking altogether. He didn't want to be the father who came home from work, cracked open a beer, and sat his butt in the recliner for the rest of the evening.

"I mean it. I'm not bringing the kids back home until you stop. You can forget about that."

"I said okay."

"I gotta go." The disappointment was there again, multiplied tenfold.

"Yeah. I'll call tonight."

"Early enough to say good night to the kids?"

"Yes."

"Okay. Bye."

"Bye."

He put the phone in its cradle and rocked back in the chair. What a mess he'd made of things. He needed his family back. He needed to ace this O'Leary case. Once he did, he'd get the big promotion and things would settle down. Then Celia would respect him again.

An idea came to him, and he scolded himself for not thinking of it sooner. It was a long shot, but if it panned out, it would seal him the O'Leary case and the partnership. He'd never stooped this low before, but if he wanted to win his family back, it was his only hope.

Loretta O'Leary was the chief operating officer for a big bank downtown. Nobody got that high on the chain without cutting a few corners. Perhaps Ken should pay some of her subordinates a visit.

CHAPTER SIXTEEN

THE CAT SCAN WAS PERFORMED without a single problem. The giant doughnut-shaped machine welcomed Nena into its center with instructions for when to hold her breath, when to breathe, when to remain still, when she could move. She'd spent the rest of the day and most of the day after that on the front porch, wrapped in her blanket, trying to ward off the panic that came in waves. Things were taking too long, happening too slowly, she kept telling herself. Why did no one feel the sense of urgency that she did?

The following day, at ten in the morning, she had her follow-up visit with the surgeon. Dr. Monroe's specialty was colorectal surgery—it said so on the door of his office—and he had an alphabet of letters behind his name. But that brought no comfort to Nena.

Floral-patterned wallpaper decorated the waiting room, the furniture was upholstered in a floral print, and framed prints of floral arrangements hung on the walls. For the office of a man who made his living (and a very good living, no doubt) by cutting people open and dissecting their colons, the decor seemed a little out of place. The flowers did nothing to comfort or calm her.

Jim was there, though, and he gave her hand a gentle but firm squeeze. "It'll be okay," he said, but it meant nothing. Jim meant well, she knew that and appreciated his support, but he was just as much in the dark as she was.

The nurse, a plump middle-aged woman, emerged from the back of the office and called Nena's name. Immediately, as if someone had turned a valve, her breath caught in her throat.

She recovered quickly, pulled herself up, straightened her shoulders, and adjusted her blouse.

The nurse had a nice smile, genuine, that showed a mouthful of straight, white teeth and an abundance of gums. She stepped aside and allowed Nena and Jim to pass through the doorway. "First door on the right, hon," she said.

The door led to an exam room, cold, sterile, lots of stainless steel. An exam bed took up most of the room, the paper covering pulled tight, without a single crease. Beside the bed sat two chairs. A magazine rack hung on the wall. Nena took one seat and Jim the other.

"The doctor will be here in just a moment," the nurse said. She bowed her head slightly and backed out of the room, closing the door until it clicked.

"I don't like this," Nena said. She looked at her watch.

"Don't like what? They're running on time."

Nena waved her hand around the room. "This room. Exam rooms. Too clinical. It's their way of reminding you that you're just a patient." "Oh, Nena. Don't be ridiculous. Some doctors like to talk in their office, others in an exam room. What's the difference?"

"In the office you're a person; in here you're a patient. There's a big difference. I don't like it."

Exactly five minutes later the door opened and a young man with shaggy hair walked in, followed by the nurse. He extended his hand to Nena. "Mrs. Hutching, I'm Charles Monroe. It's a pleasure to meet you."

After shaking Jim's hand, Dr. Monroe sat on a rolling stool and faced them. He opened a manila folder and studied the contents, his eyes dark and face expressionless. "Has anyone told you the results of the CAT scan yet?"

"No," Nena said. "I thought that's what this appointment was for."

"Yes, okay." He closed the chart and folded his hands on his lap. "I'm sorry. It appears from the scan that your cancer has spread and is in stage four. It's in your liver and lungs...significantly. I'm sorry."

Numbness overtook Nena. She knew she'd heard him correctly. *Stage four. Liver and lungs. Significant.* But it couldn't be true. The test couldn't be accurate. There had to be a mistake. "But I haven't had any other symptoms. I feel fine."

Monroe paused, looked at his hands. "You don't have to have any symptoms. I'm sorry, Mrs. Hutching, really I am. I hate being the bearer of this kind of news."

Jim's hand was on Nena's, but she couldn't feel it. His face was blank, eyes distant. He faced Monroe but appeared to be in some sort of trance.

A quick memory of her father on his deathbed flashed through Nena's mind. He was so frail, so weak and emaciated. The cancer had totally ravaged his body, spread to almost every organ, killing him one cell at a time until there was nothing more than a shell left. He could barely talk, no longer ate, couldn't even take fluids. At the end there was simply nothing left of him. He was only fifty-six.

"We're going to be aggressive in the treatment," Monroe said. "We're going to throw everything and the kitchen sink at it. Surgery first. Let's get that tumor out of you, then a full dose of chemo and radiation."

"How long?" The words tumbled clumsily out of Nena's mouth.

"Excuse me?"

Jim looked at Nena; the expression on his face begged her not to ask the question again. But she had to; she had to know.

"How long do I have...to live?"

She hoped Monroe wouldn't shrug off her question. He glanced at his hands again, set the folder on the exam bed beside him. When his eyes met hers there was pity in them, but she couldn't tell if it was genuine or a look he'd practiced over the course of his short career. It appeared authentic; if not, it was Oscar worthy. Maybe they taught doctors that look in medical school. "Honestly? It's hard to tell at this point."

"Give me your best guess."

He shook his head. "I'm sorry, I don't guess about this kind of stuff. We'll get a much better picture of how invasive the metastasis is when we get inside and get our eyes on it."

"Then give me best and worst case."

"Okay." Monroe crossed his arms. It was obvious he didn't like being pressed into answering Nena's question. "Best case, with surgery and chemo and radiation, we totally eradicate the cancer. Worst case...look..." He paused, eyed Nena and Jim as if considering whether they were strong enough to hear the truth of the matter.

Nena knew what he was going to say. It was what they all said, the glib remark about not having an expiration date. Others had gone on to beat the cancer and live out the rest of their life free of the dreaded disease. There were no guarantees, after all, only predictions, and predictions were wrong all the time.

"Doctor, please." She held up a hand. "You don't have to camouflage it with pretty colors for me. I can take the truth."

Monroe dipped his chin, again shifted his eyes between Jim and Nena, and said, "All right then. Five-year survival rate is about eight percent."

"What does that mean?" Jim asked.

"It means eight percent of people diagnosed with this type of cancer live at least five years after diagnosis."

"It means ninety-two percent of people die within five years," Nena said. "So why treat it at all?"

"Because of the best-case scenario. We just don't know how it will respond. We can't. And even with the worst case, because of eight percent there is hope, and where there is hope, we don't just give up. Besides, we need to get that tumor out."

Jim shifted in his chair, took Nena's hand with both of his, and held on like he was afraid the cancer monster would break down the door and steal her away right then while she sat in the exam room chair. "So what happens next, and when?"

"Well, we can schedule surgery now. I'd like to get you in as soon as possible. In the meantime we'll get you lined up for an appointment with Dr. Alexis, the oncologist. She'll go over the chemo and radiation with you." He paused, pushed a lock of hair from his forehead. "Folks, I'm very sorry. I know this isn't the news you wanted to hear. Believe me, it's not the news I wanted to deliver. It's a lot to take in all at once. But please don't lose hope. There's always hope. Do you have any other questions?"

Sure, she had questions, but none Monroe could answer. Nena shook her head, and Jim didn't say anything.

"Okay, well, I'll get Sue, and she'll get the surgery scheduled. We're going to do everything we can to beat this, I assure you of that."

Nena nodded. "Of course."

Surgery was scheduled for the following week, exactly five days away. They would do the colon first, then look into the liver and lungs.

On the way home neither Jim nor Nena said a word. Images of her father on that deathbed kept swimming through her mind. The hollow, gray eyes, papery skin stretched taut over sharply angled bones, the labored breathing, restless sleep. That was what the future held for her.

When they finally made it home and the truck came to a stop, she threw the door open and stumbled out. She needed air, space. The truck's cabin had felt like a vault closing in on her, getting smaller and smaller the longer she was in it.

Jim's door closed, and his voice followed her. "Nena, wait."

She held up a hand and kept walking. Gravel crunched behind her. Jim had rounded the truck and was in pursuit.

Nena stopped and turned around. "Not now, Jim, okay? I need to think."

He stopped, arms hanging limply at his sides. He looked tired and worn. Old. Worried. Scared. "We need to talk about this."

She shook her head. "I don't want to talk right now. I need to be alone."

Jim's shoulders slumped. She'd hurt him, but she couldn't deal with that right now. Her skin crawled, stomach ached. She wanted to run and run and run and never stop. Maybe she could outrun the beast inside her, get far enough away that the tests and doctors couldn't find her, that the cancer would lose track of her and leave her alone. She turned and walked away, toward the pasture where the only real freedom she had known used to play. She wished she could just keep walking and simply be no more, just fade away. A mountain higher than any she'd ever had to climb stood before her, and she didn't want to face it.

Chapter Seventeen

THE RAIN FELL WITH A steady rhythm as Barb left the office building. She stood under the portico, arms wrapped around herself, and closed her eyes. The sound of rain tapping on the aluminum roof soothed her, if only a little. A car pulled up to the curb, and its wheels splashing in the standing water brought her eyes open. An elderly man, hunched in his back, exited the driver's side and opened the trunk. Rain quickly matted what little hair he had and dotted his coat with dark spots. From the trunk he lifted a wheelchair, set it on the ground, and unfolded it. He wheeled it up to the passenger side, swung open the door, and helped an elderly woman into the chair. It was obvious he'd done this many times before. She opened a small umbrella and held it over her head. He closed the door and wheeled her up and onto the sidewalk, past Barb, and into the building. A few seconds later he returned to move the car. All without a single word of complaint.

Barb closed her eyes again, listened to the rain on the roof. She liked things to be orderly, scheduled, routine. But now her world had been shaken, everything rearranged, disjointed, uncertain. She wondered how the older couple had adjusted. Surely they once had a regular life, lived normal days with schedules and plans and places to go, jobs to work, children to raise. But over the years a new normal had to be established, a normal that kept changing, deteriorating in increments. That's what she had to look forward to.

She had cancer. Just like her mother. The same monster had found both of them and dug in its tentacles. The oncologist had just outlined the treatment plan, the chemo, radiation, then surgery. Barb was terrified of surgery. The scars, the ugliness. She wondered if Doug would look at her the same.

She reached her hand into her pocket and retrieved the scribbled note Mikey had handed her before he caught the morning school bus. *Good luck, Mom. Hope it goes okay. Love you, Mikey.* Hastily written, but so full of meaning and love. Mikey was her sensitive one, his heart as big as his world. He'd take the changes the hardest. His recent bout with bed-wetting said he already had. She folded the note carefully and put it back into her pocket.

Quickly Barb made her way across the parking lot, keeping her head low, shoulders hunched. She slipped into the car and shut the door. On the dash was a picture of Kara and Mikey, a photo from their vacation to the beach last summer. Both were smiling and squinting into the sun. Mikey held up a horseshoe crab he'd found in the surf. What if the day came when she was no longer around? What if her children had to grow up without a mother, and Doug had no wife to share the task of caring for them? The thought brought tears to her eyes. She touched the picture lightly, her fingertips lingering on the faces of her children.

She pulled her phone from her purse and dialed Doug's number. He wanted her to call him when she was finished.

He answered on the first ring. "Hey."

"Hi."

"So how'd it go?"

"All right, I guess."

"You okay?"

She faltered, the tightening in her throat blocking any words. Finally, "Yes. I'll be fine."

"Hey, I'm sorry again I couldn't be there. I really wanted to be. I needed to be."

There'd been a meeting at work that Doug simply couldn't

skip. They'd tried to reschedule Barb's appointment, but it didn't work out.

"No, it's okay. It went well. I'm fine."

"Things all set up then for chemo?"

"Yeah. I start next week. Wednesday."

"Then every week?"

"For a couple months, then every other week."

"How do you feel about it?"

Again she stumbled on her words, almost started crying. "I'm scared."

"Naturally. You'd be crazy not to be."

"More scared for you and the kids."

"Honey, don't be. We'll be fine. We just want to be there for you. You're not alone in this."

Fact was, she was just as scared for herself. "Thank you."

"Hey, I gotta run, okay? See you later?"

"You betcha."

"Love you."

"Love you too."

Then he was gone, and Barb was suddenly filled with a profound emptiness. She felt alone, stranded in a strange valley with unreachable mountains on all sides and a deepening shadow edging closer, closer, threatening to bury her in darkness. She rolled down the window an inch, breathed in the cool air. Tiny droplets of water splashed onto her face and cooled her skin.

Her phone rang in her hand. It was her father, calling about the results of Mom's CAT scan.

Chapter Eighteen

THOUGHTS OF THE PAST HAUNTED Jim. Old regrets came back like shadows in a mist, looming close then drifting away only to return again and make their presence known. He thought of his kids and the distance between all of them. He had put that same distance between himself and his own parents. After leaving the farm and finding a new life—and love— at the St. Claire ranch, he'd gone back to visit a few times, but it was never the same. A wall had been erected, even around his mother. It was as if leaving her alone with his father had surrendered her to his warped ways and altered the way she too saw the world. And his father had never returned to the man he once was. His frustration and anger so discolored his view of the world and of himself that he only worsened as the years went by. Every time Jim visited, he felt the space between them had grown a little wider, a little deeper.

They were both gone now, and he lived every day with the regret that he hadn't made more of an effort to bridge that chasm. And now that same chasm had formed between his own children, and he feared it too would only grow wider and deeper as the years passed. Because of their age differences they had never been very close, but since leaving home, it seemed they were as distant from one another as the cities in which they chose to live.

Barbara was the key, he knew that. She was the oldest and the peacemaker, always had been. Jim picked up the phone and dialed her number. Despite what Nena wanted, he was going to keep the kids informed about what was going on.

She answered on the second ring. "Hello, Dad."

"Hi, Barb."

"Did you get the results?"

He could tell by her voice that she didn't want any small talk. "We did. It's not good."

There was a long pause on the other end. "How bad?"

"Bad. The cancer has spread to her liver and lungs. The surgeon said he couldn't tell just how bad until he gets in there and takes a look."

Another pause. "I'm sorry, Dad. How's Mom taking it?"

"Pretty hard. She's not talking about it."

"Did you tell Kenny and Berta yet?"

Now it was his turn to hesitate. He picked up a pen lying on his desk and rolled it between his fingers. "Barb, I was hoping you'd call them. They'd probably take it better from you than from me."

"Dad, I don't...I haven't talked to either of them in such a long time."

"How long?"

"Over a year."

It was worse than he'd thought.

"Dad, I think you should call them. They need to hear this from you."

"Okay." He put down the pen and picked up a paper clip. When had his hands started looking so old and frail? He'd ask them again to come see their mother, but they'd refuse. And why shouldn't they? They had no ties to the ranch, nothing to lure them back.

"What's next?"

"The oncologist, then surgery next week. Barb—" He needed to ask her; she was the only one he could count on. "Could you come home after your mother has surgery, maybe stay a few days? I know it's asking a lot, and you have your own family—"

"Dad, wait."

There was a moment of silence on the other end, and Jim

almost thought she'd say yes, she'd come, help out, care for her mother.

"I can't. I–I'm sorry, I just can't."

"I understand." And he did, truly. He'd been there, distanced from his parents. He knew what it was like.

"No, you don't. It's not because I don't want to. I can't."

"Is something wrong?"

"I'm fine, Dad. I just can't right now."

"Are you and Doug okay?"

"Yes." Her answer was so quick he knew she was telling the truth. But he could tell she was hiding something.

"Doug and I are fine. It's not that. I'll come as soon as I can. I promise."

"All right. I know she'd like to see you."

"Dad, I gotta go. I love you."

"Love you too, Barb."

The phone went dead, and Jim was left once again with his memories and regrets, the shadows moving in and out of the mist.

He looked out the window of the study and saw Nena walking across the pasture. She looked old and tired. Their age had sneaked up on them, caught them both by surprise.

The St. Claire ranch had eight quarter horses for the hands to use when roaming the pastures and checking the fencing. They were stabled near the bunkhouse, apart from the thoroughbreds. On a still night Jimmy could lie in his bunk with the windows open and hear them snorting to one another. He liked the quarter horses; they were more personable than the thoroughbreds, not as high-strung. They were the workhorses, the grunts, and seemed to know they shared that in common with the hands. Jimmy had yet to ride one, though; that privilege was for the more experienced hands.

In the evening, after his work for the day was finished, Jimmy liked to visit the quarter horses. He'd been at the ranch a week and had yet to make any friends outside of Nena—if one could consider an engaged woman a friend. Jumper was all right, but after a full day of work he just wanted to collapse on his bunk and watch All in the Family or some other mindless sitcom on the little black-and-white TV set they shared. Jimmy had never been big on TV. And the Mexicans kept to themselves, to their language and their culture. Once in a while he'd overhear them saying something about the gringos and laughing, but other than that they rarely even acknowledged him.

The stables were where Jimmy felt most comfortable now. He could talk to the horses and they'd listen. He doubted they understood a single word he said, but at least they let him talk without interruption.

There was one horse in particular that Jimmy was drawn to, and the horse seemed drawn to him. He could swear that the horse perceived his hurt and felt some kind of bond with him.

Jimmy leaned over the wall of the stall and stroked the horse's muzzle. He had a white blaze that stretched from his forehead to nostrils, contrasting starkly with his dark brown coat. "It's been a week, boy, you know that?"

The horse leaned into his touch and flared his nostrils.

"One week. I wonder how Mom's doing, how Dad's been treating her."

He thought of his mother every day, wondered what she was up to, how she was holding up. The image of her face the last time he saw her, right before he walked out that door, was burned into his memory. Her red, swollen eyes and tearstained cheeks. She was so lost, so beaten down, so empty. He'd thought of going back and demanding she come with him but knew she'd refuse. She believed her place was with her husband, regardless of how he treated her. She remembered the man his father once was, the good man who was full of smiles and had a laugh that could be heard clear across the farm. She believed that man was still in there, under all the anger and hatred and frustration. She had hope that that man would live again.

Jimmy remembered that man too, but he'd lost hope of ever seeing him again. A stranger had taken up residence in his skin. He stroked the horse's muzzle again, running his palm down the blaze. "For Mom's sake I hope I'm wrong."

The horse pulled back, ears perked, and turned his head toward the stable doors.

Jimmy turned and found Nena standing there, Hickory by her side.

"Wrong about what?" She walked to where he stood, and the horse drew near to greet her, ears pricked forward.

Hickory sniffed Jimmy's boots. He looked at Jimmy, cocked his head, and whined.

Jimmy bent down to let the dog lick his hand. "Hey, boy, how ya doing?" He glanced at Nena. "What kind of dog is he?"

"Australian Shepherd. He has a great disposition around the horses. Wrong about what?"

"Nothing. Just talking to myself."

"You talk to yourself a lot?"

"Actually, I was talking to the horse."

"His name is Martin." She rested her hand on the horse's forehead.

"Martin? Interesting name for a horse."

"All the quarters are named for early presidents. Martin Van Buren. Then John"—she pointed to the stall next to Martin's—"and George and Thomas and James and James Monroe. I call him Jimmy, just like you."

She paused and smiled wide, and Jimmy thought her smile was the most beautiful he'd ever seen.

"On the end there are John Quincy and Andrew. The first eight presidents."

"Well, I'm just impressed you know who the first eight presidents were."

"I always aced history in school. You come here often to talk to the horses?"

"Every night. I guess it's more like talking to myself though."

"Nope. He understands you. Horses are great communicators."

"He understands me." Jimmy wasn't sure if she was serious or mocking him.

"Sure. They sense things. Emotions, attitudes, even motivations. Martin here probably knows when you're upset or angry even before you do."

Jimmy rubbed the horse's cheek.

"You like him, don't you?" Nena asked.

"Yeah, we've become buddies." He felt comfortable talking about the horse in this way to Nena.

"Wanna ride him?" She smiled, and her eyes held a mischievous twinkle.

Jimmy paused. He'd never ridden a horse before. Miss Molly was just a pet; she'd never even been saddled. "I, uh..."

"Have you ever been on a horse?"

For some reason Jimmy's cheeks flushed. What kind of ranch hand was he if he'd never even been on the back of a horse? "Nope. I haven't."

Nena's smile widened. "Well, Farm Boy, how are you ever going to be a cowboy if you don't learn to ride a horse?"

"All cowboys ride horses, don't they? Next you'll have me wearing a Stetson and stuffing chew in my lip."

"Now you're catching on, except the chew part. Gross." She opened the door to the stall. "C'mon. I'll give you your first lesson. Martin is about as docile as they come."

She slipped the bridle from a hook on the wall and slid it over Martin's muzzle as easily as she'd don her own jacket. When she had fastened the bridle securely, she turned to Jimmy and pointed to the far side of the stable. "Grab me the blanket and saddle over there."

Jimmy retrieved the items while Nena led Martin into the alleyway.

"Now," she said, holding a brush in one hand. "The first thing you want to do is brush his back, get all the dirt off and get the hair lying the same direction."

She proceeded to show him how to position the saddle blanket, place the saddle, and cinch it firm around the horse's abdomen. Again Jimmy was impressed with how deftly her hands handled the task. Experience had been a good teacher.

When the saddle was securely in place, she patted the seat. "Okay, Farm Boy, time to become a cowboy. Saddle up."

Jimmy placed one foot in the near stirrup and hoisted himself onto the saddle. Martin shifted his weight, shuffled his feet, nodded agreeably, and settled.

"There," Nena said. She put her hands on her hips and smiled wide. "All you need now is a Stetson and some chaps."

"Something tells me there's more to being a cowboy than the right clothes."

"Right. We forgot the six-shooter at each hip."

"Now that would be cool."

Quickly Nena saddled John Quincy and guided him alongside Jimmy and Martin. "Are you ready?"

"So long as we take it slow."

"We won't go faster than a trot. For now, just hold onto the reins. Martin knows what to do, and he'll follow us. If you want him to stop, just pull back gently on the reins and say whoa. And relax. Remember, he can sense your apprehension, and it'll make him nervous."

"That's like telling someone not to blink. All you can think of is blinking."

She laughed. "Just relax. Martin is gentle, and he likes you."

"And how do you know that?"

"He told me."

She pulled her horse around and clucked her tongue twice. "Let's *go, Martin. C'mon, boy."* Her horse started to walk, and Martin immediately caught up and came alongside her.

"You sure Ted won't mind you doing this?" Jimmy said. He could see some of the other hands around and figured word would get back to Ted. And if not to Ted, then surely to Jumper.

"I told you, Ted isn't the jealous type. He's around here somewhere, came by for the day. I'll introduce you when we get back."

When the ranch was no longer in sight, and all around them were rolling hills and pastures of unbroken green, Nena steered John Quincy near a stand of oaks. "How're you doing, Farm Boy?"

Martin instinctively stopped, shuffled his feet, swayed his head side to side, and blew a breath from his nostrils.

"I'm not a cowboy yet?"

"That's something you have to earn." Nena's eyes glistened in the sunlight. "Anyone can sit on a horse's back, but not everyone can ride a horse, be one with the power in its muscles, know its movements before it does. That takes time and hours in the saddle."

"Hours?" He looked at his watch. "We've been riding twenty minutes, and my butt's already sore." Martin had been a perfect gentleman, never once doing anything sudden or unpredictable, never once missing a step, but the constant side-to-side motion, the rhythm of the big horse's hips, had worn a sore spot on Jimmy's tail end.

Nena laughed and dismounted. "C'mon, let's have a seat here in the shade and let that butt of yours rest."

Jimmy clumsily climbed down from Martin and walked the horse to the trees where Nena waited.

She took the reins. "Like this." She looped them around a low branch, fastening Martin to a limb he could easily break if he wanted to. "He won't go anywhere."

She sat in the grass and leaned back on her hands, turning her face toward the sky.

Jimmy sat across from her, aware of the distance between them and not wanting to get too close. She was, after all, an engaged woman, and he was not to cause any trouble. He was also aware of how beautiful she was, though, and couldn't help the sudden desire he felt.

"So what do you think?" she said.

"About what?" He wouldn't dare tell her what was on his mind, that he wished she'd forget all about the prince of Arabia and be his girl.

"Riding. Being a cowboy."

"I thought I wasn't a cowboy yet. Remember? Hours in the saddle…and those six-shooters."

"Oh, right. The saddle time we can do something about. As for the six-shooters, you're on your own."

Jimmy laughed. "I like Martin. He's a strong horse."

"The strongest we have. And the most experienced. Smartest too. He's probably smarter than half the hands you bunk with, including Jumper."

They shared a laugh and a few moments of silence while they both scanned their surroundings. The grass beneath them was thick and soft, the ground cool in the shade. Above, the sky stretched out like a velvety blanket of blue, not a cloud in sight. The sun was on its downward arc, nearing the horizon. Sunset would be there soon, and then the sky would be set ablaze with every shade of orange and red and pink.

Nena picked a field pansy from the grass and twirled it between her fingers. "Back at the stable you said you hope you're wrong. Wrong about what?"

"I was talking to myself."

"You said you were talking to Martin. You can tell a horse and not me?"

What was he to say to that? Jimmy tore some grass from the ground and let it flutter from his hand. "I left home, the dairy farm, because my dad threw me out."

"What'd you do?"

"Challenged him. Stood up for my mom." He paused. This wouldn't be easy. He'd never told anyone about his home life, about the change in his father, the drunk he'd become. "My dad's an alcoholic and...gets abusive when he's had too much. He hit her, I tried to stop him, he threw me out."

"Simple as that?"

Jimmy shook his head. "No, not that simple."

Nena sat in silence, eyes on the flower in her hand. Finally she said, "And what about your mother? Where is she now?"

"She won't leave him. He wasn't always a drunk. He used to be a good man. Then the economy broke and we went bust. He's on the verge of losing the farm, losing everything." He paused for a moment and ripped some grass up by its roots, then tossed it to the side. "His drinking started slow, just a beer here and there to calm his nerves, help him settle down at night. Then the further in debt we got and the gloomier the outlook, the more he drank. He's not the same man. But she stays with him."

"She thinks that good man is still in there."

She was quick. "How did you know?"

"I'm a woman too. We think alike."

"Yeah, she's hanging on to hope. Hoping, praying, that the man he used to be will resurface one of these days and she can get her husband back."

"And you don't have that same hope?"

She was probing deeper now, digging into the depths of his mind, his heart. Normally he'd be uncomfortable with this kind of exposure and erect walls only a skilled climber could scale, but with Nena he felt at ease, like he'd known her his whole life and was never once judged. "I hope I'm wrong, for her sake."

The ride back to the stables was mostly done in a comfortable silence. The pace was slow, but Jimmy didn't complain. Their horseback seats gave them a front-row view of one of nature's most spectacular light shows. The sun was just a sliver away from melting into the horizon, and brilliant slices of mango and orange streaked the sky. Flocks of birds lifted from a nearby grove of trees, swooped as one, made a wide arc in the sky, and landed in the same tree they'd just soared from. A slow breeze wafted over the pastureland, carrying with it the scent of fresh grass and wildflowers. It was the most peaceful Jimmy had been since walking out of his parents' home—and life—a week ago. He'd never expected to land a job on the St. Claire ranch and certainly never expected to meet someone like Nena. As they rode, he felt himself becoming one with Martin, matching the rhythm of his own hips and legs with that of the horse's cadence.

Nena noticed too. "You're really finding the groove, aren't you?"

Jimmy scanned their surroundings. "Yeah, to more than just riding Martin."

"You're happy here?"

He nodded and smiled. "I am."

Nena looked straight ahead. The stables were just a hundred yards off now. "You have a nice smile, Jimmy Hutching. An honest one."

When they arrived at the stables, Nena dismounted first, and Jimmy followed her lead. She showed him how to remove the saddle, check the hooves for stones, and brush the horses down before stabling them for the night. Jimmy led Martin into his stall and made sure the water bucket was full.

And then from across the alleyway he heard Nena scream.

Chapter Nineteen

PEELING HER EYES OPEN AGAINST the midafternoon sunlight that filtered through the blinds in her bedroom, Barb rolled over and pulled the covers up to her chin. She shut her eyes and allowed images from the last remnants of her dream to stutter through her mind. She'd had the same dream every time she fell asleep for the past week. She was riding bareback on a beautiful white Arabian with a flowing mane and muscles like steel cords, gripping the mane with both hands and leaning forward as the horse raced across an open field. But this was anything but a joy ride. Panic clutched at her chest, wetted her palms, strained her breathing. They were being chased by…something, she didn't know what. Every so often she'd glance behind her, but there was never anything there but open field, grass, forested mountains in the distance. The wind buffeted her face, the horse flexed and moved beneath her, its movements so smooth and precise it felt almost like riding on air. Its breathing sounded like a steam locomotive chugging along a stretch of flat prairie with nothing to hinder its progress.

But still there was the feeling of something following, chasing, gaining ground. Relentless. Something dark and foreboding. Something intent on harm and destruction.

Barb gripped the horse's mane tighter and urged the beast to go faster, to run for the hills ahead. But no matter how fast the horse ran, no matter how hard its hooves beat at the ground and its nostrils sucked air, it made no forward progress. She looked back, feeling the presence right behind her, at the horse's hind-quarters, then the flank, the back. A hand, bony and spiderlike, reached for her. Barb screamed and pulled away, the horse's foot caught in a hole, she heard the snap of bone…

…her eyes flipped open, and she gasped for breath. She'd fallen back to sleep, had the dream again.

Forcing herself to move, Barb pushed off the covers and sat on the edge of the bed. Her head ached, thumped, throbbed, and the room spun in slow circles. She slid off the edge of the bed and into her slippers, donned her robe. When she stood, a gnawing nausea took hold of her stomach, and for a moment she thought she'd vomit. But the feeling eventually passed, and she was able to move again.

She walked to the window and pushed aside the shade. Outside, the shadows grew longer and the afternoon sun colored the field behind their house a burnt shade of orange. Barb made her way down the hall and into the bathroom. The woman who stared back at her from the mirror was a stranger, an unwanted guest overstaying her welcome.

"Who are you?" Barb asked the image. "And what did you do with Barb Mackey?"

The nausea came on so quick she barely had time to kneel over the toilet bowl before emptying the contents of her stomach.

After wiping her mouth and brushing her teeth, Barb headed downstairs and into the kitchen. Kara was at the table, working on some homework. She looked up when Barb came through the doorway. "Man, Mom, you look terrible."

"Thanks." Not only did she look terrible, she felt it too. Her muscles ached, her joints were stiff. Every movement was a chore.

"How do you feel?"

"Worse than I look."

"Is it that bad?"

"Worse."

"What's for dinner?"

Barb stared at her daughter for a second. Kara had never been the sensitive type, wasn't one for empathy. She was a kind girl, smart and athletic too, but putting herself in another person's shoes was as foreign to her as traveling to the Congo.

"I don't know. Dad will be home at six thirty. He'll have to make you something."

"But I'm hungry now."

"Then find something for yourself, Kara. You're thirteen, old enough to fend for yourself."

"Sorry." Kara slammed the book shut, shoved the chair back, and stormed out of the kitchen.

They'd all been on edge, and at times emotions ran raw. Normally Barb would have stopped her, apologized for her sharp words, given Kara some suggestions. But not today; she was too weak, too nauseated. Kara would get over it quickly; she always did. She was an impulsive girl who thrived on drama, often creating her own where none existed. Lately there had been plenty.

Barb got herself a glass of ginger ale from the refrigerator and sat at the kitchen table. Kara had been doing her math. She'd be back, and then Barb would apologize, make things right with her daughter. Until then she'd sip at her drink and hope it settled her roiling stomach.

Chapter Twenty

Dr. Alexis was a short, thin woman with a thick Jamaican accent. Her graying hair contrasted with her dark skin, but it gave her an air of sophistication and polish. She smiled a lot, and when she did, her white teeth flashed like pearls and her dark brown eyes sparkled. She spent over an hour with Jim and Nena, explaining the radiation and chemo, the side effects, the duration, and the hopeful outcomes. She assured Nena they would do all they could to extend her life, to give her more time with Jim. They were going to be aggressive and hit the cancer fast and hard. She answered all their questions. When the visit had concluded, she took Nena's hand in both of hers and smiled.

"Nena, dear," she said, "do not give up the fight. I've seen many people turn their nose up at the prognosis and live many years longer. My promise to you...we won't give up. Don't you give up."

Nena nodded and smiled politely. She was touched by the doctor's sincerity but unmoved by her promise. It was sweet, yes, and she believed her when she said she wouldn't give up, but if this cancer was going to win, which eventually it would, there was nothing Dr. Alexis or anyone else with all their drugs and magic could do for her. And after hearing the laundry list of side effects—the sensitivity to cold, the numbness in her hands and feet, the fatigue, nausea, headaches—she wasn't sure she wanted to go through with any of it. What was she fighting for? For Jim? He'd be fine without her. Her children? She'd been a preoccupied mother, and her kids now wanted nothing to do with her. They wouldn't miss her. The ranch? It was a ghost town, a remnant of a dream that faded a little more every year. Once she was gone they could sell the thing, pay off the remaining debts, and keep whatever was left.

The ride home began in an uncomfortable silence. Nena sensed Jim wanted to say something; he kept massaging the steering wheel and fidgeting in his seat.

"You know," she said, "if you're trying to get something out of that wheel, you're gonna be rubbing a long time."

Jim glanced out the side window, made a left-hand turn. "Aren't you going to say anything?"

"About what?"

"About the visit we just had, what Dr. Alexis said, the chemo, radiation, side effects, the prognosis, anything. Something."

Irritation crawled into her chest. She didn't want to be irritated with Jim. She wasn't, in fact, irritated with *him*; she was irritated with the circumstances. She hated being a victim, hated not having control, hating feeling so helpless, and hated being a burden. "I don't have much to say."

"Well, how are you feeling about it all?"

"What does it matter?" The words came out clipped and sharp.

"It matters to me."

When she didn't respond, Jim said, "Nena, I'm your husband, you can talk to me. Please, open up, tell me what you're going through, how you're dealing with all this."

"Okay. I hate it. I hate the whole thing. It makes me so scared and mad and frustrated I just feel like giving up. What's the point of going through all this surgery and chemo anyway?"

"Because it may kill the cancer, and if nothing else, it'll prolong your life."

"For what?"

A cloud of hurt moved over his face. She'd again wounded the one man who truly loved her, the one person in this world who had stuck by her all these years when she'd been so absorbed with the ranch. When he spoke, his voice was low and quiet. "For me."

Nena turned away, watched the familiar landscape of trees and pastures move by, so peaceful, so perfect, so oblivious to the storm raging inside her.

"You need to talk to someone." He said it as though he had already determined it was going to happen. Like it was an order.

"I don't need to talk to anyone."

"Yes, you do."

"Then I don't *want* to talk to anyone."

"You need to though, Nena." His hand found hers, and as always it brought some comfort, if even a little. "If…" He hesitated, swallowed. "None of us knows how much longer we have, that's the truth. Do you want to live out the rest of your life in bitterness, angry, isolating yourself away?"

She didn't answer. She couldn't. Because, of course, he was right.

Chapter Twenty-One

DAD, IS MOM GONNA DIE?"

Barb stood at the top of the stairs, hand over her mouth, silent tears spilling down her cheeks. She knew her journey would be tough on the children, especially Mikey, but she had no idea he'd been worrying about such things. But it was perfectly normal, wasn't it? She couldn't deny that she'd wondered the same thing. And Doug had too. Who wouldn't?

"No, buddy, Mom's gonna be just fine." Doug's voice sounded so certain. Like he had an inside line to God and had been told everything would work out, that the suffering was only for a season and one day they'd look back on this and chuckle that they'd ever worried in the first place. It was a nice thought, but she doubted—in fact, she knew—Doug was nowhere near as confident as he sounded.

"But she looks so sick, and all she does is sleep all the time."

She could hear the fear in Mikey's voice. No ten-year-old should have to worry about losing his mother.

"She is sick, but she's getting better. It's going to take time, and once all this is said and done, she'll get her strength back."

Barb pushed away from the wall and headed for the bathroom. She needed to make an effort not to look so sick. She could put on some makeup, wear regular clothes, that sort of thing. But the weight loss she could do nothing about. She'd lost nearly forty pounds already. The angles of her face were sharper, her cheeks hollow, eyes sunken. She barely resembled herself.

After turning on the shower, she slipped out of her robe and pajamas and stared at herself in the mirror. Ribs protruded like elongated fingers beneath her skin, pelvic and hip bones pushed out like box angles. Her skin was taut and dry and pale.

Barb got into the shower and allowed the water to pour over her face. With her eyes closed, the images came back, the dream images of the horse, the valley, the mountains, and that feeling was there again, something closing in, gaining ground, reaching for her. She pulled her head out of the water stream and opened her eyes, rubbed at them. Mikey's voice was in her head then: *Is Mom gonna die? She looks so sick.*

The tears came again and mingled with the water already on her cheeks. She'd been crying so much lately; her emotions were so sporadic and unpredictable. At times the hopelessness was almost too much to bear and the feeling of that grisly unseen hand reaching for her so real she nearly jerked away physically. She was losing herself, losing her mind, her will to fight, her will to live. Again she thought of her kids, motherless, and Doug, a widower. Her chest tightened, and her hands began to quiver.

Sobs erupted from deep in her chest, and the tears flowed freely now. In that shower, under the warm water washing away her salty tears, Barb Mackey did something she hadn't done in decades, since she was a kid...

"God, help me," she prayed. "Spare my life."

CHAPTER TWENTY-TWO

SHE KNEW THE PHOTO ALBUM was there somewhere. Under the bed, maybe. Nena got down on all fours and blew the dust bunnies from the containers stuffed under the bed frame. She slid out a box and lifted the top. Some of the kids' old school projects were in there, a few hand-cut snowflakes, some primitive drawings, a cut-out snowman. She pushed it all aside and pulled out another box. This one was stuffed with Christmas decorations, mostly homemade ornaments and old cards. Not what she was looking for either. The photo album, the one with the pictures of the kids, was in her bedroom somewhere; it had to be. An inkling of panic stirred inside her. For some reason she felt she needed to find the album, needed to see the photos she hadn't looked at in years.

Shoving the boxes back under the bed, she climbed to her feet and moved to the closet. After only a few minutes of searching she found the album under a pile of old sweaters on the shelf above the clothes rack. She ran her hand over the cover and sighed. She sat down on the bed and placed the album on her lap. Sunshine angled through the window and dusted the room in a comfortable blush. It was warm on Nena's back, bringing memories of picnics and playtime, memories encapsulated in the collection of snapshots she now held in her hands.

Nena opened the album's cover with the reverence and care one would give a century-old holy book. The binding popped and cracked like an arthritic back. On the first page was a photo of a much younger Jim holding an infant in his arms. Barbara. Nena was there too, her skin smooth, hair long, and smile wide. Her hand rested on Jim's arm, and her face was turned toward his. Page after page more snapshots greeted her, mostly of the children playing, running, making silly faces, waging water battles, riding the horses. Smiles abounded. Eyes laughed.

She turned the page, and her breath caught in her chest. There was a photo of her with all three kids. Roberta was barely a toddler, Kenny six or seven, and Barb in her teen years. Nena held Roberta in her arms, their faces cheek to cheek. Kenny and Barb sat on either side, their arms around her waist. Like floodwaters breaching a levy, the memory came back in a rush. It was Mother's Day, and they'd gone on a picnic to one of the far pastures. The sun was high in the sky and warm; a light breeze rustled through the treetops and shin-high grass. It was a perfect day, and Nena had never felt more whole, more complete. She had her horses, her husband, her children.

Lightly, as if to press too hard would smudge the memory from her mind, Nena dragged her fingertips over the photo. It was the last time she remembered being truly happy. A week later her father died and left her the ranch...and a ton of problems to deal with.

Tears gathered in Nena's eyes, blurring the image of that glorious day. Life had changed so much since then, taken so many wandering turns. There was so much hurt, so much regret.

A knock came at the door of the bedroom, startling her. She shut the album, looked up. A man stood there, familiar but strange. She knew him, but from where?

"Hello, Nena."

It came to her then, Reverend Busbey. She hadn't seen him for decades. He was much older, grayer, thinner, but the eyes were the same, and the voice. She'd stopped attending church shortly after her father died. The ranch simply demanded too much time. For months the pastor had called, even stopped by a couple times, but nothing he said could persuade her to return to church. Jim must have put him up to this.

She placed the album on the bed beside her and left her hand on its cover. "Reverend. It's been a long time."

He stayed in the doorway, his long fingers holding a ball cap. He was dressed in blue jeans and a maroon Virginia Tech sweatshirt. "Too long, Nena. May I come in? Jim told me it was okay to come up and see you."

"I have no need for church."

Busbey smiled. "I didn't suppose you did. That's not why I'm here. In fact, I'm not even at the church anymore. Retired six years now."

"And how is retirement treating you?"

"Not kindly. Arthritis in most of my joints, I need a new knee, and they tell me my back is deteriorating." He waved his hand. "The usual, I hear, for a man my age."

"I'm sorry you're not able to enjoy it more."

"Oh, I'm enjoying it okay. I do miss the church, though, the people, staying involved. At times I feel like an old racehorse in a lonely pasture, watching the young stallions run and romp."

Nena nodded. "I know the feeling."

"So I hear."

"Is that why you're here? Did Jim ask you to come?"

Busbey motioned toward a chair at the foot of the bed, near a window. "May I?"

"Of course."

He sat in the chair, rubbed his knee. "Yes, Jim asked me to come. He thought maybe you'd like someone...different to talk to."

"And did he tell you I have no desire to talk?"

The pastor smiled. "Yes, he certainly did."

"And why is it he thought I'd like to talk to you? No offense."

Busbey brushed off her thinly veiled insult. "None taken." He sat back in the chair, elbows on the armrests, and tented his fingers. "Do you remember my wife, Florence?"

"Yes, of course. She was always very kind to our family."

117

"She was very kind to everyone. She was an angel." He paused, and his eyes glazed over for only a second. "She died a year ago."

"I'm sorry," Nena said, and she was. Florence Busbey was a gem of a woman, always ready with an encouraging word and warm smile. "I hadn't heard."

The pastor's eyes dropped to the floor and followed the lines of the hardwood boards. "She battled cancer for two years. Breast cancer."

Nena could tell the wound was still very raw, far from being healed.

"It finally claimed her life."

"I'm sorry."

"Yes. We all are. She's missed dearly by everyone, especially our children and me. She loved them so much, and the love was returned."

Those pricks of guilt were there again, needling at Nena's heart. Would her children miss her dearly? She doubted it. She realized she was gripping the edge of the photo album and removed her hand.

Busbey's eyes went to the book. "Reminiscing?"

"Just going through some old photos."

"That's good. Remembering is good."

Nena didn't say anything.

"Do you know what I admired most about my wife?" He didn't wait for Nena to take a guess. "Her will to live. There at the end things got pretty bad, but still she fought. She loved life and lived it with no regrets." He stood and smoothed his pants. "Nena, not a one of us knows how much time we have left. Not a one. Don't let some doctor give you an expiration date. And don't give up. Make the most of what you have."

Tears welled in her eyes. With a quick brush of her hand she dashed at them and turned her face away. And still she said nothing. She couldn't; the lump in her throat was so large and solid it blocked any words from escaping.

Reverend Busbey approached her and put a hand, large but light, on her shoulder. "If you ever need anyone to talk to, just talk, I'm only a phone call away. I won't condemn, won't judge, won't even try to get you to go back to church. I promise."

Nena grabbed a tissue from the box on her bedside table and nodded.

"Very well. You'll be in my prayers, Nena." He crossed the open space and left the room.

Nena waited until she heard his footsteps descend the stairs and land in the foyer area, then she let the tears flow freely.

Chapter Twenty-Three

NENA'S OFFICE WAS LOCATED AT the east end of the house. It was the same size as the study but decorated in lighter, airier colors. Framed horse paintings and photos covered the walls. More trophies and ribbons adorned the bookshelves. Jim sat himself behind the desk, a trim, mission-style piece that had been in the St. Claire family for generations. Beside it sat a chunky oak file cabinet. There was no computer in this room; Nena abhorred them. No television, either. In fact, the only pieces of technology dating later than 1900 were a telephone and a calculator. This was where Nena conducted business, where she once ran the ranch and oversaw its thirty-five employees and over a hundred horses. Now the desk was mostly empty, showing no sign of any work being done here in years.

Jim opened the top drawer of the file cabinet and removed the ledger. He'd talked to Nena about computerizing the books for years, but she'd refused, saying by the time she booted the confounded thing up and worked through the maze of clicks to get to the page she wanted, she could have opened her ledger, done her business, and been finished. And for security reasons she always kept a duplicate ledger in the safe.

Opening the ledger and scanning the numbers, a knot twisted Jim's stomach. He'd never paid much attention to the business side of the ranch. That was Nena's thing. She was the horse woman who'd grown up in the horse family. Jim was and always had been a grunt, and that's the way he liked it. But he knew bad numbers when he saw them. And every time he checked the ledger, he got that same gnawing feeling in the pit of his stomach. Over the years Nena had sold the horses and some of the land. They'd trimmed the workforce until there was no one left, and they'd auctioned the trailers, trucks, and most of the tack, but he'd never imagined they'd come so close to losing everything.

He tried to push away the thought, but still it came, knocking like an unwanted guest. What would happen to the ranch once Nena was gone? Could he manage it himself? Did he want to? What was there to manage? Did he feel an obligation to keep it in the family even if none of the kids showed any interest in it? What about the grandkids? Could one of them resurrect it?

Jim put his head in his hands and massaged his temples, forcing the questions from his mind. Nena would be okay; she'd have to be. She'd beat this thing, and they could get on with their lives. They could sell more of the land, the far pastures, and pay off the remaining debt. If necessary they'd sell it all. They only needed an acre or two themselves. Some developer would surely be interested in prime real estate. As long as he and Nena were together, that was all that mattered.

Please, sweetheart, don't leave me.

He rolled the desk chair to the window and looked out across the rolling acres of green pastureland. The sky, so huge, so distant, hovered like an endless quilt, made from the bluest silk threads and pieced together with the softest cotton. In his mind he pictured Nena on horseback canvassing the area, her hair swept about by a brisk breeze. She sat so straight, so proud. She loved her horses and was never happier than when she was sitting high on one. He saw her there as if he'd been transported back in time three decades, just as real as he'd seen her then.

The horse nods its head and snorts; she pats its neck and speaks comforting words into its perked ear. A dog circles the horse's feet, snapping at a butterfly. Hickory, that silly dog.

Dropping the bucket, Jimmy followed Nena's voice and found her in one of the stalls—George's—crouched in the corner. The horse was against the far wall, eyes wide, ears laid back, snorting and stamping his feet nervously.

"Jimmy, come over here." Her voice was high and strained. "Oh, Hickory."

Jimmy approached and saw Hickory on his side, muzzle and cheek matted with drying blood, several ribs broken and deformed. The dog's chest did not rise and fall. Its lifeless eyes did not blink.

Jimmy knelt in the straw beside Nena. "Should I find the vet? Maybe—"

"No." She shook her head and wiped at a tear. "Look at him. He's—"

A voice behind them startled Jimmy. "What's going on? Nena—"

They both spun around, and Nena jumped to her feet. Ted McGovern, the prince of Arabia, accepted her into his arms and held her tight as she cried into his chest.

"What happened?" He looked at Jimmy for an answer.

"I don't know," Jimmy said. "We found him like this. We were riding and brought the horses back and—"

"Is he dead?"

"I...yes." Jimmy ran his fingers through his hair. He didn't like the way he felt, like he and Nena were doing something inappropriate and had somehow caused the dog's death, and now they'd been caught red-handed. "We found him like this."

"Shh, Nena, it's okay." Ted stroked Nena's hair. "Did the horse do it? Do you think the horse did it?"

"I–I don't—" Jimmy's mind ground to a halt. He couldn't find the words.

Nena pulled away and wiped at her cheeks with both hands. "No way. George would never do something like that."

"But look at him." Ted pointed at Hickory's broken body. "He looks like he took a few sharp kicks. How else—"

"No. Hickory has been around the horses before. They knew him." In the far corner George continued to snort and shake his head. He hoofed at the ground and bumped against the wall.

"He's still agitated," Ted said. "Maybe the dog spooked him."

"I can't…" Nena stumbled on her words. "I don't—"

"Come on, Nena." Ted tugged on her arm. "We'll find Candace and ask her to come back for the dog. I want you out of here."

"Go ahead," Jimmy said. "I'll make sure the horses are secure."

Ted left with Nena clinging to his arm. She didn't look back at Jimmy, didn't look back at the battered corpse of Hickory, her beloved Australian Shepherd, either.

Jimmy walked over to the dog, crouched beside it, and took a closer look. The poor thing had no doubt died from internal injuries, probably one of those fractured ribs puncturing a lung. George had settled some but stayed close to the wall, eyes still wide and studying Jimmy's every move. Jimmy stood but kept his distance. Something had spooked the horse, and he doubted it was Hickory.

"It's okay, boy, no one's gonna hurt you. It's all over."

George snorted and flicked his ears front to back. Flared his nostrils.

Jimmy backed out of the stall, leaving the dog where he lay. The vet, Candace, would come by later and deal with things. He closed the door to the stall and latched it, then headed back to the bunkhouse.

Jumper met him at the door of their room, hands in his pockets. The TV was off. "Gotta talk to you, Farm Boy."

Jimmy wasn't in the mood for one of Jumper's lectures. "Can it wait?" He walked past the older man and stripped off his shirt.

Jumper followed him into the room. "No, it can't. You went out riding with her, didn't ya?"

"Look, I don't want to talk about it right now, okay? I need to get in the shower." Jimmy grabbed a clean T-shirt and a pair of shorts.

"Listen here, Farm Boy." Jumper stood between Jimmy and the doorway. "There's something you gotta know."

"What, that I should stay away from her 'cause she's engaged? Got it. Loud and clear. Now get out of my way." He didn't try to hide his irritation.

The whole scene back at the stables had left him emotional and upset. The way Ted had talked to him, the accusation in his voice... The way Jimmy had fumbled over his words was just plain embarrassing. Then the way Nena...

Jimmy wanted to be the one whose arms she fell into, whose shoulder she cried on. He'd only met Ted once but already didn't like him. Why did he feel like he was competing with Ted and had just lost? He didn't want to compete. Nena wasn't his to compete for. She was engaged, taken, and he needed to remember that. She might be friendly to him, smile and laugh with him, even take rides with him, but in the end her heart belonged to Ted McGovern, the rich kid, the prince of Arabia.

"This ain't about that, Jimmy." It was the first time Jumper called him by his name.

"Then what is it?"

"I got someone you need to talk to. Come with me. You need to hear this." He stepped outside the room and waited for Jimmy.

Jimmy hesitated. "I'm done talking, Jumper."

"You don't need to do no talking then, just listen. You can listen, can't ya?"

"This better be good."

They walked down the sidewalk in front of the bunkhouse and stopped three doors down. The smell of cooking oil and spices sifted through the screened door. Jumper knocked twice. "Hey, Rick, come on out here."

A short, middle-aged Mexican man emerged. His jet black hair had been wetted and slicked back off his forehead. Two other younger men stood behind him. Jimmy knew their names—Javier and Alfonze—and nodded to them. Rick's full name was Rigaberto

Ramirez Sanchez de la Gonzalez. He was proud of his name, but apparently Jumper wasn't. Rick would have to do.

Jumper jabbed a thumb in Jimmy's direction. "Tell Jimmy here what ya seen."

Rick looked at Jimmy, then shot a glance at Javier and Alfonze. He ran his hand over his hair, smoothing it flatter against his head.

"Well, go on," Jumper said. "He ain't gonna tell no one without your permission. I'll make sure a' that."

Rick mussed his hair, then smoothed it again. He rubbed his jaw and crossed his arms. "The dog, I saw what happened." His voice was low and serious.

"Hickory? You saw who killed him?" Jimmy was ready to listen now.

"Sí. After you and Miss Nena left, I went to the stable to check on the horses." He smoothed his hair again and shifted his eyes side to side. "And he was there."

"Who?"

"Tell him, Rick," Jumper said. "Ain't no one gonna snitch on ya."

"Mr. McGovern."

Jumper put his hands on his hips. "The prince of Arabia."

"What did he do?" Jimmy asked. He didn't like where this was headed.

"Mr. McGovern, he no like the horses," Rick said. "He beats them sometimes. I see this."

Javier and Alfonze nodded in agreement.

Jumper turned his head and spit a wad of black juice on the dirt. "You watch the McGoverns long enough, and you'll figure something out, Jimmy."

"What's that?"

"Ted McGovern, the heir to the family fortune, isn't half the man his father is. And his father knows it and doesn't hesitate to remind his son of it. I've been around that family since Ted was Teddy, a spoiled little brat of a kid. He's forever trying to live up to the family name, make his daddy proud . . . and forever failing. He takes his frustrations out on the horses."

125

"Okay, so what happened in the stable?"

"After you and Miss Nena left, Mr. McGovern, he go into the stall and try to saddle George, but George no like him. So Mr. McGovern, he hit George. Hickory, he's a good dog and starts barking, going after Mr. McGovern's ankles." Rick made a barking sound and snapping motion with his hand.

"And Ted beat him?"

Rick looked at the ground and nodded. "Sí. He kick Hickory, again and again. Hickory, he try to fight back, but Mr. McGovern was too big, his foot too fast."

Anger rose in Jimmy's chest. "And he killed him?"

"Sí. He kicked Hickory until he not move no more."

"So it would look like George killed him."

"Sí."

Jumper kicked at a clump of dried dirt on the sidewalk. "Hickory was a good dog. He had no right to do that."

An image of Ted holding Nena, stroking her hair, flashed through Jimmy's mind. He ground his molars and clenched his fists.

"Don't you do it, Farm Boy," Jumper said. "I see those wheels turning, and the thoughts they're crankin' out ain't gonna do no one any good."

"You have no idea what I'm thinking."

"I know it ain't no good. Think about it; who's gonna believe you? What? You gonna go to Cricket and tell him you know Ted killed the dog, based on what, the testimony of a Mexican hand?" He turned to Rick. "No offense."

That was part of Jimmy's plan.

Rick stepped forward. "You can't tell no one I told you, man. I could lose my job."

Jumper put a hand on the stocky Mexican's chest. "Easy, Rick. No one's gonna mention any names." He turned to Jimmy. "And who's gonna take your word over Ted's? He's a McGovern, boy; do you know what that means 'round here? He's like royalty. And don't even think about going to Miss Nena—"

"Why not? She deserves to know."

"And you think she's gonna believe you over her fiancé?"

He had a point. Really, Jimmy was nobody to Nena, just another ranch hand she had a few things in common with. If she had to choose between him and Ted, of course she'd pick her fiancé every time. That much was evident back at the stable. "So what do we do?"

Jumper looked at Rick, then at Jimmy. "Nothin'. We just let it lay. Ain't nothin' we can do anyways."

That wasn't good enough for Jimmy. He had to do something. He had to find a way to tell Nena. If Ted was capable of raining that kind of violence down on Hickory, sooner or later he'd turn it on Nena. And if he ever laid a hand on her, Jimmy would make him very sorry.

Chapter Twenty-Four

BARB PACED IN HER BEDROOM, her joints aching, head feeling as light as helium. The shades had been drawn, allowing only a dusting of sunlight to filter into the room. Any bright light put her head to pounding.

The address book sat on her bed, closed. She stopped and stared at it. She didn't want to do this—not because she didn't want to talk to Berta or Kenny, but because she didn't want to talk to them about this, especially after so long. She knew old hurts would be drudged up, scabs peeled away, wounds opened. And feeling as she did, it was the last thing she wanted to deal with right now.

But she had to. She'd promised her father. And it was the right thing to do.

Making her way around the bed, she sat on its edge and lifted the address book onto her lap. She found Berta's cell phone number first. Before she could talk herself out of it, she grabbed the cordless from its cradle and punched in the numbers, held the phone to her ear.

Two rings, then, "Roberta Hutching."

"Berta?"

"Yes?"

Clearly, she didn't recognize Barb's voice.

"It's Barb."

"Oh, hey, Barb. This is a surprise."

"Is it?"

There was a pause. "No, I guess it isn't. How've you been?"

Barb quickly debated whether to tell Berta about her own battle but decided against it. She didn't want this to be about her. She'd tell Berta and Kenny about her cancer later. Right now she only wanted to talk about their mother.

"I'm okay. We're all doing okay."

"Just okay?"

Berta always had been hard to fool, even as a child. "Yeah, we have some things going on here, but we're managing. How about you?"

"Uh, yeah, yes. Fine. Doing great."

She was lying. Berta wore her emotions on her sleeve, and she never could lie past the tone in her voice. "What's going on, Berta? Something's wrong."

There was a long pause then a sniff. "Thomas and I aren't doing so well, that's all. We're having some problems. And this thing with Mom and Dad."

"Are you thinking of going to see them?"

Berta sighed. "I don't know. I don't know what to think, I don't know what to feel. I mean, she never was much of a mother to me, always so busy with the ranch and the horses. I felt like the nuisance child. But I've been having this dream lately. I'm a little girl, just a couple years old maybe, sitting on Mom's lap while she rocks me and sings me this lullaby. I remember the song for some reason—"

"'Baby, my sweet, don't you cry. Baby, my sweet, don't you fear.'"

"Yes! That's it. 'Mommy will take care of you, I'm here.' Where is it from?"

"Mom used to sing that to all of us."

"Mom sang to us?"

"All the time."

"I don't remember that. Not any of it."

"I don't expect you would." Barb stood, steadied herself, and crossed the room to the window. "You were so young. But you need to know, she was a different person then." Pulling back the shade, she squinted into the bright light, then quickly let it fall back into place.

"That's what I hear. I'm sorry I don't remember her like that."

Barb could hear the bitterness in her sister's voice. "I am too. She was a lot of fun."

"Then Granddad died, and everything changed."

"Yes, it did. The ranch had some real financial problems, and she was determined to not lose it. She poured herself into saving the ranch."

"And meanwhile she lost her family."

Barb returned to the bed, sat on the edge. She swung her legs up onto the mattress and propped her back against the head-board. "Yes. She did. But I think that at the time, in her own mind, she thought she was doing the right thing for her family. That saving the ranch, the land, the house, the horses, the business, would benefit us all."

"I needed a mother, not a bunch of land. And certainly not a horse."

"We all did, Berta. I'm not justifying what she did, and I'm not making excuses for her. Just putting things into perspective."

Berta huffed on the other end of the line. "Well, my perspective growing up was that everything was more important than me. That I was always second or third or fourth fiddle to Mom. I just wanted to be number one once."

"And you still do." Another pause. Barb could hear people talking in the background.

"Yes, I do."

"You need to go back, Berta. You need to see her. She needs to see you."

"Are you going?"

"Eventually. I have some things I have to take care of here first, some pressing needs, then I'm going to visit."

"What things? Are you okay?"

Barb swallowed. A lump had formed in her throat, lodged there like an old stubborn memory that wouldn't fade away. She decided she had no reason to keep secrets from her sister. "I have breast cancer, Berta."

"Oh, Barb, you too? How—what are they doing for it?"

"The doctors think they caught it early. I'm going through chemo and radiation now. Then surgery at some point in the future."

"How are you feeling?"

Tears burned behind Barb's eyes. "Mostly tired, light-headed, nauseated. Kinda like having the flu." Again she heard people in the background, talking, laughing. "Where are you?"

"The lobby of city hall, waiting for a council hearing to start."

"Berta, will you at least consider visiting them?"

"Uh…yeah. Hey, listen, I gotta run; the hearing's about to start."

"Okay. Think about it, okay?"

"Yes. I will. And you take care. Keep me posted on… everything."

"I will. Bye, Berta. Love you."

"You too. Bye."

Barb clicked off the phone and rested her head against the headboard. She closed her eyes and drew in a deep breath, wondering if Roberta really would consider it. Her little sister had always been unpredictable. She could also be stubborn. As stubborn as their mother.

Barb checked the time. She still needed to talk to Kenny, but it would have to wait. She had an appointment at the medical center in an hour and had to get ready for it.

Chapter Twenty-Five

THE LIGHTS IN THE PRE-OP room were giving Nena a headache. And the warmth from the thin blanket was waning, allowing the chilled air to bring her muscles to a subtle shiver. She worked her hands together, then rubbed her arms. "Can I get another warmed blanket?"

"I'll go find a nurse." Jim got up and disappeared behind the curtain.

The nurse had been in earlier to prepare her and start the IV drip. The anesthesiologist had been in to explain the procedure and have her sign a few forms. The surgeon had been in to say hi and ask if she was ready.

Was she ready? Was anyone ever ready for this? They were going to remove a portion of her colon and explore the liver (the lungs would come later). There were serious risks involved. And this surgery would kick off nine months of recovery, chemo, and radiation. Nine months of misery... if she lived that long.

No, she wasn't ready.

Jim returned with a new white blanket, folded neatly. "Here you go, sweetheart, right out of the warmer." He unfolded it and draped it over her legs, then pulled it up to her shoulders. He kissed her on the cheek. "You ready?"

Nena shook her head.

"Dr. Monroe knows what he's doing. It'll go fine. I know it will."

She knew he was saying it as much for his own benefit as hers. Jim always clammed up when he was nervous, and he'd barely spoken two sentences since they arrived at the hospital.

A few minutes later two nurses dressed in blue scrubs pushed the curtain aside. The older of the two, a thin, gray-eyed woman who had earlier introduced herself as Mary, squeezed Nena's leg. "It's time, honey. We're going to roll you down to the OR. Your husband can come with us right up to the doors. Then you're in our hands." She squeezed again. "You're in good hands, you hear? Dr. Monroe is the best at what he does. You should have full confidence in him."

Nena forced a smile and nodded. She slid her hand out from under the blanket and reached for Jim's. He took her hand and kissed it lightly.

"Okay, here we go," the other nurse said.

The bed began to roll, and a flutter of butterflies took flight in Nena's belly. From the pre-op area they rolled down a series of hallways until the bed finally came to a stop outside a set of double swinging doors.

Jim took Nena's hand in both of his and kissed it again. "I'll be waiting for you and will be right by your side as soon as I can."

Nena's hand began to shake.

The older nurse touched Nena's shoulder. "It'll be okay. Soon you'll be asleep, and when you wake up, it'll all be over."

And it'll just be beginning, Nena thought.

Jim leaned in and kissed her on the lips. "I love you, Nena Hutching."

She touched his cheek. "I love you too."

He let go of her hand, and the bed rolled again, pushing the doors open. Nena kept her eyes locked on Jim until the doors closed, separating her from anything that was familiar and comforting.

The operating room was cold and sterile, all hard surfaces and clean edges. Lots of stainless steel and tile. Bright lights, faceless people. Nena was moved from the gurney to the operating table. The anesthesiologist said he was going to start the IV, she'd get sleepy in a matter of seconds, don't fight it, just close your eyes and let the sleep come.

Nena rested her head on the hard surface and closed her eyes.

Images flashed on the inside of her lids, the photos, the memories. The children. The last image she saw just before slipping into a deep sleep was her own face and Roberta's, their cheeks pressed against one another, both smiling, happy, content. She heard her daughter's easy laughter, then fading, fading, until it was gone.

Poor Roberta.

Chapter Twenty-Six

THEY WERE TEN MINUTES INTO the trip to the medical center when Doug asked Barb how she was feeling. She looked out the window at the forest whizzing by in a blur of green. "I'm fine."

He was quiet for a moment. She looked straight ahead, and from her peripheral vision she saw him tapping the steering wheel with both hands. "You don't seem fine," he finally said.

"How does fine seem to you?"

Again, the silence. His first response had carried with it a hint of irritation, and she knew something was brewing and ready to bubble to the surface. "I wish you'd talk to me," he said. "Tell me how you're really doing with all this. Every time I ask, you just say you're fine."

"Maybe I am."

"Maybe you aren't."

"And you can tell?"

"Yes, as a matter of fact I can. You can learn a lot about a person in fifteen years if you pay attention."

"Are you saying I haven't paid enough attention to you?" Now her irritation level rose.

"You know that's not how I meant it."

The forest ended, and a stretch of barren field opened up, sprawling back all the way to the horizon. In the distance, just beyond a sloping rise, a herd of cattle grazed lazily. The angled roof of a barn was visible just behind them. Overhead two vultures carved circles in the sky.

"Look," Doug said. "It would do you some good to talk about it. I'm here to listen."

"And what good is talking going to do?"

"Well, it sure beats what you do now. You spend all your time in bed or on the recliner. You just stare off into space. You won't read, won't watch TV, won't do anything."

She turned her face toward the window again. They'd passed the farm and turned off the highway. The road now shot straight through a cornfield that had been harvested weeks ago. Stumps of stalks formed rows of bristles, perfectly arranged and curving with the rolling terrain. "I don't feel like doing anything." She said it low enough that she thought he might have missed it.

"Barb." His hand rested on her thigh. "I know you're depressed, that's normal, but it may help for you to get out of the house more, interact with some other people, laugh once in a while. You know, live a little."

How could she live when death loomed so close, in her own life, in her mother's? The weight she carried was so heavy, the burden so large and overbearing, at times she thought she'd be crushed by its immensity. She'd been struggling physically, yes, but emotionally she was a train wreck. She felt like she'd been dumped in a deep hole with no way out. No matter how hard she tried, no matter how many times she attempted to climb out of the darkness, it was hopeless. There was no escape. Doug meant well, but he simply did not understand. He had no idea what she was going through, and no amount of talking would help. It was no one's fault; it was just the nature of the beast. Doug might as well be a thousand miles away because of how removed she felt from everything she once knew.

She hated that she felt that way; she knew her family needed her, especially Mikey and Kara, but she felt helpless to do anything about it.

Again she turned and looked out the window. The fields of corn had given way to more forest, more trees and underbrush, and a winding creek dotted with fractured boulders.

"I'm so broken," she whispered, quietly enough that she knew Doug could never hear her. "I'm so broken."

CHAPTER TWENTY-SEVEN

JIM LEANED FORWARD, ELBOWS ON his knees, and looked at his watch. It'd been a little over an hour since they wheeled Nena into the operating room and out of his sight. Dr. Monroe had said the surgery would take two to three hours depending on what they found and how extensive the resection and repair had to be. It was only eight fifteen now, and at this hour the waiting room was not even half full. A couple other families were gathered in each corner, speaking in hushed tones. Tension permeated the room, thickened the air.

Jim stood, stretched his back, and walked to the water cooler to refill his cup. His mouth felt like it was lined with cotton, and a dull headache gnawed behind his temples. After downing one cupful and refilling it, he returned to his seat and closed his eyes. The prayer came easily, from somewhere deep in his soul, a place he'd rarely explored over the years. It was short and void of the flowery words and phrases often used in churches. It was just him and God, so there was no need to impress.

Praying brought memories to the surface. Jim tried to push them down, keep them under those dark waters of his past, but they kept bobbing like a buoy, coming into view and reminding him where it all had led.

Sometimes the night sky is so black and the stars so bright they seem close enough to reach out and take between your thumb and index finger. Without the glare of any kind of light pollution, the sky above the St. Claire ranch appeared to hang low like a ceiling encrusted with diamond chips. Jimmy lay on his back in the grass

on a hill, hands behind his head, and stared up at the endless display of glittery lights. He'd managed to go one day over a week without running into Nena, but every day was torture. He wanted to tell her what he knew, but he couldn't. His knowledge was secondhand information given to him by a mere ranch hand.

Ted would deny it, of course he would, and who would Nena believe—an unnamed Mexican hand or her fiancé, the wonderful Ted McGovern? Telling her would only make Jimmy look bad. He needed to stay low for a while, avoid her and let things settle down. But all the while he kept his eye on Ted whenever the prince stopped by the ranch. A few times Ted caught Jimmy watching him, smiled, and nodded cordially, but Jimmy never returned the greeting. He wanted Ted to know someone was watching, someone who didn't buy his Mr. Perfect routine.

A cool breeze blew up the hill and rustled the grass. After a day of work under the hot sun, any air movement brought refreshment. But this current brought more than that; it also carried the scent of lavender. He lifted his head and found Nena's dark silhouette making her way up the slope. She made barely a sound as she approached and stood over him. Against the ink-black sky he couldn't see her face, but he felt her eyes on him.

"Hey, stranger," she said. "Mind if I join you?"

Jimmy came to a sit. "Sure. I was getting kind of lonely out here anyway."

She lowered herself to the ground next to him and tilted her head up. "Quite a night, isn't it?"

"I was admiring the stars."

Nena was quiet for a moment then said, "You ever wonder if there's other life out there?"

Jimmy looked at her and almost laughed. "Are you a believer?"

"In what?"

"Aliens. Area 51. Abductions."

"Would that be weird?" There was not an ounce of humor in her voice.

Jimmy didn't want to hurt her feelings. "I don't know that I'd call it weird...I just didn't take you for the type."

"I'm not, really. I just wonder. So what do you think?"

"About life out there?"

"Yeah."

Jimmy thought for a moment. "I think the only life out there is God, the angels, and the saints who have gone on before us."

"Wow," Nena said. "And I didn't take you for the religious type."

"My mom used to take me to church every Sunday."

"Used to?"

"She stopped when my dad started drinking. He didn't want her wasting her time with church and those gossipy church folk. That's what he called them."

"He never went to church with you?"

"Nah. Dad always said the way a man gets close to God is by working the land, by bringing life from it, not by sitting in a pew listening to some boring preacher."

"And what do you think?"

Jimmy didn't know what he thought. Fact was, he'd never really given it much thought. He went to church because his mother said he had to, and he stopped going because his father said he had to. End of story. "I don't know. I can see my dad's point, but I can also see the benefits. What about you?"

"Dad says we're too busy for church. But when I was a girl we used to go all the time. Then my mom got sick and we just kind of stopped."

"What happened?"

"MS. It was really rough at first, you know, with all the changes that were happening, but things have slowed down now. She can get around pretty good with some help." Nena glanced in the direction of the house. "Mostly she just stays inside."

"How old were you when she was diagnosed?"

"Eleven." Nena turned her face skyward; moonlight washed over *her nose and forehead. "Sometimes I wonder why if God could make all those stars, He couldn't just make my mother better."*

"I'm sorry."

She shrugged at his apology. "We're getting along, I guess."

There was a pause in the conversation, enough time for both of them to gaze into the heavens as if pondering the wonders it held, the deep secrets hidden in the folds of the universe. Finally Jimmy said, "How're you doing with what happened…?" He knew she'd understand what he was talking about.

"All right, I guess."

The brevity of her answer said she wasn't, though. Jimmy wanted to ask her about George, if she still thought the gentle horse was responsible for Hickory's death, but he decided against it. He didn't want to ask anything that might raise suspicion. "I'm sorry about your dog."

"Why have you been avoiding me?"

Her bluntness caught him off guard. "Avoiding you?"

"Don't play ignorant with me, Jimmy Hutching. You've been avoiding me."

He sighed and studied the sky for a moment, hoping a perfectly reasonable answer would form in the clusters of stars. When it didn't, he said, "I don't know. I guess seeing you with…" His words trailed off. He sounded ridiculous and wanted to avoid making a fool of himself.

"Seeing me with Ted?"

"Something like that."

Nena's hand found his arm. He was suddenly acutely aware of the softness of her touch, the closeness of her body, the scent of her lavender perfume. "Jimmy, Ted's my fiancé. I love him in a very special way. But I see you as a dear friend."

Those were not the words Jimmy wanted to hear. He almost pulled his arm away but fought the urge. The last thing he wanted was to look like a sore loser in a game of love his opponent didn't even know they were playing. Instead he swallowed hard. "I'm glad for our friendship," he said and knew the words sounded disingenuous. She'd see right through him.

Her grip tightened on his arm. "No, I mean it. I've never been able to talk to anyone the way I talk to you."

"Not even Ted?" He hoped that didn't sound as sarcastic as he meant it.

She paused, and her hand lightened and lifted. "We have a different kind of relationship."

That was it? A different kind of relationship?

Another moment of silence passed between them, until finally Nena stood and brushed off her pants. She tilted her head upward and spun in a circle. "Jimmy, you know what I've always wanted to do?"

"Join the circus?"

"Nope."

"Wrestle a crocodile?"

She giggled. "Not even close."

"I give up then."

She spread her arms and twirled some more. "I've always wanted to dance under the stars. Slow dance, you know, with someone special."

Jimmy's cheeks grew hot, and he was glad for the darkness so Nena wouldn't see him blushing. Suddenly his pulse raced, and his palms started to sweat. He tried to think of something witty to say or maybe even romantic, but his mind locked up like dry, broken gears. He had an urge to jump up and take her in his arms, spin her around, and kiss her full on the mouth. Instead he said, "Maybe you should talk to Ted about that."

She stopped spinning and stood over him, arms at her side, chest rising and falling with each breath. "Ted's not the dancing type." The disappointment was evident in her voice. She turned to leave. "I'll see you around?"

"Sure."

"Maybe we can go for another ride sometime. You still have a lot to learn about horsemanship if you want to become that cowboy you were talking about."

"Sure. And I need to practice putting that chew in my lip and spitting like Jumper does."

"Gross."

She walked away in silence, and Jimmy watched as her form grew smaller until she disappeared into the darkness altogether. At once a great sense of loss overcame him. He loved her. He loved everything about her. He loved spending time with her. He loved the sound of her voice, her sense of humor, her smile, her freckles, the way she said his name.

But he knew it could only amount to nothing. He was a farm boy; she was a princess. That scenario only ended happily in fairy tales. This was reality, where the good guy didn't always get the girl.

Chapter Twenty-Eight

The WAITING ROOM DOOR OPENED, and Dr. Monroe, still dressed in his scrubs, walked in and found Jim. The doctor's face held a vacant expression and the color had gone out of his cheeks.

Jim looked at his watch again. "What's wrong?" It was too soon for the surgery to be over.

Monroe sat in the chair next to Jim, laced his fingers. "Jim, Nena's okay; she's in recovery. We couldn't get the tumor out. When we got in there, we found it had completely penetrated the colon wall and had its tentacles wrapped around portions of the small intestine, bladder, and left kidney. The local metastasis is significant and inoperable. Even if we did a full dissection, I wouldn't be able to remove it all. It's too risky. There may be some surgeons out there who'd be willing to take on something like this, and you're free to seek them out. My office can give you some names if you want to go that route."

The waiting room felt like it had shrunk, like the walls had closed in on all sides. Jim tried to draw in a breath, but his lungs weren't working properly, the air was too thick, too heavy. Dr. Monroe's words hammered in Jim's head...*tentacles...metastasis...significant...inoperable...too risky*. The room darkened, and the other people there became shadows, menacing, looming, elongated figures, distorted. His Nena was going to die.

The morning was cool for a change, and a heavy dew lay on the grass. With the early morning sunlight skimming the surface, the pastures appeared to be made of ice, the mountains in the distance

so many mounds of dirty snow. But truly cold weather was still a good six months away, and the forecaster had predicted temperatures in the nineties today.

As was the habit of many of the hands, Jimmy got a start on the day early, while the air was still comfortable and sweat and exhaustion didn't come so quickly. He was used to keeping these hours, rising before the sun, from his years helping his dad on the farm.

Every morning as he watched the sun peek over the horizon and that first sliver of orange orb appear, a prick of guilt jabbed at him. He had yet to check in on his mother, make sure she was okay. He could say the work on the ranch was time consuming, and it was; he could say he was totally spent after a long day in the blazing heat, and he was; he could even say he had no ride to Monroe, and he didn't; but he knew these were only excuses, poor reasons for why he had simply shirked his responsibility. He had sent his parents a letter letting them know where he was, that he was safe and had found a good job. But that was no substitute for showing up in person. He could make the time, and it wouldn't be that hard to find a ride into town, then hike the five miles to his parents' farm. He'd just failed to keep his word.

He was in the main stables, changing the water for the mares, when Jumper found him. The old guy's legs were so bowed they nearly formed a perfect O. He walked right up to Jimmy and stopped, hands on his hips, chewing something with his front teeth.

Jumper turned his head and spit out a clump of splintered sunflower seed shells. "What'd I tell you about the St. Claire girl?"

Jimmy was in no mood to be lectured. "I don't know, Paps, what'd you tell me?"

Jumper pointed a long, thin finger at him. "You want to keep your job, you watch yourself. McGovern's got his eye on you already, and he's got a lot a pull with the boss."

"I haven't done anything wrong."

"Maybe not, but that ain't the way it looks. You don't think if I could see ya up there on the hill with her last night that McGovern or one a' his boys could see ya too?"

Jimmy didn't care who saw him. He'd done nothing wrong.

"She came to me. What am I supposed to do, tell her my daddy says I'm not allowed to play with her anymore?"

After spitting another wad of shells on the ground, Jumper tilted his head and squinted his eyes at Jimmy. "You like her, don't ya?"

"What do you mean?"

"You got a thing for her."

Jimmy walked past Jumper, bucket in hand, and headed for the spigot.

Jumper tailed him. He kept his voice low. "Don't you do nothin' foolish, ya hear?"

Jimmy spun around. "Why do you care what I do? Why do you care so much if I keep this job or not?"

Hands back on his hips, Jumper slumped his shoulders. His face relaxed. "'Cause you're a good kid and I like havin' you around. It'd be just me and those Mexicans if you got canned. And they ain't very talkative, at least not in no ways I can understand."

"I haven't done anything wrong, Jumper. Honestly. And nothing's going to happen between Nena and me. She's engaged, remember."

"Yeah, I remember. That's what's got me so worried."

Jimmy turned on the spigot and let the bucket fill as Jumper walked away.

Later that morning, after all the horses had been watered and fed and their stalls cleaned out and fresh beds of straw laid, Jimmy sat on the front porch of the stud stable and ate a sandwich. A box lunch was provided to the hands every day. Nothing special, usually just a sandwich, chips, an apple, and cookies. The sun was nearing its peak now, and waves of heat danced on the stable roofs. Jimmy enjoyed catching a few moments on the porch to eat his lunch and watch the horses in the east pasture. Mares stood around and pulled at the grass while their foals frolicked and bounded here and there on stilt-like legs. One in particular, a colt, seemed born to run. He circled his mother, then dashed a straight line away from her before realizing how far he'd strayed. Looking around, he found her and ran back to her side.

A voice behind Jimmy startled him. "He's remarkable, isn't he?"

Jimmy turned and found Ted McGovern standing on the porch, hands in his pockets. He wore neatly pressed khakis and a light blue polo shirt. His hair was combed to the side with a perfect part, and his shoes, though dusty, looked expensive. He could have stepped right off the page of a popular fashion magazine.

Stepping closer, Ted extended his hand. "Ted McGovern. We met a couple weeks ago, only it wasn't much of an introduction, what with the circumstances as they were."

Jimmy didn't miss how Ted's eyes shifted when he spoke of Hickory's death. He shook Ted's hand.

"That colt"—Ted pointed to the foal, who was back to running circles around his mother—"he's the son of Mercury's Dream and Devious Driver."

The foal whose birth Jimmy had watched with Nena.

Ted shook his head. "My, my, doesn't he have some energy. He's got million-dollar blood running through him. A lot rests on that little guy."

"He likes to run," Jimmy said.

Ted sniffed, as if to dismiss Jimmy's statement as trite. "He was born to run. He's destined to be a winner. Maybe even the Triple Crown. He's going to make us a lot of money."

"And that's what it's all about?"

Ted's hands went back into his pockets. He watched the colt as he spoke. "Isn't that what everything is about?"

"Not the way I see it."

Again, a dismissive sniff. "You wouldn't understand."

Jimmy turned in his chair to face Ted. "I understand that Nena thinks you love her."

"I do love her. And when we're married, it will bring together two of the most powerful horse-racing families in Virginia, maybe

147

in the country." Ted's eyes found the playful colt again. "It will be quite the union."

"Do you really love her? 'Cause I'd hate to see her hurt." Jimmy knew his bold question would not be well received. Ted McGovern wasn't the kind of man who would tolerate being challenged by a simple ranch hand, especially one who was a transplant from a dirty dairy farm, but Jimmy didn't care.

Ted waved his hand at Jimmy as if swatting away a pesky fly. "That's sweet, it really is, but I know how to take care of a woman."

Anger rose in Jimmy's chest, the same anger he'd felt when his father brushed him aside for defending his mother. "I wonder if she'd feel taken care of if I told her you killed her dog?"

If Ted was surprised by Jimmy's knowledge of his heinous deed, he didn't show it. He stood and straightened his back, looked down his nose at Jimmy. "And where did you come up with that story?"

"I've got an eyewitness. Does Nena know about your temper?"

Now Ted's face reddened. His jaw tightened. "Eyewitness. Who? One of those Mexicans?"

"Are you worried?"

"I never touched that dog. He must have spooked the horse and got trapped in the stall with it."

"That's not what I heard."

"You've been fed misinformation."

Jimmy stood and met Ted eye to eye. They were the exact same height. "Maybe the Mexican should talk to Nena, tell her his story himself."

Ted jabbed a finger at Jimmy's chest, and his face turned a deeper shade of red. He lowered his voice. "Go back to your cows, dairy boy. Make them happy."

Jimmy wanted to hit Ted, land a solid blow right on his chin and knock the jerk on his butt. But he restrained himself. He wouldn't allow himself to become the man his father had become, to resort to violence as a way of dealing with conflict. Instead he said nothing.

Turning to leave, Ted spoke over his shoulder. "You mind your manners now, you hear?"

When Ted was out of view, Jimmy sat in the chair and dropped his head into his hands, shaken and upset. He'd backed himself into a corner now. He had to be careful. If Ted went to Cricket with any complaint, it could cost Jimmy his job, and he couldn't afford that. Not only did he need the money and a place to sleep, but he needed to be close to Nena, if for no other reason than to keep an eye on Ted and protect her. But there was another reason, wasn't there? Of course there was. He loved her.

Standing so quickly he knocked the chair over behind him, Jimmy marched to the quarter horse stable and saddled Martin. He needed to get out of this place, get away from the stables and the other hands and the work. He needed open space to cool down and collect his thoughts.

Swinging himself onto the saddle, Jimmy grabbed the reins and dug his heels into Martin's side. "C'mon, boy, let's go. Run!"

Martin's ears twitched, he snorted loudly and dipped his chin, then pushed off with his rear legs and lunged forward. They bolted from the stable like a rocket, and Martin headed for open pasture. Jimmy had no idea where they were going; he just let Martin run. The horse's power was spectacular, his muscles like perfectly fitted parts of a machine churning at top speed. At first fear tightened Jimmy's frame, but after a few seconds he relaxed, leaned forward, and urged Martin to go faster. Such power under him was like riding a tornado. Adrenaline rushed through his veins. Martin's head bobbed rhythmically, his nostrils pulled in great breaths of air, and his hooves pounded the ground with such thunderous fury it seemed they'd break through and put them both in some mythological underworld. And still Jimmy pushed him onward, faster and faster.

Finally, after several minutes of covering ground at a full gallop, Martin slowed to a trot, then a walk. His chest expanded and contracted forcefully as he filled his lungs and exhaled.

Jimmy patted the horse's taut neck. "Good boy, Martin. Good boy." He too was winded and needed a break.

Martin trotted to a stand of dogwoods and found a small creek that cut and curved through the pasture. Jimmy slid off the saddle and let Martin drink while he sat in the shade. Overhead a hawk screeched as it rode a thermal and arced higher into the sky, avoiding an annoying pair of starlings warding it from their nest.

Jimmy had never seen this part of the St. Claire land before. Martin had carried him some distance from the main stables. There were no other horses in sight, and besides the birds no other animal life at all. This was as alone as Jimmy had been since leaving his home weeks ago. Again he thought of his mother with that familiar sting of guilt. He thought of his father. He thought of the way Ted had tried to bully him. Jimmy was through with bullies. He had to tell Nena about Hickory. Whether she believed him or not was something he'd deal with at the time, but he had a responsibility to warn her of the rage that resided inside Ted. He didn't want Nena to wind up like his mother, beaten and broken, a weak shadow of the woman she once was. And if the whole thing backfired and Nena hated him…that was a risk he was willing to take. She deserved to know the truth whether she wanted to hear it or not.

Martin walked over to Jimmy and put his muzzle next to Jimmy's ear.

"Hey, boy, you ready to go?"

Jimmy stood and climbed onto the horse's back. "We'll take it easy going back, okay? No hurry."

Martin took the cue and broke into a steady trot. The ride back took three times as long. They arrived back at the stable a little after noon to find Nena there, leaning against the wall of George's stall.

"…Jim."

Dr. Monroe's voice.

"Jim."

He looked at the surgeon.

"You okay?"

Jim nodded, wiped at a stray tear that had slipped from the corner of his eye.

"Drink some of that water."

The water was cold and felt good in Jim's mouth. Rolling over his tongue, it soothed his itchy throat.

"Nena will be ready for you to see in a few minutes. One of the nurses will get you."

Again Jim nodded.

"I'm sorry, Jim. Really I am."

"Thanks."

The doctor turned to leave.

"Dr. Monroe?"

"Yes?"

"It'd probably be best if I told her. You mind?"

A pleasant smile curled the corners of his mouth. "Not at all. I'll be around this evening to check on her. If you need anything, tell the nurse to contact me."

But how could he tell her? She was already battling depression. The hopelessness of this news would push her even farther down into those murky waters. He might lose her for good.

CHAPTER TWENTY-NINE

IF NOT FOR THE HOSPITAL bed and IV tower humming in the corner, Nena would have appeared to be at rest in her bed at home. She'd been in and out of sleep for the past hour, fighting the effects of the anesthesia and pain medication. When she slept, it seemed peaceful, deep. She made no sounds, and gone were the familiar ticks and twitches that usually awakened Jim next to her. Her eyelids would flutter open; she'd smile at Jim, maybe reach for his hand, mumble a few incoherent words, then drift back into that land of drug-induced slumber.

A nurse came in, checked the IV machine and Nena's vitals, asked if she could get Jim anything, then left, shutting the door behind her. The lights were dim, the blinds turned down. And though it was midmorning, it appeared to be the middle of the night in the room.

Jim crossed his legs and shut his eyes. He prayed that God would protect his wife, that He would comfort her even now as she slept and prepare her for the news she would soon receive. It would be easier just to lie to her, tell her the surgery had gone as planned and the tumor had been removed without incident. But he'd never lied to her before, and he certainly wasn't going to start now.

"Jim."

Jim's eyes sprang open. Nena was awake. Her head turned toward him, and she looked his way with distant eyes, as if she'd suddenly acquired the ability to look not at him but through him and see the room's door, maybe even the hallway on the other side. She smiled, but it was empty, emotionless. Her hand reached for his and he took it, squeezed, kissed her palm.

"How did it go?" she asked.

Though her eyes were unfocused and cloudy, she appeared to be lucid. A knot rose in Jim's throat, and his hand began to tremble. The room suddenly felt ten degrees warmer.

"Nena, honey, I have something to tell you."

She lifted her head from the pillow, her eyebrows knitting together. "Jim, what's the matter? What is it?" Her speech was only slightly slurred, like she'd had one too many glasses of wine and was on the edge of tipsy.

He swallowed, squeezed her hand again. "The surgery...Dr. Monroe said it didn't go so well. He, uh, said..." Unbidden, tears formed in his eyes. He swallowed, collected his emotions. "He said he couldn't take the tumor out. It was larger than he thought and wrapped around too many other organs. He said it's inoperable." There. With that final declaration he felt like he'd slammed the gavel down and delivered her death sentence.

Nena's face went slack; her eyelids slowly closed and opened. Her eyes never left his, though, and still appeared to look more through him than at him. With lips parted she blinked again, slowly, as if struggling to keep her eyes open. "That's too bad, isn't it?"

Jim didn't say anything; he couldn't. For now his silence dammed the tears.

After blinking again, this time even more slowly, Nena said, "Yes, that's too bad."

Her eyes closed, head fell back into the pillow, and chin dipped. Sleep had overcome her.

Twenty minutes later she opened her eyes and reached for him. "Jim."

"Yes, hon, I'm here." He kissed her hand.

She looked directly at him, and this time there was clarity in her eyes. This was truly his wife, all of her. She looked at her gown, at the IV tower, the length of tubing running to her arm. Her eyes scanned the room as if she'd just awakened in a strange land and needed to orient herself. "Can we open the blinds?"

"Sure." Jim got up and pulled the cord to open the slats. Sunshine, bright and pure, pushed through the window and cast wide, warm bars of light across the bed.

She smiled and turned her face toward the window.

Jim kissed her on the forehead and returned to his seat beside her. She faced him, blinked twice, and said, "How did the surgery go? Did you see Dr. Monroe?"

Chapter Thirty

AKNOCK ON THE DOOR STARTLED Jim awake. He'd fallen asleep in the chair beside Nena's bed, his head tilted to one side. Spasms clutched his neck as he lifted his head and straightened his back. He rubbed it, looked up.

Reverend Busbey was there, hands in his pockets. He shrugged. "Is this an okay time?"

Nena was asleep. Jim nodded, got up, and led the pastor into the hallway. "She needs her sleep," he said. "Thanks for coming."

"I got your call." Busbey put a hand on Jim's shoulder. "Jim, I'm sorry. Such terrible news."

That familiar knot was in Jim's throat again. He'd never get used to it. "Yeah."

"Have you told Nena?"

Jim nodded. "Earlier."

"And how did she take it?"

He glanced into the room at his sleeping wife. From this distance she looked so calm, so at peace with the world around her and the cards she'd been dealt. "I think she's in shock. I don't know. She didn't say much. 'Course, she hasn't said much about any of this. It's hard to tell what she's thinking."

"And how are you doing?"

Jim sighed. "I guess as good as any husband would be. We—I—had put so much into this surgery, getting that tumor out of her, then tackling the rest with the chemo and radiation. And now..." His words trailed off.

"And now you don't know which way is up. You don't know who's on your side."

Jim knew that Busbey had traversed this exact terrain, endured these same wounds.

"Yeah. How did you handle it?"

"I gave it to God."

"You make it sound so easy."

"Oh, it was anything but easy." Busbey motioned to a cushioned bench in the hallway. "Do you mind if we sit? My knees tell me when I've worked them too hard."

They both sat, and the pastor flexed and extended his knee. "Jim, when I found out Florence had cancer, it drove me mad. I loved that woman with all my heart, and the thought of her suffering was too much for me to deal with. I wanted to fix the problem, control it. I wanted to play God."

"But you couldn't."

"That's right. She told me as much, but at the time I didn't want to hear it. I pleaded with God, even bargained with Him. Looking back on it, I'm glad He didn't take me up on my countless propositions. I made some terrible promises. Finally I gave in. Admitted to God that, as much as I wanted to, I couldn't save my wife.

"I remember the exact day and location. I'd dropped her off for chemo and had a few errands to run. I saw a mother pushing her teenage son in a wheelchair. His limbs were bent and twisted, his face was distorted. It was obvious he would be in her care for the rest of his life. She stopped right there in the middle of the store and wiped the saliva from his chin, then kissed him on the cheek. The love that mother showed her son hit me, really hit me." He tapped his fingers against his chest. "She was at peace with her son's condition. I don't know where she stood with God, but God used her to show me my own problem. And right there in the middle of the drugstore I started to cry. I'm sure people looked at me like I was some crazy old geezer, but I didn't care. Right there I gave up control and gave Florence to God. Within a year she was gone, and there was nothing I could do about it."

Tears rolled down Jim's cheeks. He did nothing to wipe them away.

"Jim, are you in that place with God? Are you comfortable giving Him control?"

Jim shook his head. "I don't know."

"Will you pray about it?"

"Yes."

"Good. That's a start. And I'll pray for both of you. You're in a hard place, a place only God can see you through. There's no doing this on your own." Busbey winced as he stood. "Do you want me to talk to Nena when she wakes?"

"No. I think it'd be best to let things settle in for right now. Thanks, Reverend."

"You're welcome, Jim. God be with you." He left Jim sitting on the bench alone with his thoughts and questions.

Jim wondered if he'd done the right thing telling Nena the truth so soon after her surgery. Maybe he should have waited a few days.

Jimmy was surprised to find Nena in the stable. The ride had left both him and Martin hot.

"How'd you know where to find me?" Jimmy dismounted Martin and went to work unsaddling him.

Nena grabbed a brush from the wall and met him at Martin's side. "Javier said he saw you leave with Martin. You know, I haven't been back in this stable since that night."

"The evening we found Hickory."

She put the brush on Martin's neck and ran it along his withers and back. The horse's skin quivered under the touch of the bristles. "It was awful."

Jimmy removed the bridle and the bit from Martin's mouth. It was covered with grass and needed a good cleaning. "You still think George did it?"

Nena paused and held the brush on Martin's flank. "I don't want to; it's not like George at all."

"No, it's not." Jimmy's pulse throbbed in his neck. "Nena, I have to tell you something. I don't want to, but I have to."

She let the brush drop to her side. "What is it, Jimmy?"

There was no easy way to say it. "Ted killed Hickory."

He might as well have said he was not really Jimmy Hutching but a man from Mars come to heal the earth's wounds. She nearly laughed.

"What? Oh, c'mon. Jimmy Hutching, if this is about you being jealous or whatever, it isn't funny."

"No, it's not about anything like that."

"Ted killed Hickory? My Ted?" Her face changed then, to something shadowing anger. "Really, it isn't funny."

"I'm not trying to be funny."

"That's quite an accusation, you know."

"I know full well what it is. Someone saw him do it. Saw the whole thing."

"Who?" Nena's voice rose an octave.

"One of the hands."

"You can't tell me who?"

"It's not my place to say who. I don't know if he wants to get involved."

"Jumper? Was it Jumper?"

Jimmy shook his head. "No. One of the Mexicans."

"And what did he see?"

Jimmy told her everything Rick had told him. When he finished, he ducked his head and said, "I'm sorry."

Nena had her hand on her hip. "Do you expect me to believe that?"

Jimmy looked up. Tears clouded her eyes, and she pressed her lips together.

"I don't expect anything," he said. "You can believe whatever you want to. I'm just telling you—"

Martin stamped his feet and snorted. Nena put the brush on his neck and stroked toward the withers. "Shh. It's okay, boy." Then to Jimmy. "We're upsetting the horses."

"And you, I can see. I'm sorry. I didn't want to upset you, but I thought you should know."

She continued to brush Martin without saying anything. Tears welled in her eyes. Finally she turned and handed him the brush. "Here, you finish. I need to go." She hurried out of the stable.

Jimmy threw the brush down and ran his hand along Martin's shoulder. "I really did it this time, didn't I, boy?"

CHAPTER THIRTY-ONE

NCE AGAIN BARB FOUND HERSELF in her bedroom with the phone in her hand, faced with a call she didn't want to make. The radiation treatments, though brief, seemed to siphon what little energy she had, leaving her feeling like a wrung-out dishrag for the rest of the day.

She held the phone on her lap, thumb hovering over the buttons. She dialed the number to his cell phone and waited. He picked up on the third ring.

"Ken Hutching."

"Kenny? It's Barb."

She could hear papers shuffling, sliding. "Oh, hey, Barb. Hi."

"Am I interrupting anything?"

"No, just, uh, doing some paperwork. How are you?" His voice was flat, emotionless, muffled with fatigue.

"I'm okay." She didn't want this conversation to get bogged down with her own issues. "How's everything going? How are Celia and the kids?"

There was a pause while more papers shifted, rustled. "Fine. Yeah, everyone's fine. Staying healthy."

"Are you all right? You sound tired."

Another hesitation. "Uh, yeah. Been busy here at work, and it's getting to me. You know."

"I do." She also knew he was lying. Neither her brother nor her sister had ever been any good at lying. "Have you heard any news about Mom? How the surgery went?"

"No," Kenny said. "Dad hasn't called yet."

"Kenny." She swallowed, thumbed the hem of her sweatshirt. "What do you think of all this?"

"The cancer?"

"Yes. Are you going to visit Mom and Dad?"

"Man, Barb, I don't know about visiting. I have so much going on here right now, a big case and…other things. I told Dad to let me help with the financial stuff. I know their insurance won't cover everything. What about you? You going to see them?"

Barb suddenly felt the urge to get up and walk around the room. Though the radiation treatment had left her fatigued, it had also left her anxious, antsy, and given her restless legs.

"I will eventually. There're some things I need to take care of here first. I'm planning to go see how Mom is doing, where I can help." She stopped by the window and peeked out from behind the closed shade. Clouds had moved in, muting the sunlight in a pale shade of yellow. It looked like a storm was on the way. "Kenny, how old were you when Granddad died?"

"I think I was about seven or eight. Why?"

"Do you have any memories of Mom before that?"

"You mean when she still acted like a mom? Not many. We took a lot of picnics in the summer, I remember that. I remember how much she loved riding, and how she tried to teach me how to ride that pony we had. Do you remember her?"

"Marvelous Marva." Barb smiled. They got Marva when Barb was eleven. Dad used to give tours of the ranch to school groups, and Marva was used for pony rides.

"And I remember Mom's smile. I always loved it. I used to do all kinds of goofy things to make her smile. She smiled a lot back then."

"I'm glad you have some good memories of her. Berta doesn't have any."

"She was only a couple years old when Mom and Dad took over the ranch."

Barb rolled up the shade and allowed the dusty light to brighten the room. "Do you ever feel sad about your childhood?"

Kenny hesitated. "Sad? I don't know. Most of the time I don't feel anything."

"I'm sorry about that."

"Why?"

"I just am."

"I know Mom was doing what she had to do. Dad tried to make up for where she was lacking at home, but he was busy too. You do what you have to do for your family, you know?"

"Sure." But she didn't. "I have to go, Kenny. Take care, okay? And let me know when you hear something about the surgery."

"Sure thing, sis. 'Bye."

Barb clicked off the phone, crossed the room, and dropped it back into its cradle. She pulled back the bedspread and slipped under the covers. The sheets were cool, and her skin puckered with gooseflesh. She could hear Doug padding around downstairs, getting ready to pick the kids up from school. She didn't mean to withdraw so completely. She needed to talk to him more, share her burden. She didn't want to lose him...or Mikey and Kara.

Chapter Thirty-Two

ENA OPENED HER EYES AND let them adjust to the muted light of the hospital room. The clock on the wall said it was five to eleven. The window blinds were turned down, blocking the light of the streetlamps below. Jim slouched in the chair next to her bed, his chest rising and falling in a steady rhythm. Outside the room only the occasional squeak of a nurse's sneaker on the tiles broke the silence.

Sleep had only come in bits and spurts since Jim told her the news. It was official: she was going to die. Dr. Monroe had come in later in the day and reiterated what Jim had said. He tried to sound upbeat, tried to assure her that nobody was giving up on her, there was still hope. But she could hear the defeat in his voice, see the pity in his eyes. It was over.

She'd do the chemo, but not the radiation. Part of her wanted to live, wanted to spend as much time with Jim as she could. But another part, the side that whispered dark things in the middle of the night, just wanted it all to end. She didn't want to suffer, and she didn't want Jim to have to watch her deteriorate. He'd been through so much in his life and had been such a devoted and loving husband. He didn't need the responsibility of caring for an invalid.

And then there were her children, scattered across the country, living their own lives, oblivious to her plight. She didn't need to bother them either. She hadn't been there for them so many times when they needed a mother; how could she expect them to come to her side now? Regret, like a shadowy specter, entered the room and hovered around her, worked its tentacles into her heart. For all her diligence and good intentions, she'd failed them all.

Reverend Busbey's words walked through her mind: *Nena, not a one of us knows how much time we have left. Not a one. Make the most of what you have.*

He was right, wasn't he? She didn't know how much time she had left. Hopefully the chemo would allow her a little more time with Jim and maybe enough time to see her children one more time, and her grandchildren. She'd like that.

Pushing back her covers, she swung her legs over the side of the bed and sat there until the room stopped spinning in circles. A subtle but persistent throb knocked under her temples. She needed to go for a walk. She was supposed to go home tomorrow, and she wanted to be able to walk to the house from the car. After standing and unplugging the IV tower, she straightened her gown and tied it shut at her side. The wheels whined when she gave the tower a push, and Jim stirred.

"Nena, are you okay?"

"I'm fine. Just need to go for a little walk around the hallway."

He started to get up. "I'll go with you."

"No. I want to go alone. I'll be okay."

"Are you sure?"

"Yes. The nurses are right out there."

He relaxed in the chair. "Be careful."

"I will."

In the hallway the nurse on night duty smiled at her and asked if everything was okay.

"Just need to move my legs. I'm fine."

The hallways formed a large square with rooms on both the inside and outside. Around the first corner Nena met a young man walking the other way, his IV tower also in tow. He couldn't have been too far into his thirties. He was thin and gaunt, and walked with short, careful steps.

He nodded at her. "How're you doing?"

"All right. I'm supposed to go home tomorrow. And you?"

He shrugged. "Not as good as I thought I'd be doing."

"May I ask what you had done?"

"Colon resection and ileostomy. Colon cancer. They say I need to walk, but my leg is killing me, keeps cramping up like a nerve is pinched or something."

"You're so young."

"That's what they tell me."

She smiled at the man. He reminded her of Kenny. "You'll make it."

"I have to. I have a wife and three little girls who need their daddy. I have to beat this thing for them."

"Then you will."

He smiled, but there was no hiding the fear in his eyes. "Have a good walk," he said, then grabbed the IV tower and was on his way.

How sad, Nena thought. So young to be battling cancer, and with three girls at home, three girls who were probably just as scared as he was. And his wife, what must she be going through? Nena watched the man leave. Every step he took looked painful, but there was determination in his gait, a resolve that she found inspiring. Again Busbey's words played in her head: *Make the most of what you have.*

The road ahead would be difficult. Chemotherapy was anything but a walk on the beach. But she could do it; she had to. For herself, for Jim, for her children.

Chapter Thirty-Three

RIVING UP TO THE RANCH house after surgery was like coming home to a stranger's place. Nena had lived in the house her entire life, and yet for some reason it looked oddly misplaced, as if while she was gone someone had sneaked onto her property and switched her home with another. Jim had to help her up the porch steps, one hand under her arm, the other on the small of her back. She took it one step at a time.

On the porch the feeling of familiarity began to return. Her father loved this spot; he'd sit on the porch every evening and puff away at his pipe. Nena liked to sit with him, smelling the sweet aroma of the tobacco mingling with that of the wisteria. In the summertime, after dark, the front lawn would be aglow with fireflies, their tiny yellow lights blinking like so many stars in the night sky. She'd sit on the top step, hands supporting her chin, and watch them dance the evening away, listening to the slow creak of her dad's rocker moving back and forth, back and forth.

Jim opened the front door, and immediately the scent of old furniture and woodstain welcomed her back to the place she felt safest, the place where she'd grown and matured and fallen in love and borne children. And the place where she'd said good-bye to her father.

Nena turned around in the doorway and surveyed the property from the porch. She could see open land to the right, the stables to the left. The pastures, now empty and overgrown, were once filled with mares and their foals, their lean muscles working gracefully as they ran and played.

She walked into the living room, the last place she'd seen her father. Barbara was ten, and they all lived in the guesthouse to the rear of the main building. Cricket, aged and bent himself, called her in to see to her father. He'd been drifting in and out of consciousness, and Dr. Peters said it wouldn't be long. She got there in time to say good-bye and kiss him on the cheek. His skin was so thin and cold he felt like he'd gone already. He opened his eyes and looked at her, studied her face.

"Nena." His voice was weak and low. He coughed, a deep rumbling hack that sounded like gravel in a bucket, and wheezed. "Nena. The ranch is yours now. Take care of it."

"I told you I would, Daddy." Tears flowed from her eyes—so many tears—and spilled onto his blanket. She recalled the argument they'd had on the porch so many years before, when she'd declared her love for Jim and refused to marry Ted McGovern. "I won't lose it. Jim and I will be fine. The ranch will be fine."

Two months later she'd met with her father's attorney and received the bad news. The ranch was in terrible debt; he doubted that her father had realized how bad it was. But Nena was stubborn. She loved the ranch and refused to let it go. They all worked so hard, she more than any of them, to save the horses and the hands. Time after time she told herself she was doing it for her family, for her children, sacrificing for them so they'd have a future. She needed to keep the ranch in the family for them.

So many lost years, so many regrets.

Nena sat in her recliner, and Jim came with a blanket for her legs. "Is there anything I can get you?"

"A glass of sweet tea?"

"Sure thing." He kissed her on the lips. "It's good to have you home."

"It's good to be home."

He turned to leave, but she grabbed his hand. "Jim."

He knelt before her, searched her eyes. "What is it? What's wrong?"

"Nothing. Just thank you."

"For what?"

"For being my husband."

He continued to search her eyes, then finally said, "You better not be saying your good-byes. This isn't over yet."

A tear spilled from her eye and caught on the corner of her nose. "I know. I'm just saying thank you."

"Okay. Then...you're welcome."

"I love you, Jimmy Hutching."

Jim put his hand to her cheek. "I love you too."

Nena smiled, but inside the tears continued to flow. Her time was almost up, she could feel it, as if it were a stalker, relentless yet stealthy, staying just out of sight. She could hold it off a little longer, but sooner or later it would catch up. Sooner or later the monster inside would claim its victory.

Chapter Thirty-Four

If the chemotherapy room was supposed to feel comfortable with its rows of recliners, potted plants, framed prints, and multiple flat-screen TVs, it was somehow missing the mark. Maybe it was the pervading smell of rubbing alcohol and chemicals. Maybe it was the abundance of sickly patients, most of whom looked as if they were two steps from the grave.

Nena followed the young nurse past several recliners. The occupants busied themselves with books or magazines. One older gentleman slept, his head tilted to one side, mouth open, a line of drool connecting his lips to his shoulder. The others said nothing as Nena passed by, but most greeted her with a nod and a weak smile. In their eyes was the look of fatigue. The battle had wearied them. Nena squeezed Jim's hand and smiled back.

"Here you go," the nurse said. She'd introduced herself earlier as Brianna. "This'll be your home for the next four hours."

Nena stripped off her coat and handed it to Jim, then sat in the recliner. Jim took the armchair next to it.

"I'll be right back," Brianna said, "and we'll get you started."

Nena reclined and looked around the room. Most of the other patients were her age or older. There was one young girl, couldn't be more than thirty, in the corner. Her skin was smooth and hairless, her face moon-shaped. She read a magazine and bopped her head to the rhythm of the music coming out of her earbuds.

To Nena's left, on the other side of Jim, was an older woman wrapped in a blanket, eyes closed. Her thin frame looked too small in the oversized recliner. Dark veins showed under almost translucent skin. Her hair was gone, eyes sunken.

From Nena's right a man said, "She's the oldest one here."

Nena turned her head. The man was elderly and thin, but not sickly-thin. His skin still had a healthy color, and his eyes were still bright.

"I'm Nick," he said.

"I'm Nena, and this is my husband, Jim."

Nick motioned to the woman on Nena's left. "Ninety-one, can you believe it? And willing to put up with this. Folks, if I made it to ninety-one, I'd be ready to go home. I'd tell them they can keep their poison."

Nena glanced at the woman again. "That's incredible."

"Incredible is right," Nick said. "She's been dealing with this mess on and off for fifteen years. And the thing is, she's still got a lot of fight left in her. She'll probably outlive me."

Brianna returned and set a tray on the small table beside Nena's chair. "We have your cocktail ready."

"You make it sound so inviting."

Brianna laughed and hooked the IV bag of chemicals onto a pole behind the chair, then she removed a syringe. "Okay, you know the routine."

The nurse worked quickly, finding a vein on the back of Nena's hand and inserting the catheter. It only pinched a little. She went to the infusion pump and hit some buttons. Immediately the pump began to hum and the steady drip-drip began.

"Okey-dokey. You're all set. Each bag takes a little over an hour, and we have three of them to go through. If you need to use the restroom, it's right down there." She pointed to a hallway to the left. "Just unplug the stand and take it along. And if you need anything else, don't be afraid to ask, okay?"

"Thank you."

"Do you have any questions?" She looked back and forth between Nena and Jim.

Nena shook her head. "I don't have any right now."

"When will the side effects start?" Jim asked.

"Most won't start until after the treatment, but a lot of people say the cold sensitivity starts almost immediately. So if you want to drink something cold, you may want to do it now before you get too far into the treatment."

Nena turned to Jim. "I could go for some sweet tea."

"There's a café on the first floor," Brianna said.

Jim stood. "Good enough. One sweet tea coming up, and I may just get one for myself too."

He left, and Nena ran her fingers over the catheter site on the back of her hand.

"Amazing, isn't it?" Nick said.

"What's amazing?"

"What they do here. Pump poison into our bodies. Just enough to kill the cancer cells, but not too much to kill us."

She'd never thought of it that way, and the idea put an eel of uneasiness in her stomach. She watched as the clear liquid dripped into the tubing.

"I'm sorry," Nick said. "I didn't mean to be negative."

"No, it's okay. It's true."

"This your first time?"

Nena nodded. "What about you?"

"I'm on my fourth treatment, but this is my third time around. Lung cancer. They told me two years ago I had six months to live." He shrugged. "I guess they were wrong... there's only one God, and the doc isn't Him."

"What's it been like?"

He looked healthy enough, but Nena had learned a long time ago that looks could be deceiving.

Nick's face darkened. "Honestly? It's been the hardest two years of my life. Everything has revolved around tests and results and scans and treatments and surgeries. It's consumed every aspect of our lives and nearly ruined us." He lifted his shoulders and let them fall. "Two years ago when I got the news, I was sure I'd leave my wife a widow. It killed me to think about it. But then I just kept on living. Five months ago she died of a heart attack. Can you believe it? Now I'm the widower. But God's been good; He's been faithful. I can't complain."

"How can you say that?"

"Say what?"

"That God's been faithful." She didn't want to get in an argument, didn't mean to be confrontational. In fact, Nena had always considered herself a religious person; she just never had time for church and sermons. But here this man sat, battling a monster for the third time, living literally on borrowed time, having gone through the hardest two years of his life, and he could say God had been faithful. Nena just didn't buy it. "Look at what you've been through."

"Right. And if it wasn't for Him, I wouldn't be here now. I know that for a fact."

"And you've never been angry with Him for allowing this to happen and taking your wife?" She'd experienced her own brand of anger, questioning God, even accusing Him.

Nick shook his head emphatically. "No way. It's not God's fault I got cancer. It's just part of the world we live in. People get in car accidents, they get abused and even murdered, they get sick. Sure, there was a time after Jeannie died that I'd wished He would have taken me first, questioned why He'd allowed me to live and not her, but I've never been angry with Him."

"But surely God could have stopped it from happening. He could have prevented your wife from having a heart attack."

"Sure He could have, but He didn't, and I didn't expect Him to. Just because He's God and I'm His child doesn't mean I get excused from the sufferings of this world. There're no get-out-of-suffering-free cards."

Jim came back then and handed Nena her sweet tea. She took a long sip and could already feel the slight tingle at the back of her tongue from the coldness. It was setting in already.

Nick wasn't finished. "All we can do is trudge through life

and take what comes at us. I let God think about the rest." He tapped his head with his index finger. "Too much for this old brain to process anymore."

The alarm on the infusion pump beside Nick's chair sounded. His IV bag was empty. A nurse came and turned off the machine and unhooked him. He didn't even flinch when she slid the needle out of the port in his chest.

Nick stood and stretched, smiled at Nena. "It was a pleasure to meet you folks. You take care, Nena, and remember what I told you."

"Will I see you next week?" Nena said.

"Lord willing, I'll be here. Same chair. I think it has my name on it by now."

"I'll look for you then."

"Good enough. Take care, folks."

"What was that all about?" Jim asked after Nick was gone.

"Nothing. We were just talking."

But it was more than nothing, wasn't it? And it was more than just talk. Nick's words had pricked Nena's conscience, stirred up feelings and regrets she'd wrestled with for years. She watched the liquid drip into the IV tubing. Nick called it poison, potent enough to kill. She needed to deal with the regrets soon; she had no idea how long she had to make things right. She just hoped it wasn't already too late.

Chapter Thirty-Five

THE CONFERENCE ROOM FELT COOLER than normal, even though the thermostat said it was the usual seventy degrees. Ken rubbed his hands together and blew on them. He'd felt cold lately, unable to get warm even in his own home. Maybe it was the fact that he hadn't gotten a full night's sleep in over a week. He glanced at his watch, looked at his client, Jack O'Leary. "You ready?"

Jack fidgeted with his necktie, smoothed his mustache. "As ready as ever. Let's just get this over with."

When Ken first told Jack what he'd dug up on Loretta at the bank, his client was hesitant. He'd been humiliated enough, he said, having his personal life exposed for all to see; exposing his wife's indiscretions would only add salt to the wound. But two days later he came back and said he wanted to use it; he wanted the house and Thor and was willing to do whatever it took to get them. Ken made some phone calls and arranged for a four-way conference, both spouses, both attorneys. This needed to be a face-to-face negotiation.

At two o'clock on the dot, the conference door opened, and Cal Tyson, dressed in his signature double-breasted suit stretched tight over his protruding abdomen, walked in, followed by Loretta O'Leary. She was well into her fifties but didn't look a day over forty. Amazing what a little Botox and hair color could do. To her credit, though, she'd kept herself in tremendous shape and still had the curves of a thirty-year-old.

Ken stood and shook Cal's hand. "Afternoon, Cal. Good to see you again."

Cal smiled. "Likewise. How's the family?" He was partner

with his wife at a rival firm across town, Tyson & Tyson. The couple, both on their third marriage and married just ten years, specialized in divorces and made quite a living off other people's misfortunes. For the Tysons marriage was a business proposition, a legal agreement that could be dissolved at any time, and whoever walked away from the broken deal with the most stuff was the grand winner. May the best man or woman win.

Cal knew of Ken's family troubles, of course he did. News traveled quickly in the cutthroat legal world. He was trying to jar Ken, knock him off balance before the negotiations even began.

Ken sat, shrugged, but never lost contact with his opponent's eyes. "They're fine, Cal. Thanks for asking."

Both attorneys took a few minutes to get their notes together and confer with their clients. Ken leaned toward Jack and whispered into his ear. "Last chance to bail out. You still want to do this?"

Jack tightened his jaw, looked at his soon-to-be ex-wife, and nodded. "Do it."

After straightening his necktie and adjusting his collar, Ken cleared his throat, hit the record button on the voice recorder, and said, "As far as my client is concerned, there are only two items left to negotiate: the house and the dog, Thor."

"Yes," Cal said, "and my client has already said she's not giving them up."

"Then we have a problem, don't we?"

"It seems we do, and we're quite ready to take this to court." Cal sat back and tilted his head enough that he appeared to be peering down his nose at Ken. "But I think we'd all like to avoid that. Since my client is currently residing in the house and the dog lives with her, it seems only prudent that those items should stay. And we believe the judge will agree."

"Prudent, why?"

"The dog is well cared for, happy in his home. He adores my client."

"And mine as well. Mr. O'Leary used to walk Thor every morning." By using names Ken was personalizing negotiation, bringing the argument to a focal point. "What does Mrs. O'Leary want with Thor, anyway?" He looked from Cal to Loretta.

Loretta glanced at Cal for his approval before answering. "Jack bought Thor for me for our twentieth anniversary."

"Did you ever spend time with him? Take him for walks? Clean up his messes?"

Her eyes darted back and forth on the table, stopped on the voice recorder. "That was always Jack's thing. I fed him every morning and when we got home from work."

"So why the resolve? Why do you want Thor so much?"

"He's a good watchdog. If I'm going to be alone now, I want a dog in the house with me."

"Why not purchase another dog?"

"I want Thor."

Cal leaned over and whispered something into his client's ear. She nodded nervously.

"Mrs. O'Leary," Ken said, "let's face it; you really don't care about the dog. You could easily buy another one. You're just holding out to get back at your husband. Isn't that right?"

"Don't answer that," Cal instructed her.

"Mrs. O'Leary, you work at CitiBank downtown, correct?"

She nodded. "That's right."

"Where you're the COO?"

"Correct."

Ken paused for effect. He knew he had both of them curious as to where he was going with this and wanted to keep them off-balance for just a bit before knocking them over. "I stopped by there a couple days ago and talked with some of your coworkers. Nice people."

Loretta shifted in her chair, shot a glance at Cal, who stared fire at Ken.

Ken reached for the voice recorder and slid it to the right so it was directly in front of Loretta. "I spoke with Gloria Winston. Pleasant lady. Is it true that you used to fudge your time sheet to make it look like you put in longer hours than you actually did?"

Cal's face went red. "Don't answer that. What's this about, Hutching?"

"And is it true that you had relations with Bruce Lennigan, the CFO, just before accepting your promotion to COO?"

Cal clenched his fist. He was known in many legal circles for having a short fuse. He punched the stop button on the recorder. "What are you doing? You think you can blackmail my client?"

But Ken didn't answer; he only stared at Loretta, keeping eye contact. She knew exactly what he was doing. He was winning. Bring on his own promotion.

Loretta's face had turned onion white. She pressed her lips together so tight her mouth became a thin line. Finally she stood, straightened her back, looked at Cal and then at Ken. Her lower lip trembled. "Tell Jack he can have the house and the dog. I never wanted either of them anyway." She spun and left the room.

Cal gathered his things and stood. His face was still red, and a single bulging vein ran a line down the middle of his forehead. "You can't blackmail her, Hutching."

"I never made a single threat. Just stated the facts as I found them. You may interpret that any way you want, but the facts stand."

Cal straightened his back and rested his hand on the doorknob. "You know, it's snakes like you that give this profession a bad rap." He walked out of the room and slammed the door behind him.

Jack extended his hand. "Thanks, Ken, really. I knew you were the man for the job."

Ken shook his hand and forced a smile.

He saw Jack out of the suite. Back in his office Ken shut the door and stood at the window overlooking Lake Michigan. Despite the cold air and brisk winds there were several boats on the water. But Ken wasn't thinking about boating. He was thinking about his big victory, the one that would seal the deal for his promotion. He was thinking about his family, Celia and the kids. Things would settle down now; he'd have more time for them. And they'd be so proud of him.

But he wasn't proud of himself. He should be excited, giddy, in fact, but he wasn't. Instead he felt cheap and dirty. He felt again like throwing himself out the window.

Chapter Thirty-Six

THE NEXT MORNING NENA AWOKE feeling nauseated and tired. She hadn't slept well, battling restlessness and dreams of her father during those last days of his life. She lay in bed staring at the ceiling for a long time before pushing back the covers and sitting on the edge of the mattress. The sun was up and shining brightly through the window blinds, coloring the room a golden orange. She loved the morning, the quiet stillness, the dew on the grass, the soft colors, the coolness in the air.

She stood, and the pain was terrible, like some little man was inside her head hammering away at her skull with an ice pick. She walked to the window and leaned against the sill. She rubbed her fingertips together. Already the numbness was beginning. The doctor had said that with each treatment it would get worse in both her hands and feet. Pulling the cord for the blinds, she rolled them up and squinted into the sunlight. The master bedroom was in the rear of the home and had three large windows across the back wall offering a panoramic view of the pastureland. Clouds dotted the sky, and in the distance, hovering just above the horizon, hung a long, low, gray storm front.

Her stomach writhed and roiled, and for a moment she thought she'd vomit, but then the feeling passed. Sitting in the armchair between two of the windows, Nena put her head in her hands and began to cry. This was only the first treatment; she had how many more? Twelve, thirteen? She couldn't remember what the doctor had said. Already the side effects were nearly debilitating. Despair tightened its grip. Maybe she'd made the wrong decision.

Her stomach turned again, and this time she was sure she'd vomit. She got up and ran to the bathroom, head thumping the whole way, knelt beside the toilet, and emptied the contents of her stomach. Tears rolled down her cheeks, and her pulse pounded in her temples like a racehorse's hooves on packed dirt. Extreme fatigue overtook her, and she rolled to her haunches and rested her head against the wall. The room spun in slow circles.

"Jim." He was downstairs, and she wasn't sure he could hear her. "Jim!"

Footfalls sounded on the steps. "Where are you?" His voice was near, in the bedroom.

"Bathroom."

He appeared and squatted next to her. "Nena, what's wrong?" He glanced at the toilet, then put his hand on her forehead. "You're hot. Can you stand?"

"I think so."

He took her under the arms and helped her up. Her legs felt like slack rubber bands.

"C'mon, hon. We have to get you to the bed, then I'm calling the doctor."

Nena put one foot in front of the other. The room spun faster, and her vision darkened. Jim's grip tightened around her arms. He was saying something, but she couldn't make out what it was. He sounded a mile away, his voice tiny and slurred. Her stomach twisted, and she thought she'd wretch again.

Then everything went black.

Chapter Thirty-Seven

ROBERTA SAT ON THE SOFA staring mindlessly at the TV, letting her bowl of ice cream melt. She hadn't eaten but a spoonful and was paying no attention to the sitcom playing out not ten feet from her. It was nearing midnight and she was alone...again. It'd been weeks, and nothing had changed. Thomas was still coming home almost every day after midnight, crawling into bed without even so much as a peck on the cheek, then getting up and leaving for the café before sunrise. There had been a couple mornings when Roberta had awakened minutes before he'd walked out the door. They'd exchanged some small talk, a quick kiss, and then he was gone. They never did have their day together.

To her credit, Tiffany didn't bug Roberta about Thomas, but she did occasionally ask how things were going. Roberta was truthful. She and Thomas rarely talked or spent any meaningful time together, but that meant they rarely argued as well. Tiffany never pushed; she'd just say that she was still praying, and she knew Roberta would make the right choice.

The right choice. What *was* the right choice? Should she give Thomas more time, or had she given him too much already? Was he playing her for a fool and using her so he could run around with Erica on the side? The café was doing great, but he still needed to pay off thousands in loans before it started generating any kind of real income. In the meantime, her meager reporter's salary was greater than his, so she carried the bulk of their living expenses. Was he simply using her for a free ride?

She still loved him; at least she thought she did. She couldn't stand the thought of being without him, even if the only time she saw him was when he crawled into bed beside her. And she could get up earlier and see him out the door. What time she awoke was her choice, not his.

Just before midnight the apartment door opened, and Thomas walked in, carrying a paper bag.

Roberta stood and faced him. "Well, this is a pleasant surprise. You're home before midnight."

"Funny," he said. He sounded irritated.

"I wasn't trying to be funny. It is a pleasant surprise."

"Don't start on the *You're never home* stuff, Berta, okay? I'm tired."

She noticed he kept his distance again. "I'm not starting on anything. What's the matter?"

He headed for the kitchen and placed the bag on the counter. "Here's some muffins for the morning."

"Thanks. That was nice of you." She walked toward him, but he quickly left the kitchen area and headed for the bedroom.

"I'm gonna jump in the shower."

Roberta rounded the counter and cut him off, blocking the way to the bedroom.

"What are you doing?" he said, an edge in his voice.

Guilt cut through her. She couldn't believe she was so jealous and suspicious. "Don't I get a hug when you come home?"

"I stink, Berta. Let me shower first, then we can sit together on the sofa."

She took two steps and wrapped her arms around him before he could back away. He didn't stink at all; he smelled like the aroma of freshly ground coffee and something else, something flowery and fresh. Erica's perfume. She knew it immediately because she smelled it each time she went in the café. Pulling away, she looked up at him.

Thomas diverted his eyes and forced a smile. "Now can I get in the shower?"

"I don't think you stink at all. Why do you smell like Erica?" She couldn't believe she was actually confronting him.

He took a step backward, the walls going up almost visibly. "What do you mean?"

"You smell like her perfume, like—"

"I work with her, Berta. What do you expect? I smell like coffee too, but you're not accusing me of sleeping in the coffee beans."

His reaction surprised her. "I haven't accused you of anything. Why so defensive?"

"Why the questions? So what if I smell like her. Don't be like that."

"Like what?"

"A jealous girlfriend who can't take her man spending time with another woman. She's an employee." His voice rose steadily as he spoke.

Things were going downhill fast. This wasn't what she wanted.

"How can I not be jealous? You spend more time with her than with me. I never see you anymore. We never talk. What happened to our day together? You canceled on our last one and promised me you'd make it up."

"I've been busy at the café, you know that." He paced the kitchen floor. "I can't believe you're holding that against me. You know I'm doing it for us, for you."

"Oh, so that's how it's going to be, that's your excuse? You're neglecting our relationship, neglecting me, for my own sake. Well, thank you, Thomas, thank you for ignoring our relationship to make it better. You're such a martyr."

She knew she'd crossed the line, but at the moment she didn't care. Months of pent-up frustration and hurt and anger poured out of her. The levy had been breached.

"I don't need this." He picked up a dish towel, threw it down, leaned against the counter, and crossed his arms. "You know, you could come down and help me in the evenings instead of sitting around here concocting stories in your head and scheming against me."

"What?" Her voice cracked with incredulity. "You told me you didn't want me to help, that you wanted to do this on your own and you didn't want me to have to work my shift at the newspaper and then turn around and work another shift in the evening."

"Well, I am, aren't I? Why can't you?"

"Because it's your café. We're only dating, remember? And every time I come down to visit, you all but ignore me…like you don't want to show me too much attention in front of Erica."

Thomas rolled his eyes and laughed mockingly. "Here we go with the Erica stuff again. Leave her out of this, okay? She has nothing to do with us or with you."

"She has everything to do with us. It's clear you'd rather be with her than with me."

There was a moment of silence while the tension between them eased a bit. Thomas stood with his arms crossed, head down. Finally he lifted his head and looked at her. When he spoke, his voice was low, serious. "Look at you, Berta. You've been reduced to a jealous girlfriend, spending her evenings alone, watching lame sitcoms and eating ice cream."

There was no real concern in his voice; his words dripped with contempt. They were meant to hurt, not console. And they did hurt—more than she ever thought words could. Tears pushed to her eyes, and that lump was back in her throat. She swallowed hard and put up her hands in a sign of surrender. "I'm done. I'm going to bed." She turned and went into the bedroom.

It was after one o'clock when she heard Thomas get in the shower. He never did slip into bed beside her.

Chapter Thirty-Eight

IM WATCHED THE RAIN LEAVE mercurial tracks on the windowpane. Here they were in a hospital room again, Nena sleeping peacefully, covers pulled up to her chest and neatly folded over.

A soft knock sounded on the room's door right before it opened, and Dr. Alexis walked in, wearing jeans and a sweater. She shook Jim's hand. "Is she doing okay?"

"Yeah, she's been asleep about fifteen minutes."

Nena had been taken to the emergency room, where they said she suffered from dehydration. They started an IV and moved her to a room in the main hospital.

"Good. She needs her rest. We're going to keep her a day for observation, just to make sure her blood counts all normalize."

"Fine. Whatever you think is best."

Dr. Alexis patted Jim on the arm. "We'll take next week off from chemotherapy, then resume the week after. Her body needs time to recover from this."

"Okay. Is this going to happen every time?"

"We'll monitor her closely during the therapy and maybe bring her in the next morning to check on things."

She shook Jim's hand again and left the room.

Jim sat in the chair next to Nena's bed and rested his hand on hers. The IV pump droned rhythmically, pushing fluids into his wife's blood. The chemicals they had given her worked to kill the cancer that had already ravaged her body. How had it come to this? He rested his elbows on the arms of the chair and rubbed his temples, fighting back the thoughts of life without Nena. He put his hand on her forehead and smoothed back her hair. He'd fight for her as he had in the past…but this enemy was one against which he wasn't sure he could be victorious.

Morning came without event. The sun rose as it always did, as it had done for thousands of years. Birds broke into song, horses grazed lazily, and dew glistened on the sea of grass that spread before Jimmy. The other hands were up and getting ready for the day, talking amongst themselves in a language Jimmy couldn't begin to understand. Long days of work and short nights didn't seem to faze them. They'd work from sunup until supper, then sit on the porch of the bunkhouse and talk and laugh and smoke until after midnight.

Jimmy stretched and wiped the sleep from his eyes. Sleep, what little he got, had come with difficulty and left him with an unsettled feeling in his chest, remnants of his confrontation with Ted yesterday morning, then with Nena later in the day. If he saw her today he'd apologize, tell her he never should have said anything about what Rick had told him. It was none of his business.

Though he believed in his heart that it was his business. If he didn't say anything and Ted hurt Nena, Jimmy would feel responsible—he would be responsible for not warning her. So what else was he to do? But still, he'd upset her, and for that he needed to make amends.

Grabbing a weed eater from the toolshed, he checked the fuel level, checked the string length, donned his safety goggles, and cranked up the trimmer. His task for the morning was to trim around the fence enclosing the near pasture and around the stables.

A little before noon Jimmy saw Nena enter the mare stable. He worked his way around the pasture fence, quickly trimming around each post, until he was positioned to see straight down the alleyway. He was still about a hundred yards away, and his view was partially obscured by the fencing nearest the stable.

Nena was in there, talking to someone. Jimmy moved to the

next post and got a better look. It was Ted. He seemed to tower over her, hands on his hips, head cocked back. She waved her arms and shook her hands. Ted raised and dropped his shoulders in a quick shrug. Jimmy moved to the next post, got an even better view. They were obviously arguing. Nena was crying, turned away from Ted. He put a hand on her shoulder, but she pulled away from him, took steps toward the stable door. Ted grabbed her by the arm and swung her around. Nena grimaced.

Jimmy shut off the weed eater and dropped it to the ground. He covered the distance from the fence to the stable in seconds, his heart thumping against his ribs. When he reached the stable, Ted and Nena were at the far end, their backs to him. Ted had Nena by the arm, practically dragging her along.

Jimmy heard Ted say, "...someplace private. We don't need everyone hearing us argue."

Nena pulled back. "Stop, Ted. I don't want to go with you."

She managed to break his grip, but he lunged after her. And that's when they both saw Jimmy standing there.

"She said she didn't want to go with you, Ted," he said.

Ted straightened, smoothed back his hair. Nena rubbed her arm. "Beat it, dairy boy. This isn't any of your business."

Jimmy stepped closer. About twenty feet separated them now. "I think it is my business."

"Oh, yeah," Ted said. "Why's that? You got the hots for my girl? My future wife? You think she could ever love you? Look at yourself, man, you're nothing; you have no future. What would she see in you?" He reached for Nena. "Come on, Nena, let's get out of here."

Nena didn't move.

"Nena, come on." Ted held out his hand, but Nena didn't take it.

"She doesn't want to go with you." Jimmy took another step toward Ted.

Ted pointed his finger at Jimmy. His eyes narrowed. "I said shut up."

Another step, and only fifteen feet separated them now. "Walk away, Ted. Leave her alone."

This time it was Ted who advanced, his face burning with rage. He shot Nena a quick glance, then drilled Jimmy with hate-filled eyes. "You don't tell me what to do. You're a ranch hand, a nobody, a vagabond who wandered in here begging for work, from what I heard."

"Ted—"

"Shut up, Nena. Let me handle this dairy queen." He took another step closer.

Ten feet now.

Jimmy tried to settle the anger clawing at his insides. Impulse pushed him to lunge at Ted, but he held back.

"And that's not the only thing I heard." Ted stepped again, and again. He was five feet away now, almost close enough to reach from where Jimmy stood. Little spots of foam had formed at the corners of Ted's mouth. "I heard you found your way here because your old man kicked you out after he beat your mother."

Jimmy clenched his fists.

"What, you couldn't protect her?" Ted was within an arm's reach now, just feet away. "And now you're trying to protect Nena? Is that it? Sweet, but she doesn't need your protection. But it sounds like your mother does, dairy boy, so why don't you go on home and try again."

Jimmy tightened his jaw. "Don't you ever touch her like that again."

"Or what?" Ted stepped forward and reached out to shove Jimmy.

But Jimmy was quick. His body uncoiled like a spring, and he struck Ted square on the jaw. Ted spun around, grunted, lost his balance, and hit the dirt floor in a clumsy tangle of arms and legs. He lay there for only a second, then shook his head and rubbed his jaw. Hair stuck to his forehead, and dirt powdered the front of his polo shirt and khakis. He stood, staggered only a bit, and felt his jaw again. His eyes shifted between Nena and Jimmy; his face burned bright red.

"Forget this," he said. Then to Jimmy, "Forget you. You're nothing. You hear? Nothing. And consider yourself out of a job."

As Ted made his way out, the stable was silent. Even the horses were motionless. The confrontation had escalated way beyond what Jimmy had wanted or expected. But what was he to do? He could have been the bigger man, should have been the bigger man. He let his rage overcome him. He was so much like his father. Too much. Disappointment moved over him like a storm cloud, blocking any ray of light. He cast a furtive glance at Nena. She had her fist to her mouth and was crying quietly. He'd frightened her.

"I'm sorry." It was meaningless, he knew, but it was all he could say. "I…I'm sorry."

He turned to leave, stopped, looked back at Nena. Her back was to him, head bowed. He'd ruined everything he had with her, even if it was nothing more than friendship. Without another word he made his way out of the stable and back to the bunkhouse. He'd go back later for the weed eater. For now, he just needed to settle his nerves and think. And pack his duffel. He was sure he'd be on the road by sundown.

Chapter Thirty-Nine

THOMAS HAD GONE MISSING.

He was gone when Roberta awoke the morning after the big blowup, but that wasn't anything out of the ordinary. What was strange was when he didn't come home that evening or the next. She was tempted to go to the café and find him, but what good would that do? *If* he gave her the time of day, they wouldn't be able to talk about what had happened, what had been said, not *really* talk about it.

His words had stuck with her, like a splinter working deeper into her flesh. *You've been reduced to a jealous girlfriend, spending your evenings alone watching lame sitcoms and eating ice cream.*

Is that really what she'd become? She looked at the half-eaten bowl of ice cream in her lap and set it on the coffee table. And the saddest part was that she actually missed him...or maybe it was that she just hated being alone. At least when he came home after midnight and crawled into bed there was somebody there, somebody she could share a bed with. Now there was no one. She didn't know if he'd ever come back.

Roberta thought about calling Tiffany and crying the blues to her, but that seemed too pathetic, so ninth grade. Roberta was a big girl and could handle this on her own. In fact, she needed to handle this on her own. She clicked off the TV, threw the ice cream bowl into the sink, and headed into the bedroom to undress and go to bed. It was after eleven, and she'd had a long day.

For the past three days she'd been covering a scandal at the courthouse. It seemed Justice Mikalotis had gotten caught texting a secretary some very seedy photos of himself. City Council was having a conniption, calling for his resignation. The press was having a field day. Roberta's editor wanted up-to-the-minute reporting.

She was just about ready to crawl into bed when she heard the front door open and close. She sat on the edge of the bed for a second, listening. She knew she'd locked the front door, so it had to be Thomas. He'd come home. For more arguing? Or to make amends. Or maybe just to clean out his belongings. Maybe he'd come back to tell her off one last time, tell her he was moving in with Erica, and get his clothes, movies, books, and coffeemaker.

His footsteps stopped in the kitchen, then moved closer to the bedroom doorway. Roberta froze. She didn't want to go through with this, didn't know how she would handle face-to-face rejection. She wanted to climb under the bed and hide there until he left.

And then he was there, in the doorway, hands in his pockets. His hair was disheveled, eyes sunken, lips drawn. His eyes met hers. "Hey."

"Hey."

"Is it okay to come in?"

He seemed to have come in peace, so Roberta nodded. "Sure. You look awful."

"Haven't slept in three nights. Been thinking a lot about you. Us. Spent the last hour just walking the Overlook, thinking."

He paused, but she didn't say anything. This was his time to talk, to get whatever was on his mind out in the open.

Thomas crossed the space between them and sat on the bed beside her. He took her hand. "Berta, I don't want to lose you. We have something special that I need. I'm sorry. I've become so wrapped up in the café, in its success and in myself that I forgot about your needs. I was so busy trying to impress you that I forgot to be with you."

"Impress me?"

"By showing you I could do this, that I could make the café a career. I'm sorry for the things I said the other night."

Tears sprang to her eyes, and one spilled over and trickled down her cheek. Thomas wiped it away with his finger and hugged her. He smelled like coffee, but there was not even a hint of Erica on him. She leaned into him as more tears came.

When she pulled away, he smiled at her and wiped the rest of the tears from her face.

"I'm sorry too," she said. "I was being so stupid, so jealous."

He shook his head. "No, you have nothing to be sorry for. I see how it looked. What you thought was perfectly normal."

"But still stupid."

He smiled. "Okay, maybe a little. To think I'd ever risk losing you, how nuts would that be?"

"Totally bonkers. I love you, Thomas."

"I love you too, Roberta Hutching, star reporter for the *LA Times*." He tilted his head and kissed her gently on the lips.

Roberta leaned into his kiss, but there was something missing in it. It didn't feel genuine.

Chapter Forty

ENA HUTCHING SAT ON THE front porch of the ranch house, wrapped in a heavy wool blanket, and sipped at her coffee. It was nothing but hot liquids for her. Not only was she cold all the time, but also her sensitivity to cold had worsened following her second chemotherapy treatment. The blanket kept her warm, though, and allowed her the freedom to spend time where she most enjoyed it, outdoors. Though the air this morning was brisk and cool, November had come rather mildly, with not one day yet to dip below fifty degrees. Odd even for northern Virginia, especially with Thanksgiving just a couple weeks away.

A gust of wind blew through the trees lining the front lane, stirring leaves from the branches. They fluttered to the ground and landed as lightly as snowflakes. Nena shuddered and pulled the blanket closer to her neck. Next time out she'd have to remember to wear a scarf and hat. She sipped at the coffee again and allowed the steam to warm her lips and nose.

In the distance she heard the sound of tires on gravel before she saw the car coming down the lane. The sound brought back a memory—she'd been doing a lot of remembering lately. She was sitting in this exact place the first time she saw Jim. He came in the truck with one of the Mexicans, she couldn't remember who. He hadn't noticed her on the porch, but she'd seen him and somehow had known immediately they'd hit it off. She remembered the first time they met, in the mare stables. They watched the birthing of the foal, the one that had cost them so much, the one that had ruined everything. Her father had risked money they didn't have on stud fees with a promise from the McGovern family that if the horse was healthy they'd purchase it and her father would recoup his investment and then some. But the McGoverns pulled out of the deal, and a year later, before her dad could find another buyer, the colt stumbled, twisted his knee, and was never the same again. They were out millions. A series of bad investments followed that, coupled with the regular expenses of keeping the ranch going for far longer than he should have, and by the time he died, the ranch was in more debt than it was worth.

As the car drew closer, Nena saw that it had a single occupant, a man. He stopped the car in front of the porch and got out. Dressed in a dark gray suit and white shirt and necktie, he held a clipboard close to his chest as he rounded the front of the car.

He stopped at the bottom of the steps. "Good morning. Mrs. Hutching?"

Nena continued rocking. "Yes, that's me."

"May I talk to you a moment?"

"Yes." Nena knew who this man was. They all looked the same. They came in their suits and ties with their clipboards and threats. She'd managed to keep them at bay now for a couple years by selling close to a hundred acres on the back side of the ranch.

The man in the gray suit climbed the stairs and reached out his hand. Nena took it and shook lightly. He looked to be in his forties, tall, slender, with thinning hair and a long, sharp nose that seemed to dangle over wide, thin lips.

"Mrs. Hutching, I'm Norman Oliver. I work for Aaron and Millhime."

"The collection agency."

"Yes, ma'am."

"Then it really isn't a good morning, is it, Mr. Oliver?"

He paused, clearly taken aback. "Well, it depends—"

The front door of the house opened, and Jim came out onto the porch. "Mornin'." He nodded at Oliver. "And you are?"

Oliver extended his hand to Jim. "Norman Oliver of Aaron and Millhime."

"The collection agency," Nena said.

Oliver laughed nervously, and his right eye twitched. "Well, yes. It seems—"

"It doesn't *seem* like anything," Nena said. "We still owe a good amount of money, we know that."

"Yes. Quite a bit, actually. And it's quite serious."

Nena shifted in her rocker, gathered the blanket tighter around her. "And so is my illness, Mr. Oliver."

Oliver looked at the clipboard, then at Nena. "Yes, I heard about that. I'm sorry, Mrs. Hutching. I'm only doing my job."

He was right, of course. This Norman Oliver with the pointy nose wasn't the one calling the shots; he was only the front man, only doing his job, as he said. He probably had a family of his own, bills to pay, kids to put through college. Taking her frustration out on him wouldn't do anyone any good.

"Of course," she said. "I'm sorry."

Jim crossed his arms. "What brings you here, Mr. Oliver?"

Oliver scuffed his feet on the porch, looked at the clipboard again. "We usually just send a letter, but I refuse to do that. I was going to call you, but I don't like telephones, either, for business like this. I wanted to come here and see the two of you, tell you in person. It seemed only right."

Nena tensed. "Tell us what?"

Oliver grabbed at his tie and loosened it. "I'm sorry, folks, really I am. You have sixty days to settle all your debts, or the agency is going to get the courts involved." He paused for a moment. "They could take your land here. All of it."

Nena's throat tightened, and tears pushed behind her eyes. He was right, she knew. The agency, the creditors, the banks...they'd all been incredibly patient for so many years. The time had to come sooner or later. Her mind spun in wide circles, searching for an alternative plan, a way out of this nightmare, but found nothing. She'd fought so hard, sacrificed so much, and now it had come to this. She reached for Jim's hand.

"Your son is a lawyer, correct?" Oliver said.

Jim nodded.

"You may want to give him a call, get his advice as to how to proceed." He looked around, surveyed the view from the porch. "If you sell the land on your own, you may get an eager developer interested and make enough to pay off the debts and save the house. It's hard to tell in this economy." Oliver took a step toward the stairs, paused, and turned back to Jim and Nena. "Folks, I really am sorry about all this, and especially for the timing. It's poor...in fact, it stinks. I'll see what I can do, but I usually don't have much of a say in these matters."

"Thank you, Mr. Oliver." Nena forced a cordial smile.

Jim shook Norman Oliver's hand. "And thanks for coming here and telling us in person."

"You're welcome. I hope it works out for you." He looked out over the ranch again. "It's beautiful land."

Seconds later the car turned around and drove down the lane. Nena dropped Jim's hand and wiped a tear from her cheek. "It's over, Jim. Everything we fought for. We're going to lose the ranch."

Jim went to one knee and took her hand back. "Now just you wait, Nena Hutching." His eyes were wide and intense and searched hers. "Don't you give up yet. We still have more fight left in us, you hear? We're not done yet."

She appreciated his enthusiasm but wasn't convinced by it. It *was* over. It tore her heart to admit it, it angered her and brought more tears, but there was simply no way they could find a buyer for the land in just two months' time. And with her feeling so weak and sick and cold, she was in no condition to continue the fight. And it was *her* fight; it always had been.

She swallowed hard and gripped his hand tighter. "It's time to give up, Jim."

Chapter Forty-One

Mom, are you ready? I'm gonna be late."

On the second floor, in the master bathroom, Barb leaned over the toilet and winced as her stomach contracted with dry heaves. Perspiration beaded on her forehead, and her hands trembled.

"Mom, c'mon."

Her daughter's impatient voice wasn't helping.

Between heaves Barb hollered, "Be right there."

She was supposed to take Kara to a birthday party. Doug had previously arranged to take Mikey to a hockey game. Barb didn't want to disappoint her daughter—Kara needed to do things normal thirteen-year-olds did. Little did she know she'd be hit with an attack of the dry heaves right before they were to leave.

Finally her stomach settled and the shaking subsided. Standing before the mirror, Barb quickly washed her face and applied the necessary cosmetics. Leaving the bathroom, she found Kara in the bedroom doorway, arms crossed.

"Mom, I'm gonna be late. Can we leave now?"

Barb grabbed a hat from her dresser, pulled it onto her head. "We'll leave when I'm ready, Kara. And if you rush me, it'll only take longer."

Kara rolled her eyes and turned her face toward the wall. "Well, is it gonna be soon? The party starts in fifteen minutes."

"Yes. And it takes fifteen minutes to get to the Hendersons'. You're fine."

"I'm not fine. We still have to go downstairs, get our jackets on, get your purse, get in the car. That all takes time. I don't want to walk in late and have everyone stare at me."

Barb brushed past her, then stopped, spun around. "Stare at you? Really? You're afraid of people staring at you?" She pulled off her hat, revealing a scalp covered with spotty strands of hair. "Try going out in public with this, Kara. People stare at this. Stop thinking about yourself for once."

She turned and descended the stairs, tears burning her eyes. Kara followed silently.

In the car the tension was as thick as gravy. Kara leaned against the door, propping her head with her hand. Barb drove a little over the posted speed limit. She knew she'd been hard on Kara, let her emotions get the better of her. Her daughter was battling those merciless teenage hormones plus the reality that her mother had cancer. Two major events. It was a lot for a young woman to handle.

Outside the sun dipped low in the sky, splashing everything in a coppery light. Trees cast long, zebra-stripe shadows across the roadway. A squirrel dashed in front of the car, zigzagged sporadically, and somehow miraculously dodged the tires.

Barb had wanted her family to be close during this time, to bond and form a union that no enemy could break. She needed their support, and the children needed her and Doug's love. But it hadn't turned out that way. Kara handled the rough patches in life differently. She withdrew, became reclusive and temperamental. Her mood swings were wide and fast, changing direction like the wind at sea. It kept them all off guard and seemed to make a bad situation only worse. But Barb knew she needed to give Kara some space, allow her room to express her fear and anxiety and worries the best way she knew how.

When she turned onto the Hendersons' street, Kara sat up straight. "Mom, wait, stop."

"What?"

"Pull the car over."

"But we're not there yet. The Hendersons—"

Tears sprang to Kara's eyes. "Mom, please, just pull the car over right here."

Barb steered the car to the curb and put it in park. "What's wrong?"

Kara was crying now, tears running down her cheeks. She wiped at them with her palms, smearing the wetness across her cheeks.

Barb pointed at the glove compartment. "Get yourself some tissues, honey. What's the matter?"

Kara retrieved a tissue and dried her eyes, but more tears came. "Mom, I'm sorry." She was sobbing now, choking out the words. "I'm sorry."

Barb released her seat belt and leaned toward her daughter, stroked her hair. "It's all right, honey. I understand."

Kara shook her head. "No, you don't." She wiped at the tears again with the tissue. "Mom, I'm scared. You're so sick. I don't want you to die."

"Oh, honey." Barb leaned in closer and put her head to her daughter's. "I'm not going to die."

"But you don't know that."

Kara was right. Barb didn't know it. No one did. She pulled her head away and looked her daughter in the eyes. "Kara, honey, listen to me. No one knows when they're going to die. I know that's easy to say, but it's true. All we can do is take our life one day at a time. I have a whole team of doctors, very smart, capable people, whose sole focus is to beat this thing and keep me alive. They're fighting for me. That's pretty reassuring. I need my family fighting for me too."

Tears continued to flow. Kara held the tissue to her eyes. "I'm sorry for being so mean to you, Mom. I hate myself."

"Oh, you don't hate yourself, honey. You're just not sure how to make sense out of any of this. We all handle it in our own way."

"But I've been so mean."

"Look at me," Barb said, lifting Kara's chin. "Take the tissue away."

Kara sniffed and obeyed.

Barb said, "I forgive you, okay? Now I want you to stop this talk about hating yourself." Down the street an SUV pulled over and Bri Harlacker stepped out, waved to the driver, and headed for the Hendersons' house. "You have a party to go to."

"I don't want to go. I just want to go home and spend time with you."

Barb smiled. "I was hoping you'd say that." She kissed her daughter on the forehead. "I love you, Kara."

"I love you, Mom."

"We'll get through this, okay?"

"All of us?"

Barb knew what she was asking. "Yes. All of us."

Chapter Forty-Two

EN SAT IN HIS OFFICE at Hertzel, DeGuardo & Shea, leaned back in his desk chair, tented his hands, and looked out the broad window over Lake Michigan. The sky was clear and blue and streaked with the contrails of jets coming and going from O'Hare. Boats made their way slowly across the water, and on the other side of the lake he could see the faint outline of Michigan City. It was a glorious day, but for a reason other than the weather and the view. At eight o'clock sharp, not thirty seconds after he'd arrived and settled into his office, he was called into John Hertzel's office. Ed DeGuardo and Paul Shea were there as well. They all stood to greet him, then didn't waste any time getting to the point. They'd been impressed with his work ethic and dedication to the company. He was an exceptional lawyer, and the O'Leary case proved that. He was dedicated and loyal, just the kind of man they wanted to join them. They offered him the position of partner in the firm. Ken didn't remember much after that. He recalled accepting the position right there and shaking hands, smiling, laughing, sharing a glass of brandy. He'd get a pay increase, of course, and a sizable bonus. He'd also get a new office, one with an even better view than the one in which he sat now.

Ken Hutching, *partner* at the law firm of Hertzel, DeGuardo & Shea, drew in a deep breath and sighed. He should be thrilled, as ecstatic as a high school football player after scoring his first touchdown. But he wasn't. He'd been victorious, yes, but he had no one to share the victory with. Celia and the kids were still with her parents. His friends all had their own families to attend to.

But that would all change soon enough. He'd called Celia right after the meeting and asked her to stop by the house this evening; he had something very important to tell her. Wouldn't she be impressed? He promised himself he wouldn't gloat, not too much anyway. But this was what he'd been working so hard for. She had to respect him now. And the kids, they'd be so proud of their dad. He'd get that yacht with his first bonus and take them all on a cruise around the lake. They'd take a cruise every Sunday morning, then eat lunch at one of Chicago's finest restaurants.

Celia's words came back to him then, words spoken in anger as they'd argued about the kids. *They don't care if you're a big-time lawyer or a ditch digger, they just want their daddy to be there.*

Well, he was going to be a big-time lawyer *and* be there now. This promotion would give him the time he needed to spend with Celia and the kids—at least that's what he'd convinced himself. Now he only had to convince Celia.

Ken looked at his watch. He had to get home and clean up. Celia would be there in two hours. Grabbing his coat, he slid a pile of papers off his desk and stuffed them into his briefcase. He had another case to prepare for and would get a head start later tonight, after Celia left.

Right on time the front door opened and closed.

"I'm in here," Ken called from the office. He stood and met Celia at the doorway. It had been a week since he last saw her. She'd brought the kids by to spend the weekend with him.

After sharing an awkward hug, he helped her with her coat and asked her to sit down. He could tell by the look on her face and her reserved movements that she didn't quite trust him, his motives, the excitement she must have heard in his voice over the phone.

Ken leaned against his desk. "How have you been? How are the kids?"

"We're all fine. The kids are good. They had a good time with you."

He smiled. "Good. I had fun too." He had set aside the entire weekend to spend with the kids and didn't do an ounce of work until they were both tucked into bed. Saturday they went to the Lincoln Park Zoo, and Sunday the indoor amusement park. He probably went overboard on the food and fun, but he didn't care. It was the least he could do after canceling on them the previous weekend. He just had too much work to do, too much to get caught up on. And it had paid off.

"So what's the news?"

Ken paused for effect; in his head he imagined a drum roll. He'd thought about this moment for months, and the time was finally here. He rubbed his hands together. "I got the promotion. You're looking at the new partner in the law firm."

If he expected her to spring from her chair and do cartwheels and throw herself into his arms, he was sorrowfully wrong. She sat there, arms crossed over her chest. "So what does that mean for us?"

Ken pushed away from the desk and threw his arms into the air. "Oh, c'mon, Celia, a little excitement would be nice. How about a 'Good job, Ken, I'm really proud of you.' Would that be so tough? You know how hard I worked for this."

"At the expense of your family. Ken, excuse me if I'm not all smiles and applause over this step up. Right now we're all feeling a little threatened by your job."

He turned both hands palm up. "But this will change everything. I already have it all worked out. I'm going to buy that yacht I've been looking at when I get my first bonus, then we'll—"

"Ken, wait." She held up both hands. "Just wait. I'm sorry, but anything that means more responsibility is inevitably going to mean more time. How does this benefit your family, besides the monetary upgrade? No matter what you think or how you look at it, it's going to mean more time at work or more of bringing your work home."

"How do you know?"

"How many hours a week do your new partners put in?"

He paused. He honestly had no idea. They were always there when he was and usually stayed late into the evening. All three of them were on their second marriage. But he didn't have to be like that.

Celia stood and smoothed her pants. She clasped her hands in front of her. "Ken, I know you worked hard for this promotion, I do. And it's a great accomplishment. But I..." She shifted her eyes around the office, chewed on her lip. "I want a divorce."

Ken fell back against the desk. "You what?"

"I want a divorce. This just isn't working out."

"But what about the promotion? What about the great time I just had with the kids?"

"It doesn't change anything. Don't you see? You haven't changed. Your job is still number one. I'm sorry. I never wanted it to come to this, but I've given it a lot of thought. I think it's the best for both of us."

"And what about the kids? Is it the best for them?"

She didn't say anything. She twisted her hands together and wiped a tear from her eye. "I'm sorry, Ken. I just can't take this anymore." She turned and left the room, leaving him alone at his desk, his briefcase full of documents behind him.

Chapter Forty-Three

NOTHING HAD CHANGED IN THE chemo room except the faces. Nena only recognized a few of the other patients from her previous two treatments. She did notice, however, that Nick was not there. She scanned the room looking for a free recliner and found one in the far corner. It was a good spot too, positioned next to one of the wide windows where she'd have a nice view of the open fields behind the building.

A cloud of depression hung in the room. There was no laughter, no excited chatter, only forced, nervous smiles and empty eyes. This was a place of gloom, where those on death's doorstep came to make their final stand. Outside a handful of horses grazed lazily, their noses to the ground, muscles quivering away flies. A dark brown stallion looked up, shook his head, and spontaneously took off at a gallop across the pasture. It was a stark contrast to the scene inside, where those weakened by disease and the poison given to fight it were bound to their chairs by IVs and monitors.

"Good morning. We meet again."

Nena looked to her left and found the young man from the hospital seated beside her. She hadn't recognized him on her walk across the room. His eyes were tired and sunken, his cheeks hollow. Any color had gone from his face.

"Good morning," she said. "I'm Nena. We never properly met in the hospital."

The man stuck out his hand to shake hers, then Jim's. "I'm Tim. How did you recover from your surgery?"

"All healed up." She didn't mention that the surgery was a bust.

A petite nurse with short, dark hair arrived with her IV

supplies and placed them on the table beside Nena. "Hi, I don't think we've met before. I'm Claire. I'll be taking care of you today."

"Good morning." Nena scanned the room one more time while Claire went to work inserting the IV and starting the pump.

"Okay, that'll do it." She rolled the IV tower behind Nena's chair. "If you need anything, just let me know, okay?"

"Thank you," Nena said. She turned to Jim. "Would you mind getting me a sweet tea? I'd like something cold before the sensitivity begins." Most of the side effects had diminished since her last treatment, but she knew within a half hour of beginning that the cold sensitivity would return and she'd be drinking lukewarm liquids for another week.

"Sure thing. One sweet tea coming up." He stood and kissed her on the cheek.

Beside her, Tim was reading a book. "Is this your first visit, Tim?" she said.

He looked up. "Yep. First time."

"Are you married?"

"For going on eleven years now. My wife is picking up the kids from my parents. I'll be finished here in a few minutes, and she'll meet me downstairs with the car. That way we can go right home and I can take a nap."

"You have three kids, right?"

A smile stretched across his face at the mention of his children. "Yeah. All girls."

"That's right. What are their ages?"

"Nine, seven, and six."

"I bet they're cuties."

His smile grew. "They sure are."

Nena's heart ached for Tim and his young family, for his little girls. They were so young to have to deal with something like cancer. How could they ever grasp the gravity of what their daddy was going through?

"How are they dealing with all of this?"

Tim closed his book and sat it on the table beside his chair. "They're doing okay. Lots of questions, most we just don't have answers for. We want them to understand that this is serious, but at the same time we don't want to scare them. It's tough, though. How do you explain cancer to a seven-year-old?"

Nena nodded. It wouldn't be easy. "And how are you doing, Tim?"

He was so young as well, too young to have to deal with something like cancer while trying to raise kids and support a family.

Tim shrugged. "I'm doing okay, I guess."

"You guess?"

He paused, looked at his hands. "I'm not afraid to die, if that's what you mean." He said it like he meant it, not like a man trying to convince himself that it was true. "I know where I'm going. The thing that scares me the most is the thought of leaving my girls without a father and my wife without a husband."

Nena's frail emotions got the best of her again. This young man was so brave, so confident, even in the shadow of death. "How can you be so sure?"

"About what?"

"You said you're not afraid to die because you know where you're going. How can you be so sure?"

"I believe what the Bible says about life after death. If there's anything that gets you thinking about death, it's cancer."

He was right, of course. She'd been thinking a lot about death lately, but she hadn't given much thought to what happened after that. "I wish I had your certainty."

"You *can* have it."

His phone rang. Tim grabbed it from his pocket and flipped it open. "That's my wife. She's back with the girls."

"Will she bring them up?"

"No. We don't want them to see me like this. She'll wait in

the lobby downstairs until I'm finished." He looked at the IV pump and the empty bag dangling from the tower. "I'll be done here any second."

The alarm on Tim's IV pump went off, a high-pitched chirp that sounded like a bird's call. Claire came over, turned off the alarm, and began unhooking Tim from the IV.

"There ya go," she said. "Is your wife here?"

"Yeah, she just texted me that she was in the lobby with the girls. Thanks, Claire."

"You're welcome. You take care, okay? And we'll see you in two weeks."

She walked away, and Tim turned to Nena. "Will I see you in two weeks?"

"I'm scheduled for the same time," she said.

"Good. So am I. We'll continue our conversation then."

"Hug those girls." She thought of all the times she could have hugged her own children and didn't…all the times she *should* have hugged them.

"I will. Bye, Nena." He left and passed Jim entering the room with two sweet teas in hand.

Three and a half hours later the last alarm on Nena's IV pump sounded. Another round of chemotherapy finished. Claire was there almost immediately to slide the needle out of the vein on the back of Nena's hand.

"Can I ask you something?" Nena said.

"Sure, anything." Claire worked on swabbing the site with an alcohol wipe.

"What happened to Nick, the gentleman who was here a few weeks ago when I was?"

The smile disappeared from Claire's face. She stopped what she was doing and held the alcohol wipe on Nena's hand. "Nick passed away last week."

"Oh, no." He'd looked so healthy, so vibrant. When he talked, he spoke like a man who had years to live.

"He'll be missed around here, that's for sure."

"He seemed like such a nice man."

Claire smiled. "He was the nicest. I never heard him complain once." She removed the wipe and placed a bandage over the pinpoint hole. "That should do it for you."

"Thank you, Claire."

Claire left, and Jim reached for Nena's hand. "You okay?"

She nodded. She wasn't okay, though. Nick's death was a cruel reminder of how deadly the beast within her was, how stealthy it could be. It was a silent killer that worked its evil in the dark corners of the body, undetected for so long, until it was too late and the damage was done. The appearance of health and vitality meant nothing with this monster. It was a swift killer and no respecter of persons.

Jim squeezed her hand. "Are you sure?"

She nodded again.

On the way home both Jim and Nena were quiet. She was tired, fatigued from the treatment, but she couldn't sleep in the car. Her mind churned and stirred with thoughts of her brief conversation with Tim, the young man who faced such an uphill climb but was doing it with such certainty. How could he be so sure? And Nick, whose life had ended too soon. Suddenly fear slipped in with cold, fleshy hands and choked her. Tears came quickly and rolled down her cheeks.

Jim slowed the car and reached for her hand. "Sweetie, what's the matter?"

She could hardly speak, hardly get the words past her throat. "I'm not ready to die, Jim."

Chapter Forty-Four

JIM HAD A HARD TIME settling Nena down and getting her to bed. News of Nick's death had rattled her, and why shouldn't it? It had rattled him as well. When cancer was involved, no one really knew what was going on inside the body. They had their CAT scans and blood work and scopes, but they only revealed so much. They couldn't peer around every corner, under every cell. How much damage the cancer had caused or how widespread its tentacles had reached was anybody's guess.

Once he'd gotten her into bed, though, and tucked her under the covers, she'd slipped into that land of dreams as quickly and peacefully as a child. She was more exhausted than she let on.

Now, sitting in the study, elbows on the desk, Jim let go of the control he'd sought and allowed his mind to wander. The only light in the study came from an oil lamp he'd lit when they got home. The soft glow of the flame cast elongated shadows across the ceiling and walls, shadows that moved and flickered, shadows that reminded Jim of other mysterious figures that menaced and seethed, inflicted violence and hate.

Two days after his altercation with Ted Jimmy was once again knocking down weeds, this time along the fence enclosing the east and northeast pastures. He hadn't seen Nena since he hit Ted and made a fool of himself. She was probably afraid of him now, afraid of his temper.

No word had come about him losing his job, so he assumed either Ted had kept quiet out of humiliation or someone, most likely Jumper or Cricket, had defended him and saved his position. As far as Jimmy was concerned, he'd continue to get up in the morning and do his work until he was told otherwise.

By the time he finished, the day was almost spent, and he was drenched in sweat and in need of cold water. After cleaning the weed eater, he returned it to the shed and was about to lock the door when he saw three men approaching—big guys, military types. Thick necks, broad shoulders, deep chests, crew cuts. Like they'd just gotten home from active duty in some faraway land. These were certainly not ranch hands come to offer help.

Straightening his back, he did his best to look unintimidated. "Can I help you guys?"

The one in the middle, the biggest man with the shortest haircut, lifted his dimpled chin and pushed out his thick chest. "You Jimmy Hutching?"

"Who's asking?"

The man turned to one of his comrades and nodded. The other opened the shed door.

Before Jimmy knew what had happened, he'd been shoved into the shed and the door closed. Two of the men stood in there with him now. One remained outside, presumably keeping watch. Jimmy's heart pounded against its bony cage, and a hot sweat broke out across his forehead.

The largest guy, apparently the leader, rolled his head and shrugged his shoulders. He had a tattoo of a panther on the side of his neck. "You upset the wrong people, dude."

"The McGoverns? Ted sent you?" Jimmy assumed as much but hoped to talk some sense into his new friends. He didn't stand a chance against them physically; they were much too large and muscular for him to defeat with his hands. His only hope was to talk them out of what they'd been hired to do. "He put a hit on me?"

The smaller of the two flexed his pectorals and squeezed his fists. There was a look of intensity, of hunger, in his eyes that was barely human. He belonged in the wild hunting for his next meal, living off the land and preying on the weak and young. "He told us not to kill you."

Jimmy backed up. "That's important information to know." His foot struck a shovel, but he caught it before it fell. Holding the shovel in front of him like a double-edged sword, Jimmy planted his feet. He could retreat no farther into the shed. It was time to stand and fight.

Unlike his partner, the leader appeared calm, relaxed, like he'd delivered these messages for Ted McGovern a thousand times. He took one step closer to Jimmy but showed no signs of fearing the shovel in his hands.

Jimmy waved the shovel back and forth. "Guys, c'mon. We don't need to do this. Let Ted fight his own battles."

Without warning the smaller one closed in. Jimmy pulled back the shovel and swung it, but his offense was short-lived. The leader had stepped in and blocked the blow with his forearm. Something hit Jimmy hard in the gut, and he dropped the shovel and doubled over. Burning nausea radiated out from his abdomen, and he gasped for breath. But the attack didn't stop. Both men's fists, the size of small cannonballs, rained down upon him, hitting him in his head, face, chest, stomach. Such a barrage it was that Jimmy had no chance of fighting back.

Jimmy's legs soon gave out and he dropped to his knees, then his side, covering his head with both arms and curling into a fetal position to protect his vital organs. Pain jabbed at him from all angles. His breath seemed to be ripped from his lungs. The assault was like being caught outside in the worst kind of hailstorm with no shelter.

While they beat him, the men rained down curses as well, but after a while their voices grew distant and the blows more numb. The men seemed to hover, strike, dart here, dart there. More than once Jimmy felt a rib pop, but even that pain seemed to dull. He thought of his mother and wondered if he'd ever see her again, regretted not making the time to visit and check in on her. He thought of Nena, wondered if she knew of this attack, if she had *agreed to it. The shed darkened. Jimmy could feel the impact of the blows but no longer felt the pain. His brain was shutting down, going into preservation mode. And now all that rang in his mind was the smaller man's words—He told us not to kill you. He hoped they were good at obeying orders.*

Seconds later the attack ceased, and the two men stood over Jimmy, breathing hard. They appeared as shadowy figures, specters from another dimension maybe. Or strangers from a distant planet come to earth to dominate it and rule over mankind. They hovered above the ground like ghosts and spoke a foreign language, their voices slurred and tinny. When they moved, they left behind a trailing image of their form, like a smudged shadow.

Jimmy didn't try to get up, didn't even try to move. He knew his best option was to be still and let this moment pass. If they were done with him, they'd soon make their exit, having delivered their message and respected their boss's decision to spare his life.

One of them, Jimmy could no longer tell which was which, stepped forward and nudged him with a foot.

"Hey, stay away from Nena St. Claire." His voice was calm, almost conversational, as if he'd met Jimmy outside this place, this ranch, and the two had shared some childhood friends. "Consider this a warning, okay?"

Jimmy said nothing.

The man nudged him again. "Okay, man?"

Jimmy grunted what he hoped they'd interpret as an affirmative.

The other one crouched next to Jimmy. When he spoke, his voice was low and serious. "There should be no need to see a doctor or tell anyone what happened here. You have a couple broken ribs, but nothing that punctured a lung. Wrap them tight, and they'll heal in time. We made sure to avoid any internal bleeding as well. You'll have plenty of bruises, very colorful ones, I'm sure, and your nose is broken. Tell them you fell off a horse at full gallop. Take some time to heal, then get lost, you hear?"

But Jimmy was fading again.

"Hey." The man tapped his shoulder. "You hear?"

Again, all Jimmy could produce was a weak grunt.

He blacked out, and when he came to the shed was dark and quiet.

Jim could still hear the man's voice in his head. For decades it had haunted him, popping up in dreams and nightmares. He never did find out who the three brutes were. They'd disappeared just as swiftly as they'd appeared. They must have been professionals, trained to do a job and vanish. He was sure Ted McGovern had paid them handsomely.

A noise from the second floor startled him, a thud, like something had been thrown or pushed over. Shoving back his chair, he stood and quick-stepped it out of the study and up the stairs. In the bedroom he found Nena still asleep and the glass of water he'd given her on the floor. The glass hadn't broken, but the water had soaked into the braided rug. Nena's arm stretched above her head at an odd angle. Her right leg twitched, jumped. Her arm came swooping down and landed by her side. She moaned, grunted, and said something unintelligible. She was having a nightmare. The nurse had said that might happen.

Jim went to her side and was about to stir her from her sleep when she mumbled, "I can't get away."

He knelt beside the bed and smoothed her hair from her forehead. "Can't get away from what, darling?"

With her eyes still closed, Nena breathed out heavily. Her legs jerked here and there; her left hand opened and closed rhythmically. She shook her head. "No. I can't get away from it. It's above me, below...it's there...in front...behind."

"What, Nena? What can't you get away from?"

"The man in the dark...he's always there. He's waiting."

Her sleep talk made no sense.

Again she twitched, breathed out, and said, "Wherever I am, I'm not for long."

Jim smoothed her hair again and kissed her on the cheek. "Hey, Nena. Wake up, darling."

Nena's eyes fluttered open but did not appear to focus on anything in particular.

"Nena, wake up. You were dreaming."

She blinked twice, and clarity came to her eyes. She focused on Jim's face.

"You were dreaming. Having a nightmare."

"I was?" Her words were slurred, drawn out like those spoken by a casual drinker who found herself one step on this side of intoxication. "I don't remember."

"It's okay." He rubbed her cheek with his thumb. "You can go back to sleep."

"Jim." She looked at him, and her eyelids drooped, closed, opened again. Her eyes were drifting, losing their connection with the present. They rolled back in her head, and she blinked slowly. "I don't want to die...but I can't get away."

He let her drift back to sleep and prayed this time it would be peaceful. Then he went back to the study and picked up the phone, punched in the numbers. A man answered.

"Reverend Busbey? It's Jim. I think we need you to come over here."

Chapter Forty-Five

NENA WAS IN BED, COVERS pulled up to her shoulders, reading a book when Reverend Busbey appeared in the doorway with Jim. She'd slept fitfully most of the afternoon, awaking several times to use the bathroom or sip at her tea, only to slip back into sleep just as quickly as she'd stirred from it. Despite her sleep, though, she still felt tired and wrestled heavy eyelids.

Jim entered the room with a fresh mug of hot tea in his hand. He set it on the bedside table. "Here you go, sweetheart. Make sure you drink it all." Jim was really pushing the liquids this time around. Neither of them wanted a repeat hospital visit. "Reverend Busbey is here."

Jim told Nena earlier that he'd called the pastor and asked him to come over. She didn't argue; she was ready to talk. "Thank you." She took a sip of the tea. "Hello, Reverend."

Busbey smiled and entered the room. "Hello, Nena. How are you feeling?"

"Tired. Thirsty. Hot liquids just don't seem to quench the thirst like a nice cold sweet tea does."

"Sweet tea is always my beverage of choice."

"You wouldn't be Southern if it wasn't."

"That is true. Do you mind if I pull up a chair and sit by your bed?"

"Not at all."

Jim lifted the armchair by the window. "Let me get it for you." He set it next to the bed.

The sun was almost gone, leaving the sky outside a deep shade of orange. Busbey sat and laced his fingers. "Thank you,

Jim." He turned to Nena. "How have you been dealing with all of this, Nena?"

She closed her book and set it beside her on the bed, shrugged. "Not very well, I guess."

"I'd think you were odd if you were handling it well. Cancer is a hard enemy to battle. It attacks you not only physically, but emotionally and psychologically as well. Even spiritually. It forces you to evaluate things most people don't like to think about."

"Like am I ready to die."

He nodded. "For instance."

She looked directly at him. "I'm not. I don't want to die."

Busbey didn't flinch. It was as if he'd been expecting her to make that declaration, as if her words were no more surprising to him than if she'd announced she was going to brush her teeth. "Not too many people do."

"No, but some are at peace with it."

"Yes, they are."

"Like your wife."

"Yes, she was."

"I'm not."

He tilted his head to the side. "Why do you think that is?"

"I'm afraid of dying." Her honesty seemed to surprise her more than it did the pastor. She had no reason to hold back, though, no reason to hide any longer. And she was glad Jim was still in the room. He needed to hear this too.

"What about death frightens you?"

She shrugged. "The uncertainty of it."

"Of death itself?"

"No. Of what happens after I die. I'm not certain."

Busbey sat back in the chair. "Nena, do you believe in God?"

"Of course."

"Do you believe in Jesus?"

"Of course."

"No." He leaned forward, rested his elbows on his knees. "I

217

mean, do you *believe* in Jesus. Not just in your head, but really believe... do you put your faith in Him and Him alone to rescue you from your sin?"

Nena dropped her eyes to the bedspread. She'd had it for years, since they were married, and it had areas on it that needed to be mended. "I'm not sure I have that kind of faith anymore."

"Anymore. You did at one time?"

When she was a young girl her parents took her to the local Baptist church every Sunday. She'd learned about Adam and Eve and Abraham and Moses, about Jesus and why He died on the cross, about His resurrection and promises. "When I was a girl, just a child, I believed with all my heart. I didn't question any of it."

"So what's changed?"

"Everything. Life. The world. Things are more complicated now, sorrow is everywhere, there's been so much hurt and pain. I've made so many mistakes."

"So things have changed, some within your control, some outside your control. Circumstances and how you've responded to them have bothered you."

She looked at Jim, who had taken a seat in an armchair across the room. Tears puddled in his eyes. He smiled at her and nodded. He'd been such a faithful husband, patient with her, strong, so sure of himself. He'd tried to make up for where she'd failed with the kids, but she knew he had regrets of his own and partly blamed himself for their distance and apathy. Her eyes went back to Busbey. "I've made so many mistakes."

Busbey reached out and took Nena's hand. "Nena, don't you see? Strip away all the circumstances, all the mistakes, all the regrets, and you're still that little girl with the simple faith who believes Jesus is the only way to heaven. She's in there still. You need to find her and embrace her. You need to believe again. Really believe. God still loves you, Nena. He's never lost faith in you."

Tears spilled out of her eyes and ran trails down her cheeks. She reached for a tissue and dabbed at her eyes.

"I'm going to pray for you, okay?"

She nodded. She knew that to open her mouth would be to unplug the flow and let the tears rush in as sobs.

Busbey stood and stretched his knee. "You can have certainty, Nena. Search your heart; find that faith again."

Nena smiled and nodded. The tears continued to flow.

Busbey left and Jim took his place in the chair beside the bed. He took Nena's hand in both of his and squeezed. "I'm proud of you, honey. So proud."

"Jim," she said through the tears. "Will you help me?"

"Of course I will."

Chapter Forty-Six

JIM'S EYES OPENED EARLY THE next morning, before the sun had fully risen and the light of day could dust the pastures. The digital clock on the table beside the bed said 6:35. He rolled over and found Nena on her back, eyes open and staring at the ceiling.

"Hey, you're awake already."

Her hands were laced and resting across her chest. She nodded but didn't look at him.

"Another sleepless night?" he said.

"I've had a thousand sleepless nights. So much going through my head. So many regrets." She turned her head and met his eyes. "I want to see the kids. I have things to say to them."

"I'll call them again. Ask them to come." He wasn't sure if they would, but he would try. He'd beg if he had to. "How do you feel?"

"Tired, weak, nauseated, the usual."

Jim pushed back the covers and sat on the edge of the bed. "I'll go get the coffee started. Do you want me to bring a cup up here, or are you going to come down?"

Nena yawned, rubbed her eyes. "I'll come down. I think I'll sit in the family room and watch the morning news."

"I'll join you then." He leaned in for a kiss, then slid into his slippers and went downstairs.

CHAPTER FORTY-SEVEN

NENA LAY IN BED FOR a few minutes, letting her mind wander back to earlier days when the kids were small and the sound of laughter and chatter filled the house. With two girls and a rambunctious boy there was never an end to the activity. She'd enjoyed it once, thrived on it even. But then she'd taken the weight of the ranch on her shoulders. At first she thought they were broad enough to carry the responsibility; she thought she could turn things around and breathe new life into the place. But she quickly learned that the damage done was far too severe to fix that easily. She'd poured everything into the ranch—all her time, her energy, her love—and told herself so many times that she was doing it for good reasons. Little did she know at the time that it would cost her everything.

Memories came back to her like lightning flashes, each one brief and clipped but powerful.

"Can you play a game with me, Mommy?"

"Not now, Kenny. Mommy's got work to do..."

"Mama, sit on your lap?"

"Oh, I'm sorry, sweetie, I can't hold you right now, I have to finish this up. Barbara! Can you get your sister? I have a few phone calls to make."

"Sure, Mom. Hey, can you help me bake some brownies later? I want to share them at school tomorrow for my birthday."

"Later? I don't know. I'm trying to settle some things here and don't know how long it will take."

"The brownies won't take long."

"Barbara, please, we'll talk about it later; just get Berta out of here."

In all her well-doing and despite her noble intentions she'd been an awful mother, neglecting her children for a piece of land. She'd lost her focus on the things that were truly important. The sound of little feet and laughter in the home would be welcome now.

Sitting up, Nena held her head to calm the throbbing. Her stomach roiled and turned; she'd have to sip the coffee slowly. She could hear the muted sounds of Jim downstairs putting the coffee on, starting the timer. She stood and waited for the room to stop spinning, balancing herself on weak legs. She thought of calling for him, asking him to hold her arm and steady her down the stairs, but she didn't want to bother him.

Holding onto the railing with her left hand, Nena braced herself with her right hand against the wall. One step at a time she descended, careful not to slip, careful not to lose her grip on the handrail. Halfway down she felt an odd pressure in her chest, and the nausea increased. One step more and the pressure built, radiating out from her chest to her neck and shoulders. She was having difficulty breathing now. The staircase darkened, and the floor below, just a few steps away, seemed to undulate. Another step. Bile surged up her throat, but she swallowed it down again. The pressure behind her ribs increased. Nena hollered for Jim but didn't know if he heard her. If she could only make it to the bottom of the steps, there was a sofa she could lie on.

Another step. Three more now.

She could do this. Again, she hollered for Jim. Her legs wobbled. The pressure in her chest was extreme now, viselike, pushing all the way up to her head. The staircase opened to the living room below, but she saw nothing. The room was dark, as if an inky mist had moved in and swallowed the furniture, the floor, the light.

She tried to say Jim's name again but couldn't.

Her legs gave out...and she went down.

Chapter Forty-Eight

Jim heard Nena call his name, then the crash. Running through the kitchen, through the dining room, heart in his throat, he hoped to God she hadn't fallen down the steps.

Please, God, let it be nothing.

When he rounded the corner of the living room and saw her lying on the floor, face down, legs sprawled, right arm bent at an odd angle behind her back, and a pool of blood around her head, he thought at first she was dead, and a sob jumped from his throat.

"Nena! No!"

He ran to her and dropped to his knees, put his hand on her back. His left hand searched her neck for a pulse. There, it was weak, but she was still alive. Thank God. He didn't want to move her for fear that she had a spinal injury, but she was bleeding badly from somewhere on her head. Ripping his phone from its belt clip, he punched in the numbers for help.

God, don't let her die. Not yet. Not like this.

Back in the hospital was not the place Jim hoped for his wife to be. They'd rushed her right there, and after an hour and a half they were finally able to stabilize her. Now, sitting beside Nena's bed in the intensive care unit, Jim held his head in his hands, fingers laced through his hair, and prayed. The machine by her head monitoring her vitals hummed quietly; an IV pump churned to an even rhythm. The lights were low and Nena slept peacefully, aided by a small pharmacy of medications. On the left side of her head, just above the eye, stitches held together a gash the length of a paper clip. Dried blood clumped in her eyebrow and matted her hair. How had it come to this? Just two months ago she was full of vigor and fight. Three months ago they'd taken a day trip to Harper's Ferry and walked all day. This person in the hospital bed was not the same woman. Fifty pounds lighter, her skin looked like it hung on her bones. Her hair was thin and brittle. Eyes sunken and hollow. She'd aged twenty years in a matter of weeks, days even. Jim still couldn't imagine life without his Nena. Though death crouched just around the corner, he didn't have to welcome it and wasn't about to go looking for it.

Please spare her life a little longer.

She wanted to see the kids, wanted to make amends. He only hoped she'd hang on long enough to do that.

The glass door to the room slid open, and a doctor stepped in, followed by three others in white lab coats.

"Mr. Hutching?"

Jim stood and shook the man's hand. "Yes."

"I'm Dr. Benson, I saw your wife in the ER, and this"—he motioned to the three young doctors behind him, two men and a woman—"is Dr. Gupta, Dr. Lynn, and Dr. Trantaforri. We will all be monitoring her condition."

"What happened? What's wrong with her? They said she had a heart attack."

Dr. Benson put his hands in the pockets of his lab coat. "That's correct. She was also moderately dehydrated and is experiencing renal failure...her kidneys are shutting down."

"From the cancer or the chemo?"

"It's hard to say, but it's probably a combination. Her body is under an extreme amount of stress right now. Her liver is also showing signs of struggling."

Jim ran his hands through his hair. "Did you tell Dr. Alexis all this?"

"Yes, she's been fully updated and should be in soon to see you."

"So what's going to happen? What are we looking at here?"

Dr. Benson dropped his heavy eyebrows and sighed, glanced back at the interns. He was a big man, broad shoulders, thick around the waist. "There's just not much we can do for her now except keep her comfortable and stable. I'm sorry. She appears to be in the end stages. She may not make it another week."

Benson continued talking, but Jim didn't hear what he said. Slowly he sat down in the chair and put his fist to his mouth. So it had come to this. Nena was going to die, and there wasn't a thing anyone could do about it except keep her comfortable. He looked at his wife, so peaceful, so frail, so close to death. Benson's hand landed softly on Jim's shoulder. The doctor expressed his regret again and said good-bye. The glass door slid open and shut. And Jim was once again alone with the humming machines and his own fears and memories. He'd have to tell her the whole story. She deserved to know. He'd kept it to himself long enough.

Jimmy had made his way back to the bunkhouse without being seen. He'd used the cover of darkness to cloak his slow, deliberate movements. Pain stabbed at his sides like knives worked between his ribs, and a jackhammer thumped away in his head. His eyes were so swollen he could barely see where he was going, but he knew the terrain well enough now to make his way around the ranch blindfolded, if needed. Stumbling through the doorway, he headed straight for his bed. He just wanted to sleep and deal with whatever wounds he had in the morning.

The TV was on when Jimmy entered the room, and Jumper leapt out of his bed. "Holy Toledo, kid, what happened?"

Jimmy raised a hand. "I'm fine. Just…" Pain jabbed at his ribs. Talking took more effort than he thought it would. "Just leave me alone. Okay?"

"No, it ain't okay. You need a doctor."

Jimmy hobbled across the room and sat on the edge of his bed. Slowly, with his arms pressed tightly against his sides to stabilize his mangled rib cage, he lowered himself to his side, then rolled to his back. A moan involuntarily escaped his harried lungs. His breaths were short and quick. Anything deeper than a gasp sent waves of pain throughout his whole chest.

Jumper leaned over him. "Jimmy. My glory, what happened to you?"

"I fell off one of the horses."

"You fell off one of the horses." He straightened and crossed his arms. "Well, that's about as good as sayin' you fell down the steps. You need a doctor."

Jimmy shook his head. "No. I'm fine, really. Just some broken ribs."

"Just some broken ribs? Son, have seen your face? You could have a concussion, internal bleedin'. I ain't havin' you die on me in this bed."

"I'll be fine."

"I'm callin' an ambulance, then I'll let Cricket know what happened." He looked Jimmy up and down. "That you fell off a horse."

"Going full gallop."

"Oh, is that how it happened?" His tone said he didn't believe one word of Jimmy's story. "Well, you're lucky you didn't go and get yourself killed. I told you to be careful."

Jimmy had no idea how long it took the ambulance to get there. He drifted in and out of sleep, each time dreaming of angry wolves attacking him, their teeth and claws tearing at his flesh, their hungry eyes penetrating his, boring into his soul. He'd awaken in awful pain, soaked in a cold sweat. One time Cricket was there, bending over him. Saying something Jimmy couldn't understand. Another time Nena was there, her soft hand on his forehead, then his cheek. She too spoke, but her words sounded garbled, disjointed.

Finally sirens, like the wail of a woman robbed of her child, sounded in the distance. Men arrived and handled him. Each movement sent jolts of pain like electric shocks around his ribs, and he'd holler out. Darkness closed in on him then, moved in and blocked out any light. He felt himself falling, as if he were climbing a muddy hill and his feet kept slipping, unable to find purchase. Down he went, and no matter how hard he struggled to slow his descent, the pull was too great.

Then total blackness moved in and swallowed him.

Jim was awakened by the sound of the room's door sliding open. He'd fallen asleep in the chair next to Nena's bed. Straightening his back and neck, he stretched the kinks out of them and pulled himself to his feet. Dr. Alexis stood in the room, hands clasped in front of her.

"I'm sorry, Jim. Really I am."

"What do we do now?"

Alexis frowned. "There isn't more to be done. We'll stop the chemotherapy, keep her comfortable. A CAT scan was done in the ER, and it showed the cancer is spreading quickly. Did Dr. Benson fill you in on the other matters?"

Jim combed his hand through his hair again, rubbed his face. He nodded. "Yes, about the kidneys and liver. And her heart, the heart attack." He looked back at Nena, still asleep, still appearing so peaceful despite the monster raging out of control inside her.

Alexis extended her hand. Jim took it, and the doctor put her other hand on top of Jim's.

"Jim." She forced a smile. "The nurse will let me know when she's awake. Then we'll talk more."

"Thanks, Dr. Alexis."

"Of course." She turned and left the room.

Chapter Forty-Nine

ROBERTA PULLED ON HER JEANS and flipped her hair over her shoulder. She looked in the mirror and wiped at a smudge of lipstick, then ran her finger under her eye, brushing away a stray lash. She was meeting Thomas at the café in an hour, and the two of them were going out for dinner. He'd started closing early on Fridays so he could spend time with her, a move she found both charming and promising. There had still been no proposal, but she couldn't help but believe it would be any week now. Since their argument and subsequent apologies, their relationship had made a complete turnaround. Thomas was more attentive, more talkative, made it home by eleven every night, and had taken the initiative to set these new hours so they could actually go out at least once a week.

Roberta pulled her hair back on one side and held it in place with an ornate silver clip. She looked at her watch: a little after eight. She'd leave now and surprise Thomas by getting there early to help him close the café. The sooner they got out of there, the more time they'd have together.

The walk from the apartment to the café took only twenty minutes. Even with the crowd on Ocean Front Walk and the congestion of the vendors, she was able to move along and make good time. When she got there, the CLOSED sign had already been hung on the door of the Sunny Bean and most of the lights had been turned off. She pushed open the door but didn't see Thomas. The chairs were on the tabletops and the floor looked swept. The air carried the aroma of the day's business. He must be in the back finishing up with the books. Maybe she could help him along by washing any last dishes.

Rounding the front counter, she called his name. The light in the back was on, and there was a small stack of dishes near the sink. The door of his office was closed.

Roberta turned the knob and opened the door.

Thomas was there.

In the arms of another woman.

Erica.

Their lips pressed tightly together, bodies entwined.

Thomas swung around, his eyes wide, mouth still parted from kissing Erica.

Blood drained from Roberta's face, like someone had sucked it out with a straw. Her head went light. She tried to say his name, "Tho–Tho–," but it wouldn't come out. She stumbled back a step or two, almost tripped over the doorway, steadied herself.

Thomas called her name, but she didn't want to hear it, didn't want to hear his voice.

He was kissing Erica. They were embarrassed. Like lovers should be.

She moved forward, forcing her feet to advance. Through the kitchen.

Thomas called her again.

She saw the knives hanging on the wall and for an instant, less than one tick on a clock, thought of grabbing one and stabbing either him or herself. Maybe Erica. She didn't care who. But she kept moving, she had to get away from him, away from the café.

She caught her hip on the counter where Erica normally stood, batting her flirtatious eyes at customers, at Thomas, and it nearly knocked her off her feet.

She ran through the dining area, but before hitting the front door, Thomas was right behind her.

"Berta, wait. Please!"

Roberta spun around and faced him, wishing now that she'd

taken one of those knives. How crazy was that? Her pulse pounded in her ears, throbbed in her neck.

His hair was mussed, and he had lipstick on his chin. *Her* lipstick. Erica's. He held both hands out, palms up. "It's not what it looks like."

"Are you serious? Not what it looks like? And what do you think it looks like, Thomas?"

"Like...like..."

He was pathetic.

"Look," he said. His eyes searched hers. "Please, just let me explain. I—"

"What? You didn't mean it to happen? You didn't want me to find out this way? You couldn't help it? Thomas, what could you possibly say to smooth this over?" She put one hand on the door's handle.

"Wait, Berta, please. Don't go." He took a quick glance behind him, but Erica wasn't there. She'd no doubt fled the scene, leaving him to fend for himself. Some woman.

"You used me." Her words were clipped, bitter. "This whole past month was an act, wasn't it? I was starting to figure things out, so you had to ease my suspicion by doing all this stuff—coming home earlier, closing sooner on Friday, actually spending time with me for once—so the heat would be off you and Erica."

"It wasn't like that. I—"

"I don't want to hear it. It's over."

He threw up his hands. "Fine, then, it's over. And you know what?"

"What?"

Both their voices rose in volume.

"I'm glad. Now I can finally be with a woman who really understands me, my passion, my drive. You...you never got me, never really supported me. Erica is confident enough to let me succeed. You're too damaged for that."

"Good!" she shouted. "She can have you. You can pick your

stuff up tomorrow while I'm at work. If it's not out of the apartment by the time I get home, I'm putting it in the hallway." Roberta yanked open the door and walked outside into a stiff evening breeze.

The sun was setting off Venice Beach, melting into the watery horizon, coloring the sky every pastel shade, but she didn't care. Tears blurred her vision as she made her way down Ocean Front Walk, dodging pedestrians and roller skaters, ignoring the calls of vendors.

Thomas's words cycled through her head like an endless loop. *You're too damaged for that. You're too damaged for that. You're too damaged...*

She *was* damaged, and now she was convinced she was beyond repair.

CHAPTER FIFTY

THE CLOCK ON THE HOSPITAL wall showed just before 6:00 a.m. when Nena stirred in her bed, opened her eyes, and looked around the room. Jim had arrived just after five and turned on the morning news. He clicked off the TV and reached for Nena's hand.

"Hey, good morning."

Eyes wide, she shifted her gaze from one side of the room to the other. "Where am I?"

"The ICU. You collapsed at home yesterday morning. Do you remember any of it?"

She stared at him blankly. "I remember coming down the steps...then nothing. What happened?"

Jim hesitated, took her hand in both of his and kissed her fingers. "You had a heart attack."

She rolled her head on the pillow and found a spot on the wall. Her throat moved up and down with a hard swallow. "Can I have some water?"

"Sure." Jim held the cup so she could drink from the straw.

"I'm dying, aren't I?"

Tears pooled in Jim's eyes and blurred his vision of her. "The doctor says your kidneys are failing, and your liver is right behind it. There's nothing they can do."

"So I'm dying."

He leaned in, pulled her hand to his lips again, and swallowed past the lump in his throat. "Don't put it that way, Nena."

"How else can I put it? It's true. How long did they say I have?" Her voice was so weak and hoarse, her hand so frail.

Jim swallowed again. "A week, maybe."

A single tear slipped from the corner of her eye and ran across her temple. She blinked rapidly, turned her head, and looked at him. "I want to go home."

"Nena—"

"Jim Hutching, don't argue with me." She stopped to lick her lips. More tears ran from her eyes. "If I'm going to die, I want to be home. And I want to see the kids one more time. Please, Jim, take me home."

He pressed her fingers against his mouth and nodded. "Okay. I'll get you home."

"What day is it?"

"Tuesday."

"Thanksgiving is in two days?"

"Day after tomorrow."

"Call the kids. Tell them I want them home for Thanksgiving. Like we used to do when they were little."

Now the tears spilled from Jim's eyes, and he let them flow. "Okay. I'll call them first thing." They *would* come; he'd beg and plead if he had to.

Chapter Fifty-One

Barb paced the exam room, absently glancing out the window at the parking lot below, watching cars come and go, other patients enter and exit. These checkups always made her apprehensive, and when she was apprehensive, she got fidgety.

Doug had been able to leave work a few hours early to be there with her. He sat on a chair, his nose in a car magazine.

"What's taking him so long?" she said. Dr. Bassler was already thirty minutes late. She watched as an elderly man closed his car door and limped across the parking lot.

Doug didn't look up from the magazine. "He's a doctor, honey; they're always late. They overbook them, and then they can never stay on schedule."

"Well, I wish he'd get in here."

The magazine dipped, and Doug turned his face toward her. "You feeling okay?"

"Yeah, sure. Just the usual." Since starting treatment she'd battled a nagging nausea. Every antiemetic that they offered her failed to do the job. She'd only vomited a couple times, but the squeamishness twisting her stomach never subsided.

"Why don't you sit down?"

"I don't want to sit down. If I sit down, my legs will bounce, and then you'll tell me to get up and walk."

Doug went back to the magazine, and she went back to pacing and window watching.

Finally the door opened and Dr. Bassler entered the room. He was a short man, balding, with little round spectacles and a cleft in his chin. When he spoke, he rarely made eye contact.

"Good afternoon, folks. Sorry for the wait." He closed the door, rolled the stool out from under the counter, and sat on it.

Barb sat on the chair next to Doug. "It's no problem. I know you're busy." Doug shot her a glance and a smile.

Bassler opened a manila folder and scanned the contents. He licked his forefinger and flipped through a few pages. His eyes found a spot on the floor in front of Barb's feet. "Well." He quickly glanced at her, then found the floor again. "Here's the situation. The blood work doesn't look good."

Bedside manner was not one of Dr. Bassler's strong points, but Barb had heard wonderful things about him, that he was one of the best in the country. As long as she knew he was competent, his oddities could be overlooked.

"Your counts are all up." He sighed dramatically. "I don't like that. In fact, I hate it."

Barb felt like some unseen presence had sneaked into the room and sucker-punched her in the abdomen. Her nausea stirred, and for a moment she thought she'd be running for the bathroom. But she drew in a deep breath, and it soon eased.

"So what do we do?" Doug said. Keeping his eyes on Bassler, he reached over and took Barb's hand.

Bassler's eyes moved along the carpet as if searching for an answer hidden somewhere in the fibers. "Now that's the question, isn't it? The question we're all asking."

"A question that needs an answer," Barb said impatiently.

"Yes, indeed." Bassler's hand went to his jaw and rubbed it. He removed his glasses, rubbed his eyes, then stood and walked to the window. For a long time he stood there, watching the activity below, hands clasped behind his back. Barb looked at Doug, who shrugged and squeezed her hand.

Finally the doctor turned and leaned against the window sill. He held his glasses up to the light, then replaced them on his nose. "I think the prudent thing would be to get another scan done; then, regardless of what we find there, we get to the surgical portion of treatment as quickly as possible."

Barb hated the idea of surgery, but she'd known it would have to happen eventually. "How bad is it?"

Crossing the room, Bassler sat on the stool again and crossed his arms. "The counts are significantly higher—"

"Which means what?"

"Which means the disease is growing in size or, at worst, metastasizing." Dr. Bassler always referred to it as "the disease"; he never called it what it was. He lifted his eyes and met hers for a moment, then found that same spot on the floor in front of her feet. "In this case? We hope for growing only."

"But either way the surgery will be worse than it would have had to be," Barb said.

He paused, thought. "More radical, not worse."

"And what if it is spreading?" Questions circled in her head so quickly she could barely speak fast enough to get them out.

"Then the full course of treatment will be more radical, more aggressive."

"Is there a conservative approach?"

"No." He was emphatic about it. "This disease demands respect. We do not play nice with it and hope it decides to leave you alone; we engage it with everything we have and destroy it."

Barb liked his resolve, but the idea of further treatment, more aggressive, radical action, put a new level of fear in her. When the appointment was over and she and Doug were in the car, she finally let the tears come. There was one question nagging her, knocking on the inside of her skull. She hadn't asked Dr. Bassler because she knew there was no answer to it, no matter how many tests he ran or how many years of experience he had: was she going to die?

CHAPTER FIFTY-TWO

NENA WAS TOO WEAK TO walk on her own, so Jim carried her into the house and up to the bedroom. He propped her pillows and pulled the covers to her chest, then kissed her on the forehead.

She blinked once lazily, smiled, and said, "I'm glad to be home. Thank you."

He kissed her again. "You're welcome. Will you be okay if I go call the kids?"

She nodded, blinked heavy eyelids again.

"Get some rest. The visiting nurse will be here soon to get us all set up." Before they'd left the hospital, a bedside commode was ordered, supplies, and homecare nursing. Nena would be placed on hospice care, which meant she'd be kept comfortable but all treatment for the cancer would cease.

"That's fine."

"Are you in any pain?"

"No. Thank God." She swallowed and winced. "Can I have a glass of water before you go? My throat is so dry."

"I'll get it right away." He started to go, but she stopped him.

"Jim, wait. Please tell the kids to come. I have to see them. I have so much to say."

He sat on the edge of the bed again and stroked her hair. "I know. They will. They'll come."

"I've been carrying this burden for so long. I have to tell them."

She knew time was not on her side; her voice held the urgency that proved it.

"They'll come, honey. Don't worry, okay?"

Again, she only nodded.

After getting her a glass of water, Jim went downstairs to the study and sat behind the desk. Home was the best place for Nena, there was no question about that, but he wondered if he could adequately care for her. He was no nurse. Yes, they'd have a visiting nurse at their disposal, but he would be the one preparing her meals, bathing her, helping her onto the commode, administering her medications. And the day would come when she fell asleep and did not awaken.

He wondered how he'd react in that moment. Part of his mind didn't want to face the reality of it, wanted to pretend it was just a possibility, not a certainty. Maybe her body would somehow reject the cancer and heal itself. Maybe God would choose to miraculously heal her. It could happen, he knew it could, if God so chose.

But what if He didn't?

The other part of his mind knew he needed to prepare himself for the inevitable. The reality that one day soon he would go upstairs or wake up in the morning and find her gone. He was so tired, and the past few weeks had been such an emotional dogfight; his nerves were frayed and splintered, as fragile as dry straw.

Jim rested his elbows on the desktop and held his head in his hands. *God, be my strength when I have none. And please work it out that our children will come, that they'll want to come. There's so much healing that needs to take place.*

When he'd finished praying, he picked up the phone and dialed Roberta's number.

Chapter Fifty-Three

OBERTA WAS STILL IN BED at 9:00 a.m. She had to
work later in the day to cover a city council budget
meeting, which meant she had the morning off. Which meant
she'd spend the morning in bed. It had only been a few days
since discovering Thomas's betrayal, and the wound was still so
raw and painful. Any movement, anything that resembled life
the way it had been, reopened the sore. The only remedy at the
moment was to stay in bed and sleep as much as possible.

Only problem was, every time she closed her eyes she saw
the image of Thomas in Erica's arms, their lips pressed together,
etched on the inside of her eyelids. She couldn't believe he'd
tried to justify what he'd done. How dare he? She hadn't seen or
heard from him since that awful confrontation. Last night she
walked down to the Ocean Walk and stood outside the Sunny
Bean. From the other side of the walkway, mingled with the
crowd, she could see him through the front window, making a
drink behind the counter. Once he looked up, and she thought
he saw her. Erica was there too, taking money and batting those
eyes of hers. Roberta had returned home in tears, scolding herself for spying on him, for the self-inflicted torture.

Rolling over, she looked out the window, at the gulls carving
lazy arcs against the blue sky. Thankfully there was nothing left
in the apartment to remind her of Thomas. He'd returned the
next day to collect his things, and he'd taken everything, even
his soap in the shower.

Her cell phone rang on the bedside table. Roberta rolled to
her back and reached for it, half hoping it was Thomas calling
to say he was sorry, he'd been tremendously stupid, he'd gotten

rid of Erica once and for all, he was begging for forgiveness and a second chance. She'd tell him no, of course, then rethink things and take him back. She hated sleeping alone, eating alone, watching TV alone, shopping alone. Even if he was gone most of the time before, at least she knew he was out there somewhere, and that he was hers. She had someone to call her own. Now she had nothing.

She glanced at the caller ID and saw her dad's name. For a moment she thought of letting the voice mail pick it up, but the thought of talking to someone who genuinely loved her seemed nice at the moment, so she hit the button to answer.

"Hi, Dad."

"Hi, Berty. How are you?" His voice sounded so distant, small, tired. But it was the voice of someone familiar, someone who represented the last thing that was right in her life, and the sound of it pushed a knot into her throat.

"I've been better. What's going on?"

He hesitated, cleared his throat. "It's your mother . . ."

For a moment Roberta thought he was going to say her mother had died, and she shut her eyes hard, bracing herself for the hurt she'd hear in his voice.

"She's not doing well. We put her on hospice care this morning."

"What happened?" She had to force the words from her throat.

"The cancer spread, she had a heart attack, her kidneys are failing. I . . . I don't know how much longer she has."

"Where is she now?"

"She's here, at home. I need you to come home, Berty. Please. She wants to see you. It'll be the last time."

Roberta's first instinct was to refuse, to conjure excuses. She had to work, it was too expensive, she'd never get a ticket with all the holiday travel. Instead she heard herself say, "Sure, Dad, I'll come."

And why not? She had nothing here. She could take a couple days off work; she had Thanksgiving off anyway. The ranch was the last place she'd felt loved, if only by her father, and the last place she'd called home. But the memories were there again, the dream, sitting on her mother's lap and listening to her sweet voice sing that lullaby. Her mother had loved her once, really loved her, and had been a real mother to her. Barb had said as much. But then she'd fallen in love with the ranch, with her mission to save it, and little Berty could no longer find mommy's lap. The lullabies stopped. The hugs and kisses and snuggle time faded away.

She'd go for her father. The sorrow and desperation in his voice said he needed her.

"Thank you, Berty. Let me know your arrival time, and I can meet you at the airport."

"No, it's okay, Dad. I'll get a rental. You need to be there with Mom."

"I love you, Berty."

Hearing someone say he loved her and mean it the way her dad did, after all the pain she'd caused him, pushed that lump farther up her throat and brought a storm of tears with it. "I love you too, Dad."

She'd go for her dad. Because he deserved it. Her mother…well, after all these years maybe it was time to set the grudge aside. She'd see when she got there.

CHAPTER FIFTY-FOUR

FOR KEN HUTCHING THERE WASN'T much thrill in victory. He sat in his new office overlooking Lake Michigan and once again entertained thoughts of throwing himself through the large panes of glass. He wasn't seriously considering it, of course, but in some morbid way the idea felt freeing, almost redemptive. And certainly vindictive. But would Celia even mourn for him?

The new office was much larger than his old one and had a private washroom and wet bar. He felt like a million bucks when he entered his sanctuary in the morning, but as the day progressed, the feeling quickly faded and was replaced by a great yawning emptiness in his gut. He wavered between thoughts that he'd ruined everything with his drive to succeed and really be somebody and thoughts that the whole divorce thing was Celia's fault. She didn't understand him, didn't even try. Her expectations were much too high, and she didn't know a good husband when she saw one.

Ken rolled his chair right up to the window, leaned forward, and put his forehead on the glass. Their suite was on the tenth floor, over a hundred feet above the street below. People hurried by on the sidewalk, cars crawled. Just a few blocks away boats buzzed along in the lake. The water was choppy today, lots of whitecaps. The smaller vessels bobbed and bounced like Ping-Pong balls in a lottery machine. Just watching them made him queasy.

He had work to do, but he didn't feel like doing it. All those years he'd put in long hours, dedicated so much energy and passion to his work...for Celia and the kids. He wanted to give them a better life. And she took it all and threw it back in his face. And now the desire was gone, the fire in his belly that had sustained him for years had been snuffed out. He didn't want to look at another case, didn't want to talk to another client. Now he only wanted to sit in his new chair in his new office and watch the world go by below. After putting in his ten hours here he'd head down to Boyle's and grab a few drinks, wash his loneliness away.

His cell phone on the desk rang. Ken spun around and grabbed it. If it was a client, he'd let it ring; he didn't want to talk legal stuff right now.

It wasn't a client, though; it was his dad. No doubt calling about his mom. Or maybe about the medical bills. Surprisingly his dad had done what Ken had asked and sent him the bills for mom's surgery and chemotherapy. Ken stared at his phone while the ring tone sounded two more times. Finally he pushed the talk button and put the phone to his ear.

"Kenny?"

"Yeah, Dad, I'm here. How are you? Is everything okay?"

There was a pause, then, "It's your mother, Kenny. She took a turn for the worse."

"What does that mean?" Surprisingly he felt a twinge of sorrow.

"She had a heart attack yesterday and...the cancer, it's spreading. She...she doesn't have long."

She doesn't have long. Those four words echoed in Ken's head, bounced around and found no resting place. What was Dad saying? Mom was going to die soon? How soon? Ken hadn't felt particularly close to his mother in a long time, but she was still his mother. Even as an adult he'd had a childish notion that she'd never die, that she'd outlive all of them and just go on living. "What do you mean by 'doesn't have long'?"

"The doctor gave her about a week."

Ken didn't say anything. He turned slowly in his chair and

stared out the window. A flock of birds flew by, battling the strong current, flapping their wings in an erratic flurry.

"Kenny, I'd like you to come home for Thanksgiving. Can you do that? And bring Celia and the kids. Your mother wants to see you."

She wanted to see him. Suddenly Ken was six again, eagerly hoping his mom would acknowledge him, want to spend time with him. "I, uh—"

"Please, Kenny, she doesn't have long."

"Yes, of course, I can come." And why not? He had nothing better to do, and besides, his mother wanted to see him. "I'll bring the kids too." Celia would have to agree.

"And Celia?"

"She...I don't know if she'll be able to make it."

"Why not? What's wrong?"

Of course Dad probably already knew what was wrong. He could always see right through Ken. But Ken couldn't admit it, couldn't bring himself to say the word *divorce* out loud. "I'll talk to her about it."

To his credit Dad didn't press the issue. "Do you need a ride from the airport?"

"No, you stay with Mom. We'll rent a car. Will Roberta and Barb be there too?" He hadn't seen his sisters in years.

"Roberta's coming. I haven't called Barbara yet."

"She'll come." Barb was always the responsible one. In fact, though she was only seven years older than he, his big sister had been more of a mother to him than Mom was.

"I hope so. Let me know what time your flight arrives. And be careful, son."

"I will, Dad."

"And Kenny...I love you."

Ken couldn't remember the last time his dad had told him he loved him. It probably wasn't as long ago as he thought, but time had a way of playing tricks on the mind. The bigger question was, when was the last time Ken said those words to his father?

"You too, Dad." That was about as close as he ever came.

Ken clicked off the phone and held it to his chin. He had no more thoughts of wasting his evening away. He had phone calls to make.

Chapter Fifty-Five

ARB WAS ON HER BACK porch watching a herd of deer rummage for food in the field behind their property. The does, four of them, had their noses to the ground while the buck kept watch for potential danger. This time of year their coloring blended perfectly with that of the harvested cornfield and leafless trees beyond that. Wrapped in a blanket, she sipped at her hot tea and closed her eyes as the warm liquid slid down her throat. It didn't matter that it was barely above fifty degrees; Barb loved the outdoors and wouldn't miss this show for anything. She and Doug had the porch built a couple years back and agreed it was some of the best money they'd ever spent on the house. They'd passed countless dusks and dawns sitting and watching the deer come and go. They'd entertained friends with barbecued meals and late nights of conversation.

Barb wondered if they'd ever do that again. They hadn't had anyone over since her treatment began; she was in no shape, physically or emotionally, to entertain guests. And with this new report from the blood work, she wondered how much longer she'd have to enjoy the porch.

Kara's laughter came from inside, followed by a loud shout from Mikey. They had half a day at school and must have just gotten home. Heavy footsteps—Doug's—vibrated the support beams under the floor of the porch. He'd taken his lunch an hour later so he could pick up the kids and run them home.

The door opened, and Doug was there with the phone in his hand, holding it out to her. "It's your father." His sad eyes and knitted brow said Dad wasn't calling with good news.

She took the phone and put it to her ear. "Hello, Dad."

"Hi, Barbara, how are you?"

"I'm doing okay. How is everything?" She almost winced after asking the question, hoping he wasn't calling to say her mother had died.

"Mom's not doing good. In fact, she…Barbara, the doctor says she doesn't have much longer."

Outside, across the field, the does stopped grazing and lifted their heads in unison. Something had spooked them. They remained motionless, watching, waiting.

"What happened?" A sudden chill took to the back of Barb's neck, so she pulled the blanket tighter.

"There've been some complications. Her heart, kidneys, liver, they're all failing her."

At once the deer took off, running and leaping across the barren field. Their graceful forms covered the ground at a remarkable speed.

Barb sat there, numb. Her mother was dying. She'd been such a strong and confident woman that Barb had it in her head the woman would never die. Nothing could beat her, not even death.

"I'm sorry, Dad. How's Mom doing with it?"

"Well, she's home now and as comfortable as she can be."

"Is she in pain?"

"She says she isn't."

"What can I do?"

There was a short pause, then, "I love you, Barbara."

"Dad, I love you too. Is there anything I can do?"

"Come home for Thanksgiving. She wants to see all of you."

"Are Berta and Kenny going to be there?"

"They both said they'd come."

She could hear the relief in his voice. It would be the first time they were all together in at least ten years. She and Doug had no plans for Thanksgiving.

The door opened, and her husband was there again. He leaned in and said, "We need to go to them."

"Okay, yeah, sure, we'll be there. We'll drive down Thursday morning, so we should get there by early afternoon."

A pack of wild dogs appeared at the edge of the woods on the other side of the field and moved into the open field where the deer had been. They sniffed at the ground and slinked around. They were rare here and extremely shy.

"Good," Dad said. "Your mother has been pretty adamant about seeing you all. She wants the family together again."

"It's been awhile, hasn't it?"

"It's been too long." Dad's voice cracked. He sounded so tired and weary. Beaten down in every way.

"Are you doing okay, Dad?"

"Sure, honey. Don't worry about me. I'll be fine. I'll see you Thursday."

She knew he wasn't fine, but she also knew she'd never get him to talk if he didn't want to. "Okay. Love you, Dad."

"I love you, too."

And then he was gone. Doug pulled up a chair beside her. "So what do you think?" he asked.

"I think we're doing the right thing."

He reached for her hand. "Yeah, me too." Leaning in, he gave her a peck on the lips. "Gotta get back to work. You all right here with the kids?"

She nodded. "Thanks for picking them up. I could have done it."

"Nah, it was nothing. You need your rest."

Doug left, leaving Barb with thoughts of her past, of the last time she hugged her mother, the last time she'd said "I love you" to her, the last time she held her hand, kissed her cheek...the last time she felt a bond as strong as she did now.

Chapter Fifty-Six

HE KIDS WERE COMING HOME. Jim stood from his chair and walked over to a window. The study only had two windows, both protected by café-style wood shutters. At the moment the shutters were pushed open, allowing the early afternoon light to wash through the panes of glass and warm his skin. He could hardly believe they were all going to be together again, the kids, the grandkids, the whole family. Rubbing his jawline, he whispered a prayer of thanks and relaxed against the window frame. The kids had surprised him by how quickly they'd agreed to come. He only hoped they'd make it on time. Nena was so weak and frail, and she was eating next to nothing. She looked as thin and fragile as one of the leafless saplings outside.

The windows looked out over the east pastures, now empty and overgrown. At one time he could stand here and watch thirty horses graze and run and play in the fields. The white-washed fencing once glistened in the sun. Now witchgrass and thistles had overrun the pastures, and the fence had faded and chipped. Some of the rails had warped and even broken under the scourge of rain, sun, heat, and snow. Beyond the pastureland a gray line ran along the horizon, stretching as far right and left as Jim could see. That was where field met forest and the woodlands began. He used to like to ride his horse out there and explore the tree line where deer and foxes liked to hunt for food.

Despite the chilly temperature outside, Jim opened the window and leaned on the sill, drawing in a deep breath of the cool, moist air. The smell of dry grass and dead leaves was in the air, the smell of autumn, usually Jim's favorite time of year. In the ranch's heyday, every Thanksgiving the St. Claire family would gather all the hands and employees and celebrate their thankfulness with an outdoor feast followed by a blazing bonfire. After Nena's dad died, Jim carried on the tradition until most of the hands had been dismissed and the other employees had moved on. There just weren't enough horses to support a crew.

A fox leaped from the field, changed direction in midair with a flick of its tail, and landed, disappearing in the high grass. Thoughts of the good days, of laughing with the ranch hands, of spending hours on horseback, surveying the ranch's perimeter, dug up other thoughts, but they were memories best left buried.

Jimmy awakened to the sound of Nena's voice. His eyelids fluttered open, and there she was, those green eyes, those freckles. She'd never looked more beautiful. At the moment he felt no pain, but after trying unsuccessfully to move, sudden panic gripped him. The realization that he could have been killed overwhelmed him. He tried to speak, but his tongue felt glued to the roof of his mouth.

"Here." Nena spooned a few ice chips into his mouth.

They melted almost instantly but succeeded in loosening his tongue. He tried again. "I'm sorry."

Nena's hand went to his head and smoothed back his hair. Her touch was so soft and warm he wanted to lean into it, but he couldn't move.

"Don't say anything. You don't need to. Just rest."

He did need to rest—already his eyelids were growing heavy, urging him to sleep again—but he didn't want to. There was one more thing he wanted to tell her, one more thing he had to say. "I love you."

She smiled, and a single tear spilled from her eye and slipped down her cheek. "I know."

He was overcome once again by sleep.

When he awoke, Nena was still there in a chair next to his bed.

Outside it was dark, but in the hospital room a single fluorescent bulb above his bed burned. Nena appeared to be asleep, her head lolling to one side, propped by her hand. Jimmy found the bed control and pushed the button to raise the head. The bed squeaked and Nena stirred, opened her eyes. In an instant she was by his side.

"Hey, you're awake."

He felt more alert this time. Gone was the fog in his head, but his mouth still felt like it'd been stuffed with cotton balls.

"Can I have a drink?"

Nena reached for a cup. "The nurse said no drinking yet, but you can have ice chips." She spooned some into his mouth.

He let them melt, then swallowed. "Thanks. How long have I been out?"

"A little over a day."

"Wow. Feels like a week. How do I look?"

She paused and put her hand on his. "Like you fell from a horse at full gallop."

He wasn't sure if she believed his story or not, but he decided not to press the issue. If he were a betting man, which he wasn't, he would have put his money on her knowing full well what had really happened.

Nena patted his hand. "Your mother stopped by."

"She did? How—"

"Cricket called Mosley and got their address. We tracked down their phone number. She's a very nice woman."

"How did she look?"

"Fine." Her hand left his and found his cheek. "Worried about you, but fine."

Jimmy forced a little smile. "Good." And it was good. Better than good. It meant his leaving hadn't made things worse for her. "How long have you been here?"

"The whole time. I haven't left that chair."

"What about Ted?"

She shrugged. "What about him?"

"Won't he—"

She touched his lips with her finger. "Ted's done. We're finished." Her eyes searched his face, and again tears welled in them. "You're my hero, you know that?"

"I'm not exactly the hero type."

"Yes, you are. You're exactly the type of hero I've been dreaming about my whole life."

"I thought you wanted a real cowboy."

"You're so much more than any cowboy. There's something I didn't get to tell you before." "You got me a pair of six-shooters?"

She leaned forward and put her lips to his. They were so soft and gentle, he barely felt them there. When she pulled away, she looked deep into his eyes, past everything external, past his bruises and cuts. "Nope. I love you too, Jimmy Hutching. Just the way you are."

"With my bruises?"

"Oh, especially with your bruises."

"So does this mean I'm not going to lose my job?"

She laughed. "I told Cricket everything about Ted and Hickory and how you protected me. Rick spoke up too. He came to your defense. Your job is fine."

"Good."

"Yeah, it is good."

CHAPTER FIFTY-SEVEN

BY THANKSGIVING MORNING NENA WAS so weak she could barely move herself in bed. She had declined faster than Jim thought possible. She was strong enough to sit (if he propped her up on pillows) and still sharp enough mentally to hold a conversation, but anything beyond that and she was as helpless as an infant. Yesterday she started losing control of her bladder, and Jim expected the bowels would not be far behind. The nurse had warned him that providing care for Nena at home would not be easy; it was a twenty-four-hour job. But Jim never once entertained the thought of putting his wife, his precious Nena, back in the hospital or in some nursing home. She belonged on the ranch, the only home she'd ever known, the place she'd given her life to.

It was near eleven o'clock in the morning when he heard the first knock on the door. After kissing Nena on the forehead, he left her side and padded down the steps. On the porch he found Roberta and Kenny and Celia with the two children.

Roberta stepped into his arms and gave him a kiss on the cheek. "It's so good to see you, Daddy."

He hugged her tight and drew in the aroma of her hair. It was good to have his baby girl so close again. She smiled, which always pushed her eyes into crescents like Nena's, but in them he saw the sorrow she was trying to hide. He'd sensed it in her voice the last time they spoke. His hand went to her cheek. "Are you okay?"

She nodded. "I am now."

Kenny extended his hand and smiled. "Hey, Dad."

Jim took his hand and pulled his son close for a hug. "I'm glad you came, Kenny. And Celia, you too."

Celia, who held Maddy in her arms, hugged him with one arm. He kissed her on the cheek, then sneaked one in on Maddy, who only looked at him with strange ambivalence. She didn't know her own granddaddy. Robby stepped up and stuck out his hand for a shake.

"Well, hello, Robby," Jim said, shaking his grandson's small hand. "Aren't you the little man."

"You'll never guess what happened, Dad," Kenny said.

"I bet I wouldn't."

"Berta's connecting flight at O'Hare was the very same flight as ours to Baltimore. We were three rows apart."

Jim laughed. "What are the chances of that?" It *was* good to have the kids home again. "Well, come inside."

Roberta motioned toward the SUV sitting in front of the house. "Our luggage is still in the car. Kenny was kind enough to let me hitch a ride with them."

"Aw, don't worry about that," Jim said. "Kenny and I will get the bags later. Come in and let me get you something to drink. Your mother is upstairs, but she wants to wait until everyone is here to talk to you. She gets tired so easily."

Kenny was the last one in and shut the door behind him. "Did Barb say when she'd get here?"

Jim looked at his watch. "She said they'd shoot for a little after noon. How was traffic?"

"Not bad," Ken said. "Once we got out of the Baltimore area, it moved quickly."

"Why don't you make yourselves at home and I'll go get some tea for everyone."

Jim went to the kitchen to get the drinks. He was surprised by how mature Roberta looked. The sadness in her eyes bothered him, though, and awakened his fatherly instincts. He wondered what or who was the cause of her unhappiness. And then there was Kenny and Celia. Jim hadn't missed the tension between them—the way they avoided eye contact and kept the children as a protective barrier between them. They danced that awkward waltz of two people at odds. It was obvious to anyone who had been there. And Jim and Nena had been there more times than he'd like to admit.

After pouring the tea, he gathered the glasses on a tray and headed for the living room. Halfway down the hall he heard what sounded like arguing. Celia's voice. As he drew closer he heard part of the conversation.

"How can you say that?" Celia said. "You know I wanted to come. I wanted to be here for your family."

Kenny started to reply, but Jim entered the living room abruptly. He didn't want their arguing to reach Nena upstairs and upset her. Kenny stopped midsentence, his cheeks flushing. Celia took Robby by the hand and left the living room. There were tears in her eyes.

He set the tray of glasses down on the coffee table and offered one to Kenny.

Kenny took the glass and slumped his shoulders. "Sorry, Dad."

Jim sipped his tea. "You want to talk about it?"

After taking his own sip, Kenny said, "Not really, but I guess you're going to find out sooner or later." He looked around the room and finally found a spot on the floor. "Look, Celia and I, we're getting divorced. It's her idea."

"Sure you don't want to talk about it?" Jim said again.

"Not really. I just thought you deserved to know before you found out some other way."

"Is it final?"

Kenny shook his head. "Yeah, I guess. I don't know. Like I said, it's Celia's idea. I don't know what's going through her head anymore."

Jim's heart felt like it had dropped out of his chest and landed in his stomach. He and Nena had seen hard times. They'd fought and argued and bickered. They'd been each other's worst nightmares at times. But they'd never once considered divorce.

Jim rested his hand on Kenny's shoulder. "Son, marriage isn't something you just undo. It's worth fighting for. *Celia* is worth fighting for."

Roberta entered the room then and hesitated. "Am I interrupting?"

"No, no." Jim picked up a glass and handed it to her. "Join us, Berty. Tell me about California."

At twelve thirty Jim called Barb's cell phone. She said they were stuck in traffic—an accident had happened on the freeway—and she had no idea how much longer it would be. They should get started, and she and the family would join in when they got there. Jim clicked off the phone and set it on the table.

"Barbara's stuck in traffic," he said to Roberta and Kenny. "No telling how late they'll be. Let's go up and see your mother awhile."

Celia had come back with the kids but kept her distance from Kenny. "Should we come also?"

Jim walked to her and kissed Maddy on the forehead. "You're part of the family, aren't you? Nena's been waiting to see her grandkids."

CHAPTER FIFTY-EIGHT

ROBERTA WASN'T PREPARED FOR WHAT she saw. Her mother looked like a corpse exhumed from the grave. Her ashen skin was stretched taut over angular bones and had a translucent quality not unlike onion skin. Her eyes were sunken and gray, her lips thin and pale. An image of that woman who used to rock her and sing lullabies flashed through Roberta's mind. The loving arms that held her, the sweet breath on her face, the smell of shampooed hair, it all came rushing back. How she wanted to collapse in those arms again, especially when the wounds inflicted by Thomas were still so raw. As she approached the bed, she felt as though her legs were going to give out from under her.

Her mother reached out a bony hand and smiled at her. Roberta hadn't seen that smile for years and realized suddenly how much she'd missed it, even longed for it. All the years of neglect and *Not now, Berta, I'm too busy; Later, Berta, don't disturb me;* and *Oh, Berta, can't you find something else to do?* tried to force their way into her mind, but how could she feel anything but pity for the wisp of a woman in this bed? How could she hate the fact that for most of her life she had had no mother?

She took her mother's hand and held it.

"Roberta, my baby. It's been a long time since I've held your hand, hasn't it?"

Surprisingly, her mother's voice was still clear.

"Yes, Mom, it has been. Too long."

"I know." Her mother swallowed and winced. "I wasn't much of a mother, was I?"

"You did the best you could." Roberta didn't believe that, of course, but this was not the time to pour on the guilt.

Her mother shook her head slowly. "No, I didn't. I lost so many years trying to save this place, thinking I was doing it for my family. For you, my Berta. When all along I was neglecting you and never even noticed. And now here I am, dying in this bed, and all I can think about are all the regrets I have…all the memories I could have had. I was never there for you, never gave you the love you needed."

Tears pooled in Roberta's eyes. She wanted to be angry, wanted to shout at her mother, tell her now was a fine time to be admitting all of this. Why couldn't she have come to her senses decades ago when Roberta needed a mother, needed to be loved and held and played with, needed someone to teach her how to live and love and raise a family of her own someday? But she couldn't find the anger. All she felt were sorrow and pity.

"I'm sorry, Berta. I know it doesn't change anything, but I am. I'm so sorry. Can you ever forgive me?"

Tears flowed freely down Roberta's cheeks now. "Yes, Mom, I forgive you."

Her mother reached up with her free hand and wiped a tear from Roberta's cheek. "I love you, my baby girl."

"I love you too, Mom." And she did. At that moment she loved her mom more than she thought she was capable of loving anyone.

Tears pushed their way out of her mom's eyes now too and made silvery tracks across her temples and into her thinning hair. She squeezed Roberta's hand tight and pulled her close. "There's something else, Berta." There was intensity in her eyes that hadn't been there before. "You deserve so much more than what I gave you. I know you're searching for love. Don't settle for just anyone. You deserve a man who will love you for who you are, one who will adore you and be willing to give up everything for you. Wait for him, Berta. Promise me you will."

More tears streamed from Roberta's eyes. "I promise." She swallowed a sob and nodded; it was all she could do. Then she turned, crossed the room, and threw herself into her father's strong arms.

CHAPTER FIFTY-NINE

HATEVER EXPECTATIONS KEN HAD UPON entering the bedroom were quickly dashed when he saw his mother for the first time in four years. This was not the woman he remembered. Gone was the determination in the set of her jaw, the fight in her eyes. Gone was the fullness in her cheeks and lips. When she looked at him it was with tired eyes that had all but given up the battle. He could see it as plainly as if the words had been written across her forehead: she was nearing the end of her journey.

Ken approached the bed and took his mother's hand in his. The last time he held her hand was when Granddad died. He remembered it clearly. He was only seven. It was such a hot day for October, an Indian summer day, and she took his hand as he stood by the grave and wept. Her touch brought comfort and security, a promise that she would never abandon him.

Now it meant nothing. It was just the bony, frail hand of an old, dying woman. But that woman was still his mother, and behind all the apathy he'd felt toward his parents and the hurt of his past, he still loved her. A son always loved his mother, no matter what.

She tugged on his hand and motioned for him to come closer. When he leaned in, she reached her other hand up and pulled his head to her face to give him a kiss on the cheek. "Kenny, my only son." She licked her lips. "Hand me my water, dear. Please?"

He gave her the glass, and she drew in a long sip from the straw. "Thank you. How has your job been?"

Ken hesitated. He didn't know if Dad had told her about the

impending divorce. "It's great, Mom. I just made partner in the firm. It's a pretty big deal."

She smiled, but he didn't miss her glance to Celia and the kids standing across the room. "Kenny, you're the one most like me. Determined and stubborn. A hard worker." She paused, and tears welled in her red-rimmed eyes. "I made so many mistakes thinking I was doing the right thing for the family. For you kids."

"Mom, you don't have to—"

"You hush now, Kenny." She shook his hand. "I'm doing the talking now. Nothing is more important than your family. No job, no piece of land, no reputation. I know that now. It's too late for me to do anything about it"—she paused and glanced at Celia again—"but it's not too late for you."

Ken felt heat in his cheeks. Dad must have told her. "Mom, we'll make it okay." He didn't want her worrying on her deathbed.

"No!" Her voice rose, and lines appeared across her forehead. "You listen to me, Kenny. I'm not just some old rambling woman to be patronized. I know you're looking for approval, the approval I never gave you as a child. You feel that by getting more promotions and earning more money that Celia and the kids will appreciate you more, maybe even love you more. But it backfired, didn't it?"

She was right, of course, about everything. He had been seeking their approval, and when it didn't come, he thought he only needed to work harder, longer, climb higher on the ladder of success. Surely they'd see his accomplishments sooner or later, and then they would really love him. But it hadn't worked out that way, not at all. His palms grew sweaty and his face flushed even more, not because he was angry or embarrassed, but because of the guilt he felt. He'd been exposed.

"Son." She pulled him close and whispered into his ear. "Fight for them. They're worth it. The children need their daddy, and Celia, she needs a man to love her. Look what happened to us. You don't want that to happen to your family."

She released her grip on his hand, and he pulled back. Tears built in his own eyes now, but he tried hard to dam them.

"Now, there's one more thing I have to take care of." She looked at her hands, then at him. "Kenny, I'm sorry for not being the mother I should have been, for leaving you alone so much, for not loving you the way a mother should properly do. Will you forgive me?"

Ken could no longer stop the tears as they pushed their way over the rim of his eyelids and spilled down his cheeks. "Yes." That was all he could say.

"Now go love your family, son. Love them like they've never been loved before."

He backed away from the bed, turned, and took Robby in his arms, glad his son was still small enough to hold and hug. Ken held on tight, as if letting go would somehow mean losing his son, his family, for good. He wouldn't let that happen. And things needed to change.

Chapter Sixty

WHEN BARB OPENED THE DOOR to the bedroom, the first person she saw was her father. His red eyes and the weariness in the lines of his face made her think for an instant that she was too late. Roberta was there, as were Kenny and Celia and the kids. Robby was getting so big, and Maddy was just darling.

Barb opened the door all the way. Her eyes met her mother's, and immediately the tears came in waves. She tried to stop them, tried to be strong, but it was as useless as preventing rain from falling from the sky. She grabbed Doug's hand, and he squeezed hers, told her she could do this.

Her mother smiled. "Barbara, come here. Let me look at you."

Barb walked to the bed and removed her hat, revealing her hairless scalp.

Tears spilled from her mother's eyes. "Oh, my girl." She reached for Barb's hand. "No, not you too."

Barb knelt beside the bed and kissed her mother's hand. "I'm so sorry I couldn't come earlier, Mom."

Her mother reached out and wiped a tear from Barb's cheek. "No, you have to take care of yourself. Barbara, please take care of yourself."

"I am, Mom. We're doing all we can." But it wasn't enough, was it? Barb couldn't help but see herself lying in that bed, emaciated, weakened, dancing with death.

"What is it, dear? What kind?"

"Breast cancer."

"Barbara, I'm sorry. Why didn't you tell us?"

"At first I just didn't see the point. And when I found out about your cancer, I didn't want to worry you."

"I'm sorry. I'm so sorry." The tears came quickly now. "I haven't been the mother you needed."

Barb put her hand on her mother's cheek. "Mom, don't. I forgive you; I already have."

"Be strong, Barbara. Don't ever give up. Promise me you won't give up."

A sob jumped into Barb's throat. "I won't, Mom. I promise."

"Doug needs you, and so do your children." She looked across the room at Kara and Mikey. "You've always been the strong one. Don't give up."

"I love you, Mom."

"Oh, my Barbara. I love you too."

Barb walked back to Doug, who took her hand and held it close to his chest.

Chapter Sixty-One

JIM STOOD AGAINST THE WALL and watched his family gather around the bed of his wife. The grandkids were all in front, from the smallest, Maddy, to the oldest, Kara. Nena smiled, she laughed, she talked; she reached her hand out and took Maddy's tiny fingers in it. Doug had an arm around Barb's waist; Ken and Celia stood shoulder to shoulder. It was a start. He was sure they'd find reconciliation. It wouldn't be easy, especially for Ken, but it would make them both stronger. Trials had a way of doing that.

No one mentioned Thanksgiving dinner. There was no talk of turkey or dressing or cranberry sauce. They were content just to be together, to enjoy the company of those they loved. For Jim there could be no better Thanksgiving celebration. This was all the sustenance he needed, and it would keep him going for months, even years.

He turned and faced the window, listening to the medley of familiar voices behind him. The sky was nearly black. Only a sliver of the horizon could still be seen, just a crooked line illuminated by the waning light of evening. A few stars were present already, making an early appearance to welcome in the night.

As the voices behind him faded, Jim's mind wandered to a time in the past, a time he'd just as soon forget but somehow felt he needed to remember.

Jimmy kept Martin at a walk as they made their way across the pasture. Any movement faster than that sent waves of dull pain around his rib cage. It'd been nearly five weeks since the beating,

five weeks of bed rest and lots of time with Jumper. Jimmy's mother wanted him to come home to recover—his father had even agreed to it, as long as it was temporary—but Jimmy declined. The ranch was his life now. And besides, Jumper and Nena proved to be capable nurses, Nena more so than Jumper. The bruises were mostly gone now, and only that dull ache was left in the ribs. The past week Jimmy had spent more time walking the grounds, building up his stamina again.

This morning he'd gotten the idea to ride Martin. He'd wrapped his ribs tight, so tight he could barely draw in a deep breath, and quickly found that anything faster than a walk brought on the ache. He could tell Martin wanted to run, needed to run. The horse was like a steam locomotive with no release valve. But Jimmy kept a tight hold on the reins and held the horse to a brisk walk.

He patted Martin's neck. "It's okay, boy. Give it a few more weeks and I'll be able to run with you."

Up ahead the pasture met a wooded area. Jimmy had never been to this part of the ranch and didn't know how deep the forest ran. The shade looked enticing, though. It was almost noon, and the sun was high and hot.

At the forest's edge Jimmy dismounted and tied Martin's reins to the branch of a dogwood. A boulder protruding from the ground made a nice place to sit and rest. To his right, a little over a hundred yards away, a handful of deer emerged from the forest and foraged along the tree line. Two does searched for food with their fawns while a thick-necked buck kept watch.

Suddenly the buck's head turned toward Jimmy, then the does'. They all stood statue still and watched him, sniffing the air, determining if he meant any danger. Jimmy stared back, not moving. Martin grazed lazily in the shade, his nose to the ground, indifferent to the showdown taking place.

By the time Jimmy heard the footsteps behind him it was too late to run. He spun around and saw Ted sitting high on a jet-black horse, pistol in hand. He was no more than fifty yards away and closing at a fast trot. Jimmy looked back for the deer, but they were gone. Martin snorted his protest.

"It's okay, boy. Settle." Jimmy stood and walked to the horse, put a hand on his neck. "Easy."

Jimmy hadn't seen Ted since hitting him five weeks ago. He knew from Nena that the engagement was off. She'd told Ted she wanted nothing to do with him.

Ted approached and pointed the gun at Jimmy. "Well, look at this. I'm glad to see you're feeling well enough to ride again."

Jimmy had nothing to say to him. He didn't know Ted well enough to judge whether he was capable of using the gun, but from what he'd seen, he wasn't writing it off.

"You ruined my life, do you realize that?"

When Jimmy didn't answer, he hollered, "Do you? I lost my girl because of you. I lost a merger that would have made me one of the richest men in Virginia because of you. I lost my reputation because of you." He jabbed the gun at Jimmy. "Because of you."

Jimmy squared his shoulders. He didn't want Ted to see the fear clawing up his throat. This was not the same Ted he'd encountered before. This Ted had spent five weeks fuming and feeding his hatred. In his eyes was something malevolent and vile. At that moment Jimmy realized Ted was indeed capable of using that gun on a human being.

"No, because of you," Jimmy said. "But it doesn't have to go on. You can stop it now."

"Oh, I'm going to stop it." The gun wavered in Ted's hand. Jimmy wondered if he'd been drinking; he could see that Ted was a hairbreadth from pulling the trigger.

Jimmy raised both hands to shoulder height. "Whoa, c'mon, man. Easy now. This isn't the way."

Ted lowered the gun. "No, it's not. It'd be too easy." He adjusted himself on the saddle. "I'm going to count to twenty, give you a little head start."

The man had gone mad. Did he intend to hunt Jimmy like an animal?

"One...two..."

Jimmy lifted his foot to put it in the stirrup.

Ted lifted the gun. "Uh, no. The horse stays. You go on foot. Three..."

Jimmy looked around, his heart in his throat.

"Four..."

The open pasture would be certain death. His only hope was to lose Ted in the forest.

"Five..."

CHAPTER SIXTY-TWO

THE KIDS HAD ALL GONE out to eat, and Nena was alone in her bed. Across the room Jim stood facing the window, his back to her, his mind a million miles away. She didn't want to disturb him, not yet. He needed his own time to think, to reminisce, to sort through all the memories and hopes and fears. They'd come such a long way together, shared so many times, both good and bad. And he'd always been her rock, the one consistent thing in her life.

Nena pulled the sheet to her neck and shivered. She still couldn't believe all the kids had come home, but she was so thankful she got to see them one last time. And it would be the last time. She'd said her good-byes, made her peace. Now death was right around the corner, tapping, tapping, beckoning her.

She wasn't afraid; she had nothing to fear anymore. Her words spoken just days ago to Jim—*I'm not ready to die*—were born in fear, but the fear had since been vanquished, chased away by the glorious light of hope and love and salvation. She welcomed the transition from this life to the next.

Suddenly a great sense of fatigue overcame her, and for a moment she thought it was time. She closed her eyes, then slowly opened them, found Jim's back. He'd carried so much weight on those shoulders over the years, so much of *her* burden. He was exactly the man she'd needed, the man God had for her.

Bowing her head, Nena folded her hands over her chest and thanked God for the life He'd given her. She prayed for Jim, that he'd have the strength to go on without her and find happiness, that he'd continue to mend the wounds between the children. She prayed for Roberta, that she'd find love, real love, the kind that gives everything and asks for nothing in return. She prayed for Ken, that he and Celia would fight for their marriage, for their children, for each other, that they'd find joy in togetherness. She prayed for Barb, that she would find the strength and resolve to battle the monster within her, that her health would be restored. And she prayed for herself, that God would quicken her entry into eternity...for she was ready now.

Nena opened her eyes and smiled. Peace like she'd never felt before poured over her like warm water. It was as though God Himself had put His mouth to her ear and whispered words of comfort and security, promised her that everything would be as she had prayed for her family. His arms were around her, holding her, preparing her.

"Jim."

He didn't turn around, didn't acknowledge her voice. He was so deep in some memory he'd barely noticed when the children slipped out.

"Jim."

He stood motionless, watching the stars in the evening sky.

"Jimmy Hutching."

Jim started and turned around. His face still so much resembled that boy of just twenty-one whom she'd fallen in love with. The vitality was still there, the fire. He had so much more living to do.

"Jimmy, I'm ready, honey."

Chapter Sixty-Three

JIM STEPPED AWAY FROM THE window and sat on the edge of the bed next to Nena.

"Where were you?"

"Far away. Just remembering."

"I hope they were sweet memories."

"Mostly." He smiled.

"Thank you," she whispered.

"For what?"

"For bringing my babies home. It was so good to see them."

"Do you feel better now?" He brushed a hair from her forehead.

"I'm at peace...so happy the children came."

"Good." He stroked her cheek. "That's all I ever wanted."

She reached out her frail hand and cupped his face. "I love you, Jimmy Hutching."

"I love you too, Nena. I always have."

"Do you know what I want to do?"

"What's that? You name it."

"Go outside and get my dance under the stars."

Jim glanced at the darkened window, then back at his wife. "I think I can make that happen." He stood, pushed back the blankets, and scooped her into his arms. She felt no heavier than a sack of grain.

Carefully Jim navigated the steps, walked through the house and out the back door onto the patio. The chill in the air nipped at his nose and ears, momentarily burned his lungs. Above them stars like grains of sugar splashed across a black countertop dotted the sky a million deep and wide and far.

Nena sighed. "It's cold out here."

He kissed the top of her head. "Really? I hadn't noticed."

She turned her face toward his, and for an instant, the briefest of moments, she was twenty again, and he was young and in love. They had the world before them and all the time they needed to explore it.

"Right now," Nena said, "I think I'm more content than I've ever been in my life. There's no place else I'd rather be than in your arms."

Holding his wife, Jim began to dance. He floated around the patio, gliding his feet to a song in his head, while the rest of the world around him disappeared.

Nena put her head to his chest and held onto his shoulder with one hand.

Without further hesitation Jimmy ducked into the forest and began running. With each step pain shot through his sides, like taking punches unprotected. He ignored the pain, pressing on through tangled undergrowth and over rocky ground, taking short, shallow breaths and changing direction often. The forest's canopy was high and thin, allowing plenty of sunlight to filter to the floor. It wasn't long before the pain in his sides was too great and forced him to stop. He leaned against a tree, arms wrapped around his torso, and took slow breaths. The muscles of his legs felt like overstretched rubber, and his diaphragm was on the brink of spasming.

Had Ted reached twenty yet? He must have. Jimmy held his breath and listened. Then why didn't he hear anyone advancing through the forest? He couldn't have put that much distance between himself and his pursuer.

Then he heard it, a broken stick, rustling leaves, a horse's hoof-beats. Jimmy pushed off from the tree and started running again. The pain in his ribs had intensified, and he wondered if the fractures had displaced again. He needed to get to an area of thicker growth, to slow the horse down or force Ted to take to his feet. But everywhere Jimmy looked it was the same. Trees were ten, fifteen feet apart. The undergrowth was thick, but that would only slow down the runner on foot, not the man on the horse. His only hope was to either make it back to the ranch before Ted caught him—unlikely, considering the distance they were from the ranch and the pain in Jimmy's sides—or double back to Martin without Ted noticing.

Pushing onward, brushing through stands of serviceberry, around thick-trunked oak and elm, Jimmy endured the fire in his chest. He didn't stop again until he reached a large boulder jutting from the forest's floor. To his left the terrain sloped up; to his right it remained fairly level. He had no idea where he was, which way the ranch was, or where he could find Martin. For all he knew he was running farther and farther away from the ranch, deeper into the forest. Holding his breath, he listened. In the distance he could hear that ominous sound of Ted approaching, relentless, steady.

Jimmy only had one chance: make a stand. He raced around to the backside of the boulder, grabbed a broken limb the size of a baseball bat, and found enough footing to climb to the top. His only hope was to wait until Ted passed, jump from the rock, and tackle him. He'd use the stick if he needed to, but his main objective was to get the gun from Ted. Unarmed, he was just a man with a chip on his shoulder.

As he waited, Jimmy slowed his breathing and settled the pain in his ribs. He knew the attack would hurt like crazy, but his life depended on it.

Finally Jimmy caught his first glimpse of Ted on the horse's back. He was holding the handgun shoulder high, ready to fire. Jimmy had one chance; he'd have to make this perfect. If not...

As Ted drew near, Jimmy crouched behind the crest of the boulder. When the horse was even with the rock, he pushed off to launch himself but lost his footing and slipped. Ted swiveled in his saddle and fired a shot, hitting a tree just beyond Jimmy's head. Acting on instinct, adrenaline surging, Jimmy threw the stick at Ted, forcing him to lift both arms and duck to protect himself.

Seeing his opportunity, Jimmy leaped from the boulder and hit Ted square in the chest. Both men tumbled from the horse and hit the ground hard. Jimmy felt his ribs pop, and pain shot through his chest like a gunshot. But the pistol hadn't discharged. He rolled over and scrambled to his feet, searched the ground for the gun.

Ted lay on his right side, not moving. The gun was nowhere in sight. Still Ted didn't move. Jimmy approached him cautiously, thinking maybe this was a trick, a trap. He nudged Ted with his foot. But there was nothing. Getting closer, Jimmy noticed the blood on the leaves around Ted's head. He hooked his foot under Ted's shoulder and rolled him over. His body fell limply into place. Bile surged up Jimmy's throat. The right side of Ted's head was caved in and smeared with bright red blood. A rock, the size of a basketball, now covered with blood, protruded from the leaves. Jimmy placed his fingers on Ted's neck and felt for a pulse. He leaned close and listened for breathing, watched the man's chest. Nothing.

Ted McGovern was dead.

Jim stopped dancing and kissed her again. "Nena, there's something I have to tell you, something that happened a long time ago and I've never told anyone. I'm sorry I kept it from you. You deserved to know."

"Shh." She put a finger to his lips. "You don't have to tell me."

"Yes, I do. I've been carrying it around for way too long."

"No. I already know."

"What do you know then?"

"About Ted and how he really died."

The story the coroner settled on was that Ted had lost control of his horse and was thrown, hitting his head on a rock.

"How—"

"Do you think I didn't know how much he hated you? How much he wanted you gone? And besides, Ted was the best horseman I've ever known. He didn't just get thrown from any horse. I also knew the man I loved wasn't a murderer."

Jim paused. He couldn't believe she'd known all these years. "Why didn't you ever say anything?"

"There was no need to. It was in the past. What was done was done." Her voice was fading, growing weaker. She tried to lift her hand, but midway to his face let it drop. "Jim, you fought for me then, and you've been fighting for me ever since."

"I don't want to lose you."

"Only for a time, my sweet Jimmy, only for a time."

She closed her eyes, and Jim felt a shock of panic run up his spine. "Nena, no, don't leave me. Please."

Her eyes opened. "I love you, Jim. From the moment I saw you get out of that pickup, I loved you. I knew you were the one."

Jim kissed her forehead, her cheek, her lips.

Nena's eyes closed again, and this time they did not open.

Chapter Sixty-Four

T HE CONFERENCE ROOM HAD NEVER looked so big or felt so intimidating.

Ken sat across the table from the three partners, *his* three partners. John Hertzel laced his fingers and rested his hands on the large, mahogany tabletop. "Ken, I speak for all of us when I offer you our sincerest condolences on the passing of your mother. I'm sure she was a wonderful woman to raise a man such as yourself. Now what's this meeting about?"

Ken fidgeted in his chair. He couldn't remember the last time he'd felt this nervous. Maybe right before taking the bar exam. Maybe right before taking Celia as his wife.

"Yes, thanks. And thanks for coming. All of you." He drew in a deep breath. "I'm very grateful for all you've done for me here at the firm. Making partner was a lifelong dream come true, a real career milestone. I couldn't ask for anything more. But I'm going to have to resign as partner. In fact, consider this my official resignation from the firm." There, he'd said it. He held his breath, awaiting their response.

Paul Shea raised his eyebrows and crossed his arms. "This is certainly a shock. I know how much you've wanted this, Ken, and how hard you've worked for it. Why the change of heart?"

"My family, Paul."

Ken didn't miss the glance between Paul and Ed DeGuardo. "What does your family have to do with this?" John asked.

"Everything. Yes, I've worked hard for the promotion, the partnership, for everything I've accomplished, but at the expense of my wife and children. And I almost lost them. It's time I started fighting for them."

"So what are you going to do now?" Paul asked.

Ken drew a circle on the table with his finger. "I'm going home to Virginia, moving my family to my father's ranch. I think I'll help him rebuild it, maybe practice law on the side for a while, do some *pro bono* work. I'm going to spend time with my family, teach my kids how to ride a horse, work with my hands, love my wife."

"Sounds like something out of a country song," John said.

Ken smiled. "Something like that. It's the next best thing to paradise."

He pushed back his chair, stood, and pulled his shoulders back. He wasn't going to go out like a quitter. This was his decision, and it was the right one. "Gentlemen, thank you for everything." He turned and left the conference room.

Halfway down the hall he was stopped by a voice. Ken turned and found Ed behind him, hand extended. He took the senior partner's hand and shook it.

"Ken, I just wanted to say I admire you. You're taking a risk, you know, but I think you're making the right decision. I learned the hard way—and maybe I'm still learning—that nothing is worth losing your family over. I wish you the best."

"Thanks, Ed. I appreciate it."

And then he left…left his office with the great view, left the practice, left the building, left his old life behind to start a new life and a new adventure.

Chapter Sixty-Five

I THINK WE CAN BEAT THIS, Barb." Dr. Bassler closed the manila folder and sat back in his chair. He glanced between Barb and Doug, then found his usual spot on the floor to settle his eyes on. "It'll be the fight of your life, but you can do it."

Barb reached for Doug's hand. "What's it going to take?"

"I won't sugarcoat it. Radical mastectomy, radiation, aggressive chemo."

Barb looked at Doug, who smiled and nodded and squeezed her hand. He'd been with her the whole way so far, no need to question his loyalty now. If she ever had an advocate, a friend, a partner, a lover, it was Doug. And the kids, they would be strong too. They'd already been so strong. They amazed her.

"Whatever it takes," she said, and she meant it. She wasn't fighting only for her own health, but for Kara and Mikey, for Doug, for her father, and, yes, even for the memory of her mother who'd fought valiantly herself.

"Great," Dr. Bassler said. He clicked his pen and jotted something down on a piece of paper. "Let's get the ball rolling then."

In the parking lot Doug put his arm around Barb's shoulders. "You amaze me, you know that?"

"No, I didn't. Why's that?"

"You're so strong."

"I put on a good show."

"No, I mean it. Your strength is inspiring."

She leaned into him. "I couldn't do it without you...and God, of course. How do people handle something like this without faith? The hopelessness they must feel."

"We were there."

"I suppose we were. It's not a pretty place to be, either. You know, I think once we beat this thing, I'd like to make it a point to help others going through this same valley. To point them to the truth, show them there is hope."

Doug kissed her on the cheek. "That sounds like an excellent plan."

Chapter Sixty-Six

ROBERTA LEANED AGAINST THE FENCE and drew in a deep breath of the cool country air. Pastureland spread out before her like a brown sea that went on forever. There was nothing like this in Los Angeles, not even close. After the funeral she'd gone back to California, quit her job at the *Times*, said good-bye to Tiffany, packed up, and moved back to the ranch. This was where she truly belonged, where she'd find new life, and perhaps, in God's good time, a new man. For now, though, she'd enjoy spending time with her dad and Kenny and his family. She'd enjoy rebuilding the ranch and caring for horses again.

"What are you thinking about?"

Her dad came up from behind and stood next to her, both arms resting on the top rail.

"New beginnings. Starting over."

"Pretty deep stuff."

She surveyed the land, the rolling hills, cloud-dotted sky. "Being here, it's like being born again."

"Every day."

"And I'm looking forward to each one."

"How'd the interview go?"

She'd applied for a job as a staff reporter with the *Monroe Daily Record*. "Better than I could have imagined. They said I was overqualified for the position."

"And that was great?"

"Sure. They asked me to be their primary feature writer, which includes a daily column."

"And you turned it down, didn't you?"

She nudged him with her elbow. "Not in a million years."

Her dad put his arm around her shoulders. "From the *LA Times* to the *Monroe Daily Record*. Does it feel like a step down?"

Roberta shook her head and laughed. "No way. It's a step up." She kissed her father on the cheek. "Definitely a step up."

COMING FROM MICHAEL KING
IN WINTER 2014—

A Million Miles From Home

CHAPTER ONE

I FELL IN LOVE WITH ANNIE Fleming when I was thirteen. We were neighbors, had been since we were in kindergarten and her family moved to Boomer, North Carolina, from Detroit. Her daddy had been transferred there, some new position at the local bookbinding plant that apparently needed a big city goon to fill it. Annie's daddy beat her on a regular basis. The first time I met her, she was hiding in my tree house. At six years old I had no idea what it meant to be beat by your father. My dad was a drunk, but he wasn't a violent one. He'd holler and occasionally toss a toaster or dinner plate across the kitchen, but he never once laid a hand on either me or my mother. It just wasn't his style.

When we were thirteen, I found Annie again in my tree house. She'd climbed up there after another thumping from her daddy. Her right eye was a little puffy, and she had a nasty blue and green bruise on her left arm, just above the elbow. She usually did a pretty good job of hiding the bruises but didn't care if I saw them. I was the only one who knew of her secret, of the pain she hid from the rest of the world. I didn't know if her momma was aware of what went on in that home of hers. I figured she was either as dumb and blind as an earthworm and had no clue, or she knew very well what was going on and chose to look away and pretend she didn't. Either way, I hated both of Annie's parents.

That evening I climbed up into my tree house after dinner and found Annie sitting there in the corner, both knees pulled to her chest, her hair matted and frizzed, her cheeks stained with tears. I walked over and sat next to her, touched the bruise on her arm. "Does it hurt?"

She shook her head. Annie always shook her head when I asked if her bruises hurt.

Pulling my knees up, I reached for a baseball card on the floor beside me. It was a 1975 George Brett. Kansas City Royals. Holding the card between my thumbs and index fingers, I tore it in half, then in quarters.

"I hate him." And I wasn't talking about George Brett. I'd never told Annie how I felt about her daddy. Part of me wanted to reach out and take those words back as soon as they left my mouth, and part of me wanted them to hang out there, to float all the way down the tree and across the yard and into the Fleming living room where Annie's father was no doubt perched in front of the TV, beer in hand. I wanted him to know I hated him.

"Don't," she said, and her voice cracked. "Hate never solved anyone's problem."

"Killing did. I want to kill him."

Annie turned and shoved me in the arm. Tears poured from her eyes again. "Don't you dare say that, Benjamin Flurry. You'd be no better than him then, and you are better. You're a good person, the best I know. Don't let hate make you no better than him."

It was right there at that moment that I fell in love with Annie Fleming. It hit me so hard I almost started to cry. I wanted to take her into my arms and hold her, protect her, erase her pain. I wanted to run away with her and start a life of our own. But I was thirteen, and what did a thirteen-year-old know about making his way in the world? Instead I said, "I hope we can be friends the rest of our lives."

Through her tears and red-rimmed eyes she smiled at me. She had a beautiful smile. I always thought I could look at it all day and never get bored. "I'd like that, Ben." That was all she said, but it was enough to keep me going for five more years.

When I was eighteen, I told Annie I loved her.

We'd remained friends through middle school and high

school, the best of friends. She'd dated a few other guys, and I'd gone out a couple times with other girls, but I think deep down we both knew we were destined for each other. Some day.

Our senior year I was accepted into the environmental science program at Penn State University. Annie never planned on going to college; she'd always said her only ambition was to be a wife and mommy. I couldn't have admired her more.

It was late August, and I was leaning against my jam-packed F-150 when Annie walked over from her house. She didn't have a bruise on her. Her daddy had stopped beating on her when she became quick enough to dodge his blows and make him look foolish. Instead he'd resorted to the verbal brand of abuse; I think he came over and took lessons from my father.

Annie's hair was swept back in a loose ponytail, and she wore a pair of jeans and a snug T-shirt that accentuated her slender, athletic figure. Normally she smiled a lot when she was around me, but this time the smile was nowhere to be found.

"I can't believe you're actually leaving." She leaned against the door of the truck and folded her arms in a pouty kind of way.

I shoved my hands in my pockets. "I can't either. Kinda snuck up on me."

She patted the truck's rusty exterior. "You think this 'ole gal is up for the trip?"

I'd wondered too if my aging Ford would make the fifteen-hour trek north. "We'll find out, I guess. I may be calling you to come rescue me along the side of the highway somewhere in northern Virginia."

There was her smile. "I'd be there in a heartbeat."

"Even at two in the morning?"

"Even if you were halfway across the world."

A moment of comfortless silence hung between us while I suppose we both tried to put off the inevitable good-bye.

My palms had taken to sweating, and my pulse suddenly thumped in my ears. I hadn't planned on saying it, I was anything but impulsive, but it just seemed the time was right. I blurted the words out. "I love you, Annie."

If she was surprised by my awkward declaration, she never showed it. She glanced at me then looked straight ahead. "I wondered when you'd get around to saying it."

"What?"

"Oh, c'mon, Ben. You've loved me since middle school. You know it."

"How could you tell?"

"A girl knows when she's loved."

"Really?"

She faked a look of surprise. "Guys can't tell?"

I shook my head. "We're clueless."

Annie slid closer to me, so close her arm touched mine. "Well, since you're so clueless, I guess I have to spell it out for you. The feeling is mutual."

I was paralyzed, didn't know what to say. My mouth suddenly went dry. "Hmm." It was all I could muster.

She nudged me. "Is that all you're gonna say?"

Finally my voice came. "How long?"

"How long what?"

"Have you felt this way?"

Another nudge, this time harder. She smiled again. "Ben Flurry, you act like it's some disease. I've loved you since we were thirteen, that time you threatened to kill my dad. I was so mad at you for saying it, but at the same time I knew you only wanted to protect me. It was probably the sweetest thing anyone's ever said to me. Until now."

I never told her that was the exact time I fell in love with her too. I figured I'd have all the time in the world to tell her.

Again, on impulse, I turned to face Annie, put my hands on her shoulders, and kissed her soundly on the lips. She didn't pull back, didn't push me away. Instead she leaned in and returned my kiss.

We were married four years later, a month after I graduated and landed a job with the Pennsylvania Department of Environmental Protection. It was a simple wedding, outside, with a picnic reception. Annie's parents offered to pay for a big fancy deal, spend thousands on their little girl, but Annie refused. She didn't want any part of her father's generosity knowing it always came with a price. We lived in a two-bedroom apartment where the furniture was sparse but the smiles and laughs were abundant. We were happy and madly in love.

Two months after the wedding I came home from work one rainy day and found Annie sitting on the floor of the bathroom crying. I feared the worst, though I had no idea what the worst could be.

"Annie, what's wrong? What is it?"

She held up a little white stick and pointed to the pink lines. It was then I realized her tears were not tears of sorrow or pain but of happiness and expectancy.

The time rolled by, and the months were filled with shopping for baby supplies and measuring Annie's growing belly. And as her belly grew, so did her appetite. Late-night runs to the local Waffle House became the norm. She'd sit up until midnight eating a Texas melt with hash browns and watching the late-night shows.

One morning, a month before her due date, I was awakened by Annie jumping up and stumbling out of bed. "My water...my water..."

I stirred and turned over. At first I thought indigestion had finally gotten the best of her. But after feeling the wet sheets on her side of the bed, I realized what happened: her water had broken.

It was as if someone reached inside my head and flipped the panic switch. I was out of bed faster than my feet could find the floor and landed on my butt. The clock on the dresser said it was 4:52. The outside world was dark, but rain tapped on the windows. It had been raining for four days straight, and nearly every secondary road in our area was flooded. Alternate routes to the hospital ran through my mind. I hadn't planned for this, for our baby to be a month early. I wasn't prepared.

Fortunately Annie was. She was calm too. She stood at the foot of the bed, holding her belly, legs spread and glistening in the light of the small lamp. Sweat dappled her forehead and upper lip. "Ben, get the bag."

I found my legs, got them under me, and stood. "What bag?"

"The hospital bag. It has all my things in it, and the baby's too." I didn't even know she'd gotten a bag together. "It's in the closet."

Bag in hand I led my wife into the bathroom. "Call the doctor's office," she said as if she were giving directions to a five-year-old, "and tell them my water broke and we're on our way to the hospital. The number's on the fridge."

Leaving her standing in the bathroom, I stumbled down the stairs and found the number.

The next few hours are still a blur. Somehow we got to the hospital. It took us all of six tries with different routes before we found one that wasn't flooded. Annie was given a room, and things started happening. Contractions hit her hard and heavy. The nurses kept commenting on how well she was handling it for her first labor and how quickly things were progressing. We watched the monitor beside her bed, and I tried to prepare her for every contraction, but she could feel them before I spotted the little line beginning to slope upward. The line below it was the baby's heart rate. It pulsed fast and steady...until one particularly strong contraction hit Annie out of nowhere, and the heartbeat slowed noticeably.

I pushed the button for a nurse, and within minutes the room was full of people in scrubs hurrying about and talking in hushed tones. The doctor arrived soon after, all business and straight-faced. He had Annie lie back and checked her.

"Dear," he said, "you're fully dilated and effaced." And after glancing at the monitor and the sluggish pulse line, he looked at Annie and raised his eyebrows. "Okay, now, on the next contraction push with everything you have. We need to get this little darling out."

Annie pushed and strained until I thought the veins in her forehead and neck would pop. But not much happened. When the contraction passed, she dropped her head back and panted like a woman who'd just run a marathon. Sweat stuck her hair to her forehead and ran rivulets down her cheeks.

Thank God a nurse was by her side to comfort and instruct her, because I proved to be useless. I'm not usually squeamish about pain and body fluids and such, but there's something about watching your wife suffer that tears at your heart. I'm a fixer, a problem-solver, and this was one valley I couldn't carry her through. I gripped her hand and wiped her tears and prayed. Man, did I pray.

On the next contraction the doctor said he could see the top of the head.

Two contractions later Annie let out a guttural moan and bore down.

I could have sworn the hands on the clock stood still at that moment and the world stopped spinning on its axis. I heard the doctor say something about notifying the NICU, heard one of the nurses let out a pitiful moan, heard Annie grunt and sigh deeply. But it was what I didn't hear that scared me. There was no crying. No sound of a healthy baby gasping for its first breaths of air. No sound of life. The doctor cut the umbilical cord, and that's when I caught a glimpse of our baby girl, as blue as a Smurf, with the umbilical cord wrapped around her little neck like a tentacle from some otherworldly creature. She was as limp as a wet blanket in the doctor's big hands.

Annie kept saying, "What's wrong? Why isn't she crying?"

A nurse took our daughter, wrapped her in a blanket, and swept her away. At that moment I thought I felt the floor shift and almost lost my balance. My heart was in my mouth, and I couldn't even speak. All I could do was take Annie in my arms and cry with her.

A little over a week later I stood behind the glass doors at the rear of our house, the ones that overlooked the patio and a sprawling field, and held my daughter, Elizabeth Grace. Lizzy. She was beautiful, pink, plump, and fully alive. Our miracle. The doctor's all told us she may have some cognitive deficiencies and motor control problems as she matures and develops because of the lack of oxygen to her brain during those harrowing minutes when the umbilical cord was compressed, but at the moment we didn't care. She was our daughter, and she was alive.

I loved the view out the back of our house. Where the green grass of the yard ended, a cornfield, harvested and ready for winter, spread out like a brown ocean as far as I could see. I knew that beyond the horizon was a woods that ran the whole way to the neighboring farm because I'd walked it many a time. It was my place to be alone and think and pray, to allow the world to fade away and just be who I wanted to be, who I was born to be. Just Ben. No pressure, no expectations, no schedules or bosses or reports to finish.

I felt that way holding Lizzy too. To her I was just daddy, even though she didn't know it yet. I could look into those baby blues all day and see in them the kind of innocence and trust and faith the world of adults knew nothing of.

Annie came up behind me and kissed the back of my neck. "Hey, daddy. Whatcha doing?"

"Just admiring our perfect little baby girl."

She touched Lizzy's cheek with her finger. "She is perfect, isn't she?"

"I'm going to spoil her; you know that, don't you?"

"I suspected as much."

"I've a right to."

"Every daddy does."

Annie rested her cheek on my arm and worked Lizzy's tiny hand around her finger.

My eyes lifted and found the horizon again. From our home to the edge of the world the sky was blue, streaked with wispy clouds and criss-crossing contrails. But beyond the horizon a long, low, gray storm front inched closer like an army marching to battle. And at that moment I had the feeling that what we'd just been through was only the beginning, that some devious, malevolent force was tracking our happy little family, stalking us, gaining ever so slowly, intent on causing mayhem and leaving hearts broken.

I tightened my hold on Lizzy and tensed as if the force would suddenly materialize and snatch her from my arms.

Annie noticed and lifted her head. "What's wrong?"

"Nothing. Just my imagination toying with me." Only it wasn't.